BOOK 5

CLANS
OF
MULL

THE
DEFIANCE OF A
Scottish Heart

KEIRA
MONTCLAIR

CHAPTER ONE

TASKILL

Autumn, 1316, Isle of Mull, Scotland

THE YOUNGER GUARD'S form was all wrong—shoulders too high, weight on his heels instead of the balls of his feet. Taskill circled him slowly, watching for the moment the lad would inevitably overcommit.

"Keep your guard up, Boswell. A Norseman won't wait for you to—"

The boy lunged. Taskill sidestepped easily and tapped the flat of his blade against Boswell's exposed ribs. "Dead. Again."

"How do you move so fast?" Boswell panted, resetting his stance.

"Practice. And I don't think about it anymore. My body knows what to do." Taskill raised his sword. "Again."

The clash of steel on steel filled the practice yard, the familiar rhythm settling something restless in his chest. This, at least, made sense. Attack, parry, reset. Clear rules. Honorable combat. No lies, no betrayals, no—

"Rider approaching!" The shout from the gates cut through his thoughts. "Chief Rankin!"

Taskill's sword arm faltered. The name hit him like a fist to the gut.

Rankin.

Which meant Dermot, most likely—the old chieftain who'd been growing stranger since his wife's death. Or possibly Sloan, Dermot's son and the current chief, a man Taskill actually respected.

But Dermot had only one unmarried daughter.

Only one daughter Taskill had spent five years trying not to think about.

"Go on, then." Boswell bent over, hands on his knees. "I need the rest anyway. You fight like you're trying to kill something today."

Every day, Taskill thought but didn't say. Fighting kept his mind occupied. Kept the memories at bay. Kept him from thinking about copper hair and green eyes and a laugh he hadn't heard directed at him since—

He sheathed his sword and strode toward the gates, nodding to the guards as he passed. Cold autumn wind cut through his tunic, but he welcomed the bite of it. Pain was honest, at least. Pain didn't smile and lie and pretend vows meant something when they didn't.

"You'll marry her now, Taskill."

The words stopped him dead three paces from the gate. His heart slammed against his ribs so hard he felt it in his throat.

Marry.

He must have misheard. Had to have misheard. Taskill forced his feet forward, forced his expression blank—a skill he'd perfected over the years, hiding what roiled beneath the surface. Dermot Rankin sat atop his mount just outside the gates, still every bit the warrior despite his sixty-odd years. Broad shoulders squared, sharp eyes missing nothing.

"Excuse me, Chief?" Taskill's voice came out steady. Good. "You called for me?"

"I did. Get on your horse now." Dermot's gaze locked onto him with unsettling intensity. "I've waited long enough. She's nine and ten now, and it's time."

The ground tilted beneath Taskill's feet. *She.* There was only one "she" Dermot could mean.

Sheona.

Heat flooded through him, followed immediately by ice-cold dread. "Chief Rankin, I think there's been some misunderstanding—"

"No misunderstanding. Your father and I agreed years ago. You'll agree to marry my daughter, then we'll find the priest."

The world narrowed to a pinpoint. His father. A promise. Marriage.

All the things Taskill had sworn to avoid, crashing down on him at once.

"My father's been dead two years." The words came out harsher than intended. "And he made no such promise to my knowledge."

Liar, a voice whispered in his head. *You're lying just like he did. Saying whatever serves you, truth be damned.*

Taskill's hands clenched into fists. No. He wasn't lying—his sire hadn't told him about any

betrothal. But the ease with which the denial
came, the practiced smoothness of it...

God help him, he was his father's son.

"Taskill?" Lennox's voice cut through the
roaring in his ears. His brother strode toward
the gates, assessing the situation with the swift
calculation that made him a good chieftain.
"What's happening here?" Lennox had been
chieftain of Clan MacVey since their sire's death
two years ago.

Thank Christ. If anyone could handle Dermot's
madness, it was Lennox.

Taskill stepped back, letting his brother take
the lead. He needed space. Air. Distance from the
words still echoing in his skull.

You'll marry her now.

Movement at the corner of his vision made
him turn. Sheona stood near the practice field
with Eva, her face pale as moonlight. Their eyes
met across the courtyard—green eyes wide with
shock—and Taskill's chest constricted so sharply
he nearly gasped.

Five years. Five years since he'd let himself really
look at her. Five years of training himself to turn
away, to ignore the pull that had nearly destroyed
his carefully constructed walls.

She was more beautiful than his memories
allowed. The girlish softness had given way to
elegant cheekbones, a determined jaw, copper
hair that caught the autumn sun. She wore men's
trews and a practice tunic, an axe in her hand.

Still fierce. Still herself.

Still everything he couldn't let himself want.

Her expression shifted from shock to something that looked like pain, and she turned away sharply.

That old, familiar ache twisted in his chest. The same ache that had lived there since the day he'd walked away from her at the water's edge. The day he'd chosen to break her heart once rather than break her soul slowly over a lifetime.

"Dermot Rankin, stop acting like a fool and close your mouth!"

His mother's voice rang across the courtyard like a battle cry. Rut MacVey stood on the keep steps, her posture rigid with fury. Even at her age, she carried herself like a queen—tall, willowy, beautiful, and utterly unwilling to tolerate any man's nonsense.

She'd tolerated his father's for years, though.

The thought came unbidden and bitter. Had she known? Had she looked the other way, pretended everything was fine while Douglas MacVey smiled and lied whenever it suited him?

Taskill forced the darkness down. His mother deserved better than his poisonous thoughts.

"Mother, I will handle Chief Rankin." Lennox's voice carried an edge of exasperation.

But Rut was already moving toward them like a ship in full sail. "Dermot, did you hear me? You wish to talk about my dear Douglas and what he agreed to? Then you better plan on talking with me, because I'm the only one who is aware of his dealings.

"Are you listening?" She came to a stop directly in front of Dermot's horse, finger pointed like a blade. "Stop yelling at my sons and stop blaming them for all your problems. It's not their fault that Sheona can't find a husband. If she'd start acting like a woman, mayhap she'd find one."

Anger spiked through Taskill's veins, hot and immediate. *Don't.* Don't insult her. Don't suggest she needs to change, to be less than she is, to diminish herself to fit some man's narrow idea of what a woman should be.

But he bit his tongue. He had no right to defend Sheona. No right to speak for her, not when he'd spent five years avoiding her.

"What the hell does that mean, Rut?" Dermot's face flushed red. "How dare you insult my sweet lass."

"She may be sweet, and she is beautiful, but she dresses like a man. And I heard what you said. Douglas did not agree to have Taskill marry Sheona."

Relief flooded through him so powerfully his knees nearly buckled. His mother would end this. She'd send Dermot home, and Taskill could go back to his careful distance, his managed pain, his solitary life.

The life where Sheona was safe from him.

"He promised," Dermot insisted.

"And how many casks of the sweet amber brew had the two of you imbibed when he made said promise?" Rut shivered in the cool air, arms crossed over her chest.

Dermot grinned. "Mayhap a few."

"Doesn't hold when you have enough in you to keep you from mounting a horse. You were making plans you shouldn't have been making."

Rut's voice softened slightly. "And Taskill is not marrying Sheona. Lennox, take him back home."

"I don't think Sheona would agree to the match, Chief Rankin." Taskill kept his voice level, respectful. Anything to end this nightmare. "With all due respect."

She'd be horrified, he thought. *She'd remember the boy who was her friend and wonder what happened to him. She doesn't know I'm protecting her. She thinks I just ... stopped caring.*

Better that than the truth.

"She doesn't need to agree," Dermot snapped. "I'll choose her husband, and I choose you. Now get on your mount and follow me back to Rankin land. Stop arguing with me, lad."

"Nay, Dermot." Rut's voice rose. "And he's not a lad anymore! He's five and twenty."

"Stop giving orders on my land, Dermot." Lennox's tone carried the weight of authority now. "Your behavior is more than insulting."

The argument escalated around him—his mother's fury, Lennox's cold authority, Dermot's stubborn insistence. But Taskill barely heard it. His gaze kept drifting back to where Sheona had been standing.

She was gone now. Vanished.

Running, probably. From the humiliation of being bartered like livestock. From the rejection of hearing that he wasn't interested.

I'm so sorry, Sheona. You deserve so much better than this. Better than him. Better than me.

The old man finally grumbled something about contacting King Robert and turned his horse to leave—the wrong direction, naturally. After the arguing ended, and Lennox mounting up to escort him home, the courtyard finally began to clear.

Taskill stood rooted to the spot, his mind a storm of memories he couldn't suppress.

Sheona at ten, beating him at archery and crowing with delight.

Sheona at twelve, swimming in the loch, daring him to dive from the highest rock.

Sheona at fourteen, laughing at one of his terrible jokes until tears streamed down her face.

Sheona at fourteen, standing on the bank in her wet chemise, the afternoon sun turning her into something ethereal and dangerous and utterly forbidden.

And him, walking away. Choosing to walk away rather than risk becoming what his father was.

"Task." Lennox's hand landed on his shoulder, making him flinch. When had his brother returned? "You all right? Jasper is with Dermot. I'll catch up in a bit."

"Fine."

"That's shite and we both know it." Lennox moved to stand in front of him, forcing eye contact. "Talk to me."

"There's nothing to discuss. Dermot's mad. You sent him home. Its' done."

"Is it?" Lennox's eyes narrowed. "Because from where I'm standing, it looks like you just watched the one woman you've ever cared about get humiliated in front of the whole clan, and you're about to snap."

Taskill's jaw clenched so hard his teeth ached. "I don't know what you're talking about."

"Brother." Lennox's voice gentled. "I've known you your whole life. You haven't looked at another woman with real interest since you were twenty years old. You train like a demon, your smiles aren't genuine, and you've built walls so high even Mother can't scale them. And it all started the summer you stopped swimming with Sheona Rankin."

The observation landed like a blow. Taskill forced himself to breathe. "Your point?"

"My point is that Dermot might be mad, but he's not entirely wrong. You and Sheona—"

"There is no me and Sheona." The words came out too sharp, too fast. "There never was. There never will be."

"Why not?"

Because I'm my father's son. Because I saw what he was, what men really are beneath the vows and smiles. Because I have his blood, his weakness, and I'll be damned before I inflict that on her.

But he couldn't say any of that. Couldn't explain without revealing the truth he'd buried two years ago, along with his father's body and his lies.

"I have my reasons."

"Reasons you won't share?"

"Reasons that are mine alone." Taskill stepped back, breaking his brother's hold. "Dermot won't push this again. He's not that far gone. It's over."

He walked away before Lennox could argue, heading for the stables. He needed to ride. To think. To breathe without the weight of everyone's expectations crushing his chest.

His brother mounted up and waved at him. "This isn't over!"

The stableboy had his horse ready by the time he arrived—a gray stallion with a steady temperament and enough speed to outrun his thoughts. Or at least tire them out.

Taskill mounted and rode hard toward the coast, the wind stinging his eyes as the castle disappeared behind him. He didn't slow until he reached the cliffs overlooking the sea, where gray water churned beneath a grayer sky.

This was where he came when the memories got too loud. When the fear that he was becoming his father overwhelmed the walls he'd built to contain it.

He dismounted and stood at the cliff's edge, letting the salt spray wash over him.

You'll marry her now, Taskill.

What would happen if he did? If he ignored every instinct screaming at him to stay away? If he let himself have what he'd wanted since he was old enough to understand wanting?

He'd already seen that story. Knew exactly how it ended.

"This changes nothing, boy. You'll tell no one."

His father's voice, cold and commanding, in that moment when Taskill's world had shattered. When he'd understood that the man he'd admired was a lie.

Taskill had been twenty. The same age he'd

started noticing Sheona differently. The same summer he'd walked away from her rather than risk becoming what his father was.

Five years of distance. Five years of careful control. Five years of fighting the pull toward her like a drowning man fighting the tide.

And now Dermot wanted to force them together.

Nay.

He wouldn't do it. Couldn't do it. Even if some traitorous part of him whispered that maybe, possibly, he could be different.

But what if he couldn't? What if the weakness was in his blood, waiting?

Better to be alone than to become the man who destroyed Sheona Rankin's spirit.

Better to break her heart once than to watch it wither slowly over years of marriage to a man who couldn't keep his promises.

Movement in the distance caught his eye. A rider, heading along the coastal path. Even from here, he recognized the copper braid, the straight-backed posture, the way she sat her horse like she was born to it.

Sheona.

His heart contracted painfully.

She was riding alone, one guard as her protector. *He* should have been her protector.

Still fierce, he thought. *Still refusing to be caged.*

He should look away. Should mount his horse and ride inland, put distance between them like he'd done for five years.

But his feet stayed planted on the cliff's edge, and his eyes stayed locked on her retreating figure until she disappeared around the bend.

"I'm sorry," he whispered to the wind. "I'm so damned sorry, Sheona."

For the distance. For the hurt. For being too much of a coward to tell her the truth—that staying away from her was the hardest thing he'd ever done, and the most necessary.

For being his father's son, and hating himself for it.

The wind carried his words away, and Taskill stood alone on the cliff, watching the empty path where Sheona had been, and wondering how long a man could keep running from the one thing he wanted most in the world.

CHAPTER TWO

SHEONA

THE AXE FELT good in her hands—solid, honest, real. Sheona adjusted her grip and let it fly, satisfaction singing through her as the blade thunked into the center of the target.

"Beautiful throw!" Eva clapped, her eyes bright with admiration. "You'll have to teach me that technique."

"It's all in the release." Sheona retrieved the axe, running her thumb along the blade's edge. Still sharp. Good. "You can't hesitate. The moment you doubt, your aim suffers." She loved it the day Eva had married her brother, but loved it even more when Eva volunteered to teach Sheona how to throw an axe. Sheona had learned quickly.

"Is that advice for axe-throwing or for life?" Eva asked with a knowing smile. She'd married into Clan Rankin but still returned to Clan MacVey to visit her family often. She'd brought Sheona with her this morn.

Sheona laughed. "Both, I suppose." She lined up for another throw, finding the familiar calm that came with practice. This—the weight of the weapon, the focus required, the satisfaction of hitting her mark—this made sense. This she could control.

Unlike everything else in her life lately.

Her father had been acting strange for weeks now, muttering about duty and marriage and time running out. As if Sheona were a cask of wine about to turn to vinegar. As if her value decreased with every passing season.

She was nine and ten. Not exactly ancient.

And more importantly, she had no interest in marriage. Not since she'd learned—

"Sheona, look." Eva touched her arm, nodding toward the gates. "Is that not your father?"

Sheona's stomach dropped. Dermot Rankin sat astride his horse just outside Clan MacVey's gates, his posture rigid with purpose. The set of his shoulders, the way he held the reins—she knew that stance. He was here for something, and whatever it was, it wouldn't be good.

"What's he doing here?" Sheona murmured, dread creeping up her spine like cold fingers.

"I don't know, but he doesn't look happy."

When did he ever, these days? Since Mama's death a little over a year ago, her father had become someone else entirely. Angry, controlling, desperate to maintain order in a world that had turned upside-down.

And Sheona had become his favorite target.

"You'll marry her now, Taskill."

The words carried across the courtyard like a thunderclap. Sheona froze, her axe halfway to the target.

Marry. Taskill.

Nay. Nay, she must have misheard.

But Eva's sharp intake of breath confirmed she'd heard the same thing.

Sheona's hands went numb. The axe slipped from her fingers and thudded to the ground. Her feet moved without conscious thought, carrying her closer to the gates, closer to the nightmare unfolding before her.

Taskill stood just inside the gates, his expression carefully blank. That expression—she knew it well. Had memorized every variation of it over the years. The slight tightening at the corners of his eyes. The way his jaw set just so. The absolute stillness that meant he was feeling everything and showing nothing.

She'd spent five years learning to read him from a distance, since he'd made it clear he wanted nothing to do with her up close.

"I've waited long enough," her father continued, his voice carrying to every corner of the courtyard. Guards stopped their training. Servants paused in their tasks. Everyone was watching now. "She's nine and ten now, and it's time."

Heat flooded Sheona's face. *She.* As if she were livestock. As if she weren't standing right here, hearing herself discussed like a problem to be solved. She picked up her axe and moved it from one hand to the other, anything to help her get past being made a spectacle at Clan MacVey.

Taskill's gaze swept the courtyard and landed on her. For one heartbeat, their eyes met, and something flickered in his expression—pain?

Regret? But it vanished so quickly she might have imagined it.

Then he looked away.

Always, he looked away.

The old wound in her chest—the one that had never quite healed—split open anew. Five years since that day on the shore. Five years since the day her mother had called her out of the water, scolding her for being too old for such games. Five years since Taskill had said nothing in her defense, had simply turned away and let her go.

She'd waited all evening for him to come find her, to tell her it was all right, that they'd figure out a way to stay friends even if they couldn't swim together anymore.

He never came.

And the next day, when she'd sought him out, he'd looked through her as if she were made of glass. Transparent. Inconsequential.

Forgettable.

"Chief Rankin, I think there's been some misunderstanding—" Taskill's voice was steady, controlled.

"No misunderstanding. Your father and I agreed years ago."

Sheona's breath caught. Her father had arranged this? Years ago? While she'd been pining for a boy who could barely stand to look at her, there'd been some secret agreement hanging over her head?

Fury warred with humiliation in her chest.

"Dermot Rankin, stop acting like a fool and close your mouth!"

Rut MacVey's voice rang out like a battle horn. Sheona had always admired Taskill's mother—a woman who took shite from no one and made no apologies for it. The kind of woman Sheona's own mother might have been, if she'd been allowed.

The argument erupted in earnest then. Rut marching forward like an avenging angel. Lennox emerging from the keep, his expression thunderous. Dermot shouting about promises and honor.

And through it all, Taskill stood silent. Passive. Letting others fight his battles while he remained carefully, deliberately neutral.

Just like at the coastline.

"She may be sweet, and she is beautiful, but she dresses like a man," Rut said, gesturing at Dermot. "And I heard what you said. Douglas did not agree to have Taskill marry Sheona."

The words hit like a slap. *Dresses like a man.* As if there were something wrong with her. As if she needed to change, to become someone more palatable.

Sheona's hands curled into fists at her sides.

"I don't think Sheona would agree to the match, Chief Rankin," Taskill said, his voice infuriatingly calm. "With all due respect."

Something inside her cracked.

He wouldn't even look at her while he rejected her. Couldn't be bothered to acknowledge her presence while discussing her future. Just stood there with that blank expression, as if the whole thing were a minor inconvenience instead of her entire life being debated in front of the whole clan.

Of course he wouldn't agree to the match. Why would he? You're not worth fighting for. You never were.

The thought was poison, but she'd carried it for five years. Ever since the day Taskill MacVey had looked at her—really looked at her—and decided she wasn't worth the effort.

"She doesn't need to agree!" her father roared. "I'll choose her husband, and I choose you. Now get on your mount and follow me back to Rankin land."

"Nay, Dermot," Rut shouted. "And he's not a lad anymore!"

The argument spiraled, voices rising, tempers flaring. Sheona stood rooted to the spot, her heart hammering so hard she thought everyone must be able to hear it. Her vision narrowed to Taskill's profile—the strong line of his jaw, the fair hair catching the autumn sun, the careful distance he maintained from everyone and everything.

Especially her.

She'd loved him once. Loved him with the uncomplicated devotion of a girl who didn't know better. Who thought friendship meant forever, and that the boy who made her laugh until her sides ached would always be there.

She'd been a fool.

"Stop giving orders on my land, Dermot," Lennox said, his voice cold with authority. "Your behavior is more than insulting."

Her father finally grumbled something about

King Robert and turned his horse—the wrong direction, naturally. Even in his fury, he was lost.

Lennox mounted to escort him home, and gradually, the courtyard began to return to normal. Guards went back to training. Servants resumed their tasks.

But Sheona couldn't move. Couldn't breathe past the humiliation choking her.

Everyone had heard. Everyone knew. Her father had tried to barter her like a broodmare, and Taskill had rejected her without even doing her the courtesy of meeting her eyes.

"Sheona." Eva's hand touched her arm gently. "Are you all right?"

No. She wasn't all right. She was shattered, mortified, furious.

But she couldn't say that. Couldn't fall apart in the middle of the MacVey courtyard with half the clan watching.

"I'm fine." The lie tasted like ash. "I need... I need to go."

She turned and fled before Eva could stop her, before the tears burning behind her eyes could fall. Her feet carried her around the perimeter of the courtyard out to the stables. The Rankin guard, Miles, helped her mount and followed her out. She couldn't get home fast enough.

As soon as they made it to her home, she hopped of her horse, handed the reins to a stable lad and hurried away. She had to find a place where she could let go. Let the awful hurt out that stabbed her so much that she had to fight the tears begging to flood her face.

She ran inside the keep, up the stairs to the end of the passageway to her favorite place. The parapets. Empty, usually. The one place she could breathe.

She shoved through the door and stumbled out into the wind, gulping air like a drowning woman breaking the surface.

He doesn't want you. He never did.

The thought was a knife between her ribs, twisting.

She'd known it, of course. Had known it for five years. But hearing it spoken aloud, announced to everyone—that was different. That made it real in a way it hadn't been before.

"What's he done now, MacVey?" Sloan's voice drifted up from below. He must have been near the gates.

"I did naught wrong!" Her father's voice, belligerent. "Just went calling for what was promised to my daughter long ago. Lennox won't hold to his father's word. We may have to declare war on him, Sloan. It's only right."

Daughter. War. Promised.

The words barely registered through the roaring in her ears. She tore back down the stairs and out to the courtyard.

"Da! Please stop!" She hadn't meant to shout, but the words tore out of her anyway.

Her father turned, his expression shifting from fury to dismissal in an instant. "This is not your affair, Sheona. Go back inside."

That gesture. That careless wave of his hand, as if she were a serving girl to be dismissed. As if her own future weren't the very thing being discussed.

Rage, white-hot and clarifying, burned through the humiliation.

"Is it about me?" She moved down the steps, her voice shaking with barely contained emotion. "Because if it's about me, then it is my affair, Da."

"Sheona Rankin, you'll hold your tongue—"

"Keep your mouth closed until we are in your son's solar, Dermot," Lennox said to her father, his voice sharp with warning.

"Don't tell me what to do, MacVey. This is my land now."

"I'm telling you so you won't embarrass your daughter further."

The words hit like a physical blow. *Further.* As if she weren't already humiliated enough.

Sloan grabbed their father's reins. "Get your arse down, Da. And you'll do what Lennox says until we're inside. Close your mouth."

They disappeared into the keep, still arguing.

Sheona shook her head, unable to speak past the tightness in her throat. She followed them inside on numb legs, her mind spinning.

Taskill. Marriage. Promise.

The words jumbled together, making no sense and perfect sense at the same time.

She reached Sloan's solar just as her father tried to bar her from entering. His hand caught her shoulder. "Not you."

"Oh, Sheona needs to be here, Dermot," Lennox said firmly. "I insist."

"MacVey, you sure are ornery. Is your new wife mad at you?"

Sheona slipped past the men while they argued and took a chair in the back corner. Sheona gripped the arms of the chair, her knuckles white, and waited for her world to finish crumbling. Eva appeared inside a moment later. Her friend must have followed her home.

The door closed. Sloan rounded on their father immediately. "What now, Da?"

"You know what. I told you that Douglas gave me his word a long time ago on that issue, and I'm not letting it go. Lennox will do what his sire promised me. It was his sire's word, and we agreed on it."

"I'm not willing to commit to a promise made by a dead man," Lennox said coldly. "A promise that exists only in your mind, Dermot. Da said naught to me about this, so I'll not be honoring it."

Sheona wanted to scream. They kept dancing around it, speaking in circles, while she sat there with her heart in her throat.

"Lennox, you'll not be expected to honor it." Sloan's voice carried the weight of exhaustion. "We'll handle this."

"Aye, you will, MacVey. If I have to drag him to the chapel, I'll do it."

"Da, he already rejected me." The words exploded out of Sheona before she could stop them. "I know you are talking about me, but I should have a say in this."

Her father spun around so fast it startled her. "You'll sit down and be quiet. This is a discussion among chieftains, and your thoughts have no bearing on it."

"I will not sit down!" Every muscle in her body trembled with rage. "This is my life you're discussing! I have every right—"

Her father charged. Three chairs went flying as he barreled toward her, his arm raised, fury twisting his features into something unrecognizable.

Sheona's back hit the wall. Her hands came up instinctively to protect her face. *He's going to hit me. My own father is going to—*

Sloan and Lennox caught him before he reached her, wrestling him back. Her father struggled, his voice raw with anger. "Let go of me, Sloan. She's got that slap coming. This is not her affair. Women do what they're told."

Sheona's legs gave out. She slid down the wall, her hands still raised, her whole body shaking. This wasn't her father. This was a stranger wearing his face. A man who'd been slowly disappearing since Mama died, leaving behind this angry, unpredictable shell.

"It is her affair, Dermot." Lennox's voice cut like ice. "Hers and mine. I'll not force my brother to marry your daughter. He's not interested. Get over it!"

The words landed like arrows, each one finding its mark.

He's not interested.
He's not interested.
He's not interested.

"Taskill." The name came out as barely a whisper. Her throat had closed around it.

"Aye, he's your betrothed, and it's time to announce it," her father said, finally stopping his struggle. "Douglas and I agreed on it long ago."

The room tilted. Sheona's vision blurred at the edges. She heard more arguing—Sloan's voice raised, Lennox's cold fury—but the words meant nothing.

Taskill.

The only man she'd ever loved.

The man who'd rejected her five years ago without explanation.

The man who wouldn't even look at her today while her father tried to force him into marrying her.

He's not interested.

She had to admit that once her father had left, perhaps Taskill would rethink the betrothal. They'd known each other forever. But his brother spoke the words that he knew in his heart.

She shoved away from the wall and ran. Stumbled through the door, down the corridor, her vision swimming with tears she refused to let fall. She needed air. Needed to be anywhere but here, with everyone's pity following her like a stench.

Her feet carried her to the parapets—the highest point, where the wind was strongest and the sea stretched out forever. Where she could breathe.

She burst through the door and stopped short.

Her dear sister Marta sat on a stool, her newborn daughter nestled against her shoulder, patting the bairn's tiny back in a gentle rhythm.

"Marta?" Sheona's voice cracked. "What are you doing here?"

Her sister looked up, her brown eyes warm despite the exhaustion written in every line of her face. "Trying to get her to sleep. I think she likes to listen to the water lapping against the shore. Rowan is with his father, so I thought I would try this spot. It's peaceful here." Then her gaze sharpened, taking in Sheona's face. "What's wrong?"

The kindness in her voice shattered what little control Sheona had left. She burst into tears—ugly, gasping sobs that she'd been holding back for what felt like years.

"Da," she managed between gulps of air. "He's having a fit. He went to Clan MacVey and told Lennox he was going to announce the betrothal that his father agreed to."

Marta's eyes went wide. "What betrothal, Sheona?"

"Da claims Douglas MacVey promised that Taskill would marry me." The words tasted bitter. "Can you believe it?"

"Oh, Sheona." Marta's expression melted into sympathy. "Sit down, love. I'm sure Lennox told him nay. Da is getting up in his years—"

"I know, but he's so mean now." The words came out small, childlike. Because that's what she felt like—a small child who'd lost her father and didn't know how to get him back. "He was going to hit me. Marta, he raised his hand to me. Sloan and Lennox stopped him, but he would have—"

"What?" Marta's voice went hard. "He tried to strike you?"

Sheona nodded, hugging herself against the cold. Or maybe against the memory of her father's rage-twisted face. "I don't understand what's happening. It's like he's not himself anymore. Not since Mama..."

The door banged open. Their father stormed out, saw them, and opened his mouth to bellow—

"Don't you dare wake this sleeping bairn, Da," Marta hissed, somehow managing to sound like a protective wildcat while barely raising her voice. "Or I'll wake you up tonight to walk her. Do you hear me? Take your loud mouth away from here."

Their father actually retreated, hands raised in surrender. "Calm down, Marta."

"I will not calm down. How dare you pull this now?" She stood, cradling the baby protectively, and thrust the sleeping bundle into Sheona's arms. "You'll follow me back inside. If Mama were still here, she'd never allow this to happen."

To Sheona's amazement, their father did what Marta said. Meek as a lamb, he followed her sister back into the keep.

Sheona settled onto the stool, arranging wee Margret Ailis in her arms. The baby sighed in her sleep, one tiny fist escaping the plaid wrapping to flex against Sheona's chest.

"Don't you worry, wee one," Sheona whispered, her throat tight. "Your mama will protect you from the ornery man. And so will I."

She pressed her cheek against the baby's impossibly soft skin, breathing in that sweet newborn scent that smelled of milk and hope and new beginnings.

Would Sheona ever have her own? She'd dreamed of it once—a wee lass with copper hair and bright blue eyes, like her Da. A boy with Taskill's smile, his laugh, his gentle strength.

Impossible dreams. Foolish dreams.

The baby's tiny hand found Sheona's finger and gripped tight, the simple gesture somehow grounding. Life went on. Hearts broke and healed and broke again, and life just... went on.

"I loved him, you know," she whispered to the sleeping bairn. "He could have been your uncle Taskill. Loved him since I was old enough to know what loving meant. But he doesn't want me. Mayhap he never did."

The wind carried her words away, out over the sea, where all the broken dreams went to die.

She'd been nine when she first realized Taskill MacVey was special. Not just another boy to play with, but someone who made the world brighter. Who understood her in a way no one else did. Who never made fun of her foolish questions and taught her to skip stones and never once told her she should act more like a lady.

At fourteen, she'd understood she loved him. Real love, the kind the bards sang about. The kind that made her heart race when he smiled at her. The kind that made her imagine a future— marriage, children, growing old together.

At fourteen, she'd lost him. One day at the

water's edge, one scolding from her mother, and everything had changed. He'd looked at her like a stranger. Walked away without a backward glance.

She'd waited five years for him to come back.

He never did.

And now, hearing it spoken aloud—*he's not interested*—that was somehow worse than the silence. Worse than the distance. Because there was no ambiguity anymore. No room for hope.

He didn't want her. Had never wanted her. And now everyone knew it.

A tear splashed onto baby Margret's blanket. Then another. Sheona let them fall, too exhausted to hold them back anymore.

She'd never marry. That much was clear. Because Taskill MacVey was the only man she'd ever love, and he'd made it abundantly clear that the feeling wasn't mutual.

So be it.

She'd rather spend her life alone than settle for someone who wasn't him. Even if it meant watching from a distance as he eventually married someone else. Even if it meant dying an old maid with nothing but memories of what might have been.

And after what she'd found out about married life, she had to admit that it was probably for the best. She had no desire for that life. Even with Taskill.

Some losses you never recovered from.

Some wounds never healed.

The baby stirred in her arms, making soft mewling sounds. Sheona rocked gently, humming an old lullaby their mother used to sing. The one about the selkie who loved a mortal man but could never stay on land.

Another story about impossible love.

Another reminder that some things were never meant to be.

"I'll be all right," she whispered to the baby, to herself, to the wind. "I'll survive this. I always do."

But even as she said it, she wasn't sure she believed it.

Because surviving wasn't the same as living.

And she'd been merely surviving for five long years.

CHAPTER THREE

SLOAN

SLOAN ENTERED THE solar after he heard Marta yelling at his father. Poor Marta functioned on little sleep these days. Gideon came up behind Sloan and said, "I'm getting her out of there."

"Great idea, Gideon. I'll talk to Da."

Gideon set his hands on his wife's shoulders and slowly turned her away. "Your brother needs to talk to your sire, love."

"You hear me, Da. Be nice to Sheona." She gave him one last glare before heading out of the solar while Sloan came in, kissing the top of her head as he passed his sister. Then he closed the door behind him.

"Sit down, Da."

"I was chieftain first, so don't give me orders, son." His father was still all riled up over something and he wouldn't leave until he found out what had him so upset.

"It's not meant as an order. I can see how upset you are. I think you'd feel better if you were sitting down. Are your hips bothering you more?" His father often complained about his hips, sometimes his knees, and sometimes just because he missed his wife.

"Nay, not my hips." He finally yanked a chair to a different spot and sat down.

"Then what? You're upset about something."

His father leaned over and set his elbows on his knees, his hands rubbing his face. He'd give the man the time to gather his thoughts, but something was bothering him.

After a long pause, his father said, "All right. I'll tell you because you're the chieftain and you should know."

"I'm listening." Sloan leaned back and folded his hands in his lap.

"I was in the stables brushing my horse down the other day when I heard three men laughing about something. I moved closer and overheard one of them bragging about taking someone's maidenhead."

"That happens, Da. I'll take care of it for you. Who was it?"

"Nay, it doesn't happen," his father shouted, jumping out of his chair. "Not to my daughter."

That got Sloan's attention. "They were speaking of Sheona?"

"He was. I heard him say he was going to be the one who took it. But by the time I rounded the corner, they'd disappeared. I think I cursed rather loudly, and they disappeared. I want to kill him with my bare hands."

"I'll do it for you, Da," he said, keeping his

voice level. He didn't wish to get his father any more excited. "Just give me a name."

His father closed his eyes and cursed, "Shite. I don't know. My ears aren't what they used to be, Sloan. No matter how hard I try, I cannot identify the voice and it's killing me. I couldn't sleep last night, trying to think of every guard and their voice. I couldn't decide."

"So you thought it best to force a marriage on Sheona?"

"Aye, before she loses it. If she doesn't have it anymore, they won't talk about her. Don't you see? If they take her maidenhead, no one will have her. I have to stop it from happening." He leaned forward, the misting in his eyes clouding his vision.

Sloan sighed. "I do see, Da. But I don't think your solution is fair to Sheona."

"She doesn't need to choose her husband. I didn't pick Ailis. And Taskill is a fine man. He lives on the isle. Why not Taskill?"

"Da, will you let me handle this? I'll talk to the guards I trust and see if I can't find out who it is."

"And lock her up, Sloan."

"Nay, I'm not locking my sister up, Da. Stop it."

"If you don't, I will."

"If you do, I'll lock you up, Da."

"Hellfire, nay, you won't."

He left, slamming the door behind him. Sloan had to set Ingelram on him, or he'd get in trouble for sure.

CHAPTER FOUR

TASKILL

———————

TASKILL PACED AT the top of the wall, waiting for his brother to return. Jasper said, "You're pacing like an old maid, T. Let it go. Lennox won't marry you off to someone you don't approve of."

The sound he hated to hear caught him. His mother. "Taskill, is Lennox back from visiting that old bird yet?" She wore her mantle this time, the rich red woolen garment wrapped tightly around her.

"Nay, Mama."

"Come and get me when he returns. No point in him repeating himself."

Meg flew up the staircase to the top of the curtain wall. "I'll go tell her when he returns, Taskill. Don't worry. I'll handle her."

"My thanks, Meg. What did I do without you? I lost Eva, but I gained you, thankfully." He glanced at Meg, wondering why she looked as though she had eaten a mouse. "What?"

She hopped from one foot to the other, then

glanced from Jasper to Taskill. "You don't see it, Taskill?"

"See what?" Taskill asked, confused.

Jasper grinned. "I surely noticed earlier." The man who was second to the laird when Taskill was busy had an expression on his face that appeared as if he carried the secret to the sea tides.

"Noticed what?" Taskill felt completely ignorant now. What had those two seen that he hadn't? "Tell me. I'm too worried about being forced to marry on the morrow to see clearly."

Jasper nodded to Meg, who chuckled and whispered, "Your mother and Dermot."

"Oh, they do love to argue. I saw that. Just like when Eva and Sloan were the issue. Mama loves to put him in his place."

Jasper tipped his head back and laughed. "Oh, I think she'd have loved to put him exactly in his place. And the place would be underneath her. I think she would love to be on top."

"What?" Taskill couldn't believe what he'd heard. "Mama and Dermot?" He jerked his head back and forth between the two grinning faces.

Meg let out a giggle that didn't stop, and Jasper guffawed more than he'd ever seen him. "Those two? You think?" Taskill couldn't have been more shocked.

"Oh, the tension in the air when those two go at it is powerful. Dermot would love to throw her down in a pile of hay and mount her like a Grant stallion takes its mare ..." Jasper's sides shook from his laughter.

"Nay, nay, nay!" Taskill yelled. "That's my mother you are talking about." He covered his ears and said, "I'll never believe it. You are both daft."

"She's a woman, Taskill," Meg said.

"I don't care. Never, ever say that again. Never." The very idea nearly made him spew over the edge of the wall.

Jasper pointed, noticing Lennox and his well-known gallop coming down the path toward them. "There he is."

"Thank the Lord above. Does he look pleased or pished?" Taskill asked.

"Taskill," Meg asked. "Before he gets here, I have to ask. Why aren't you married? I know your brother was fussy, but you don't seem to be."

Jasper choked on the sip of water he'd just taken from his skin. "I'm going down to get Lennox's horse."

Taskill knew why Jasper ran. Because no one understood him—Taskill had always been referred to as the more handsome of the two brothers. And true, he was five and twenty and should be married or at the least, betrothed. But he'd had no urge to do so. Oh, he'd been with a few, and many had tried to talk him into marriage.

But something held him back.

Some liked to call him a big flirt, but he didn't feel that way. He never pursued a lass unless she came to him first. Fear of rejection caused that. He couldn't help it if he was friendly and happy most of the time. He kept his hair thick, and it turned quite golden in the summer, something he hated to cut. So, he let the loose waves grow, and women loved it.

But lately, he tired of it all. The lasses were pretty, but they all seemed to blend into the same person. They asked the same questions, thought the same way.

Where would they live if they married? Would he take her to Edinburgh for her gowns? Could she have a maid to tend to her needs? Could she choose the menu?

It was as if they all dreamed of being married to a chieftain, but they weren't interested in Lennox. They'd been like that before Lennox met Meg, so nothing had changed much.

Lennox was serious, and his responsibilities made him short at times. Meg had been the best thing that had ever happened to him. Taskill would love to find his perfect match in the same way his brother had. It was like a bolt of lightning came down from the sky and struck Lennox in the heart when Meg arrived.

Was there such a lass out there for him?

As Lennox's second-in-command, Taskill had plenty of responsibilities. And he adored bairns. In fact, he couldn't wait to see the first child born to Lennox and Meg. Or to Eva and Sloan.

But Taskill was unlikely to have any. He didn't think he could do the right thing by any lass. There was something inside him, something that ate away at him, that said he'd never be a good husband.

And he wouldn't do that to any lass. If he couldn't love them with all his heart, be completely devoted to his wife and his family, then he couldn't stand in a chapel and say the vows.

He couldn't marry someone like Sheona unless he could give her his full attention. She deserved that much. They'd played together as youngsters, and he'd always admired Sheona because she never acted like a girl. She swam and fished and rode on horseback when her father wasn't around. She loved obstacle courses, and he heard her ask Sloan once if he'd teach her how to throw a dagger.

But Sloan had denied her. Sheona was unlike any of the lasses who fawned over Taskill, begging him to court one lass or another. She was quite unique and he had always admired her for that.

But he still couldn't marry her.

There was a time when they were younger that Taskill had thought he and Sheona would make a fine couple, though she was nearly six summers younger than he was. But there had been times when he, Lennox, and Sloan had played together, pulling the three lasses in to join them, ignoring the age difference. Lennox had been the eldest at ten and six, Taskill, ten and four, Sloan a summer and a half younger. Then Sheona had been nearly nine. Of course, the lasses always played the enemy and lost to the stronger clan that the lads represented, but it had inspired a feeling in Taskill he hadn't had before.

He'd begun to feel like Sheona's protector. Every time her brother or sister ordered her about or criticized her, Taskill found himself standing up for her. Lennox had often teased him about it, but Sheona was brighter than anyone gave her credit for.

But his favorite characteristic of Sheona had been that she had no fear of anything they asked her to do. Eva and Marta would never play in the mud or touch a frog or a fish. Sheona didn't mind any of it.

So, when they'd reached the point of choosing partners, Taskill had chosen Sheona first. Lennox always worked with Marta while Sloan matched with Eva. Taskill's favorite activities had been racing across the meadow on their strongest horses and preparing obstacle courses. But then everything changed. Eva and Marta didn't wish to play with the lads any longer, so Sheona had to give up the same.

They'd all continued to swim together until Sheona had developed. Then her mother stopped everything. He'd thought that odd because no one had told Eva or Marta they couldn't join the lads, but Sheona had grown breasts at a young age.

And her mother had ended all swimming with the boys.

Staying apart hadn't set kindly with Taskill. He didn't find the separation the least bit respectful. He'd grown fond of Sheona, even though there were nearly six summers between them.

But he got over it once the lasses had begun to flirt with him. And flirt they did. More than he wanted, if the truth were known. Now he had a reputation that he'd never desired or deserved.

Lennox entered through the gates, so Taskill wiped the sweat from his hands and proceeded down the steps to determine if he was betrothed. Oh, he liked Sheona well enough. She certainly was a beauty and smart too. But he couldn't do it to her. He'd not marry her. She deserved a man who would be faithful, loyal, and one who loved her.

He liked Sheona, but that was it.

If he were forced, he'd leave the isle rather than force himself on the poor lass. It just wasn't fair.

With that decision made, he moved to learn his fate. "Well?"

Lennox pulled him into the stables to the back stall. "Lads, do not let anyone near this section. Even my mother."

"Aye, Chief."

Taskill followed his brother through the passageway between the stalls, the horses nickering along the way, but it wasn't until the very end when Lennox turned around and said, "I calmed him for now, refused him, but he'll not agree for long. Either you have to find a lass or Sheona needs to find a husband, because he's angrier than an otter protecting its cubs. He'll be back for you in less than a sennight, if I were to guess."

"Shite."

"Lennox, I need to hear all of it." His mother came down the passageway toward them.

Lennox was about to yell at the stable lads, but Taskill stilled him by placing his hand on his brother's shoulder. "Do you think they could stop her? They're good lads."

Lennox grumbled but agreed. Meg came along behind their mother, hiding a smirk.

The woman waited until she was close, then barked, "If he won't listen to you, then I'll go. That ornery bastard is not going to order my sons around. Douglas made no such agreement. I knew everything they discussed, every plan he and Dermot made together."

Taskill knew that wasn't true, though his mother liked to think she knew everything their father did. Men kept secrets.

He knew it better than anyone.

"Mama, I've calmed him down for now. Sloan will talk to him. I don't want you to go there. Leave it be for now, though I just warned Taskill that Dermot will probably return in a sennight."

His mother narrowed her gaze at her youngest son. "Then Taskill should find himself a wife. It's about time. I'd like to see all three of you married with bairns before I pass on. Have you someone in mind, Taskill?"

"Nay, Mama. No one at all."

"What think you of Sheona?" she asked warily.

"Nay."

"Why not? I mean, I don't think you should simply because Dermot wishes for it, but she is a lovely lass and she's still unmarried," his mother suggested.

"We were friends for so long, playmates, that it just doesn't seem right, Mama. I don't look at her that way."

"Who do you look at that way?" she asked, clearly doubting his words.

"I don't want—I mean, I wouldn't do that to
her." What exactly was he trying to say, anyway?
He could not describe what weighed heavy like
a rock in his gut.

"What the hell does that mean?" Lennox asked.

Meg said, "You would make a lovely couple,
but if she's not right for you, just say so, Taskill.
No need to explain."

"She's not right for me," he said, letting out a
breath.

"Then who is?" his mother asked, her arms
now crossed the way she crossed them when you
didn't dare cross *her.*

"No one. There is no one right for me. And I
cannot explain it."

Taskill didn't understand it himself, so how
could he possibly explain it to someone else? He
wasn't right for anyone.

They all left him alone, but he couldn't handle
the guilt raging through him. He knew exactly
how it all had looked to Sheona. She'd been
humiliated by everyone for one reason.

He'd rejected her in front of the entire MacVey
Clan.

He mounted his horse and headed out, not
knowing exactly where he'd go, but he rode
toward the sea. A short time later, he found
himself outside Clan Rankin.

Sloan was at the gates, but Dermot was not
anywhere to be seen. "Sloan, may I speak with
Sheona, please?"

"Are you sure you wish to see her after all that
happened?"

"I owe her an apology, and I'd like to do it face-to-face. Please."

Sloan said, "Come in. I'll bring her to my solar. I'll leave you two alone, but I'll be in the hall listening."

"And your sire?"

"I'll keep him away."

"My thanks," he said, following Sloan inside, wiping the sweat from his hands onto his trews. The lass did the strangest things to him.

He paced, but he didn't have to wait for long. She entered, her eyes red, but no visible tears. Even upset, she was the most beautiful woman he'd ever seen. Sloan closed the door behind her.

"Sheona, I came to apologize. I'm sorry everything happened the way it did. I didn't mean to embarrass you, but I had no idea your father would do what he did."

"Nor did I. I know it's not your fault that it happened the way it did, but…"

"But what?" He stepped closer, a mistake because he took in her scent, the one he called the gift of the pines with a touch of lavender. His Sheona.

"Tell me the truth, Taskill," Sheona's voice cracked. "Why did the denial come so easily to you? We were such good friends for so long. Until that day in the sound. We'd always spent so much time together and it just ended."

"Sheona, you deserve someone better than me. You'll find someone and live a wonderful life."

She put her hand up to stop him. "Taskill. Stop hiding behind excuses—"

"I'm not hiding behind excuses." He cursed.
"I'm protecting you!"

"From what?"

"From me!" The words tore out of him. "From
what I am. From what I'll become." She stepped
closer, her eyes fierce.

"You're not making sense."

"I'm my father's son, Sheona." His voice
dropped to barely a whisper. "In every way."

"Your father was a good man—"

"No." The word came out harsh. "He wasn't.
To everyone else, aye, he was the perfect chieftain,
the devoted husband. But I saw the truth. The day
we stopped swimming, the morning before—I
learned something about him that I've never
shared with anyone, but he was not the man
everyone thinks he was. I caught him in a lie."
Sheona's face went white. "And do you know
what he said after that? He said, 'This changes
nothing. You'll tell no one.' I haven't been the
same since then."

"Taskill—"

"I have his blood, Sheona. His weakness. Every
day I fight it, but what if I can't? What if I marry
you and then—" His voice broke. "I'd rather cut
out my own heart out than hurt you. I'd rather
die alone than become the man who destroys
you with lies."

Sheona fell into a chair, her shoulders slumped.
"You are not your father, but you've made your
wishes clear. My thanks for taking the time to let
me know. Sloan will see you out."

His heart was totally ripped in half now.

CHAPTER FIVE

SHEONA

~~~

SHEONA HADN'T MOVED inside yet from the parapets after Taskill had left. True, it was getting chilly, but she didn't mind. She knew she was in a bind. A true bind that she had no way of getting out of if she knew her sire well enough.

She'd escaped everyone's mind for long enough, and in that, she'd been fortunate. They'd lost their dear mother, Ailis, over a year ago. Her father still hadn't adjusted to her loss because Ailis had done so much for their clan.

Then Lennox fell in love with Meg, and Sloan married Eva. Her father had been so involved with Sloan and Eva. Then he'd had to deal with losing his son, something Sheona still didn't think he was over, even though he'd declared that he no longer had a son named Rinaldo. He'd denied him, put a blade in his own son's heart, and was so upset, no one was allowed to mention her dead brother's name. Dermot had disinherited his own son.

Then there was Marta and Gideon's loss of two bairns in the past couple of years. Everyone had taken it hard because Marta had suffered so. And when she'd finally kept the last pregnancy for so long, everyone had been on tiptoes praying the bairn would survive.

And Margret Ailis did survive. Like a wee warrior, she'd been born with a cry that had echoed to the rafters in the middle of the night, and everyone had cheered. Marta had named her after their dear mother, and their father had cried for an entire day.

Then there was the constant attacks on the different clans on Mull and the addition of the Granthams at Duart Castle. The isle had been in such turmoil with the assault on the different clans, the missing bairns, that they'd had to gather together to fight off the evil one named Kelvan.

But they had, and everything had returned to a usual pace. Except her father had to have something to focus on.

And Sheona was the something he'd chosen.

Damn it all to hell and up to the tip of Ben Buie.

Now everything had quieted down, and winter was nearly upon them. The cold had come along, with the snowflakes due to be here soon. Yuletide would be here before they knew it. Sloan and Eva were ecstatically happy, as were Gideon and Marta, and Lennox and Meg.

That left all the attention on Sheona, something she'd dreaded. She wouldn't tell anyone the truth—that the thought of mating with a man made her ill. So she had to come up with a good reason to stay single.

She appreciated that Taskill had come to explain his reasons, even though they were foolish. But actually, he'd given her another reason not to marry. She couldn't imagine being in love and finding out your husband was with another. That confirmed everything.

She would not marry anyone.

The door opened, and she'd expected to see Marta or Eva, but instead, her father sauntered across the parapets, finding a stool to set beside hers.

"Greetings to you, lass."

"Da." Sheona fumbled with the fur she had across her lap, something to keep her hands busy.

"Lass, I apologize for yelling so at you. But you know how I feel about chieftains' business."

"Nay, I don't. Please tell me why I shouldn't be involved when you're discussing my life. This wasn't some minor issue, Papa. You wished to choose someone without asking me. Why?"

"Och, because that's the way it's always been done. We made arrangements that would guarantee our allies for years to come. It's the way of the Highlands. You know it, lass."

"Da, do you really think MacVeys would ever turn against us? Especially when Sloan is married to Eva?"

He sighed. "Nay, but I'm not going to be around forever, Sheona. I'd like to see you happily married with bairns of your own."

She considered her words carefully before saying what was on her mind, trying to offer the best explanation her father would accept. "But what if I don't think I'm right for marriage?" She had no desire to marry anyone else but Taskill, and since he wasn't willing to marry her, then her choice was no marriage at all, for more than one reason.

"Oh, horse bollocks. Every lass should be married. Why would you wish to spend your life alone? I've been lost without my Ailis, and you know it."

"I just don't think I would like married life." She dropped her gaze, hoping her sire wouldn't see the fear in her eyes. After all, she knew what would happen when one got married. She was fully aware of maidenheads and how they got ripped out of one's insides, making a lass bleed and cry in pain.

Scream in pain.

Nay. Not for her. Why would she want that forced on her just to have a bairn? And the pain of childbirth? She'd heard Marta and decided that wasn't for her either.

Her mind was made up. She would never marry.

"Well, if you're going to be that stubborn about it, then your choices are limited, lass. You have to become a nun." He stood up, not waiting to hear her response, something that surprised her.

She could have guessed a hundred different responses, but none of them would have come close to this. "A nun? You mean live in a kirk?"

"Aye, if you cannot be married with a man, then you must devote your life to the Lord. Those are your choices, Sheona. I'll not allow anything else. A spinster's life is no life for one of my girls. Find a husband or become a nun. You think on it and let me know by the morrow." He got up to take his leave and headed to the staircase.

"Da, wait." She stood, waiting for him to turn around because she wished to see his expression.

It took him a while, but he finally turned back to her. "What is it?"

"You wish to get rid of me? Send me off to the nunnery? Just because I don't wish to marry Taskill MacVey?"

"Nay. I wish for you to marry and have bairns. Live on the isle. The only one is Taskill. I don't think Brian MacQuarie is right for you, so its MacVey or the nunnery."

"What about the Granthams? There are others. Broc MacNicol is betrothed to Merryn MacClane."

"Fine. You find a Grant who will marry you and I'll agree. None of those Ramsays. Anyone with Logan Ramsay blood in them is no good. I don't want my granddaughters acting like Gwyneth Ramsay either. You've got one sennight. I'll contact the nunnery, just in case that's your choice."

Sheona fell back onto her stool after her sire left. She had three choices—a nunnery, Taskill, or find a Grant to marry. Her life was falling apart.

She had to find Marta and see what she thought.

Marta would surely be in her chamber feeding

wee Margret. It was nearly the bairn's bedtime, though the wee lass did not sleep through the night yet.

She knocked on Marta's door. "May I come in to chat with you, Marta?"

"Of course," she called out.

Sheona peeked her head around the corner.

"Come in, Sheona. Gideon is with Sloan and Da, checking the curtain wall. Some area that needs repairing. I'm glad Gideon is familiar with Da's ways. Anything upsets Papa these days, including you, poor sister." Margret suckled quietly while Marta sipped on some wine.

"I surely have upset him. I just came from a conversation with Da, and I wish to hear your thoughts."

"Oh dear. I can tell it was not a pleasant conversation, was it?"

Sheona shook her head, fighting her tears. "Nay. Not good at all." She lifted her gaze to the ceiling, hoping her tears would stay at bay. "He said I must marry."

"Well, that's not so bad. So, he's not forcing you to marry Taskill? I thought that would please you."

"He said I could marry someone else on the isle, but who is there? I don't care much for Brian MacQuarie, so he said my only other choice was a Grant. He said marrying a Ramsay wasn't allowed. And I don't know any Grants other than Broc, and he's pledged to Merryn MacClane now. Do you know any other Grant men of age? Nice ones?" Not that it mattered to her. It wasn't that she was set against Taskill as she was set against any man at all.

Marta said, "Let me think. Grant men. So, Connor is a Grant, and his daughter is Dyna. Doesn't she have a sister and two brothers? She has a sister Astra, and a younger brother. I think there's a blond lad who's older. Hagen, I think? He has those blue eyes that see right through you. Like Dyna and her mother. Isn't it fun to see how their bairns all came out? Sela is white-haired, blue-eyed, and Connor has the darkest hair ever with blue eyes. And Dyna is like her mother. And the youngest one, Morgan, looks like Connor. But Hagen is fair-haired, not white-haired, but golden. They say Connor's mother was golden-haired. Mayhap you should consider Hagen."

"I'll speak with Dyna when we go. But how do I go ask her? Wouldn't it seem unusual to approach and inquire about her brother's marital status?"

"I know. I heard they are having a festival on the morrow. A big one. We can go. I'll go with you. Dyna told me once they all have brothers when I asked about Broc. She said Broc has two brothers and two sisters. And Alaric has a brother, and he is handsome, is he not? I met him once. His name is Jowell, I think. I wonder if he's here. You could have your pick. I'll help you." She reached over and patted Sheona's hands.

Sheona couldn't fathom walking into Clan Grantham and asking Dyna if there was an available bachelor. What a ridiculous thought.

"Where is the nearest nunnery? Mayhap I should consider becoming a nun."

"A nunnery? There aren't any on the isle. There's one on Iona near the abbey. They say it's lovely. Isn't that where Magni stayed with his parents? And I think that's where Simone and Artan live too, though Artan goes back and forth because he's Quade's second. I would bet that Simone comes to MacQuarie Castle soon. I heard she loves the beaches and likes to lie in the nude in the sun, and no one sees her …" Marta giggled, then looked at her sister.

Sheona couldn't stop the tears from falling. Where did she belong?

"Sheona, you might enjoy visiting the nunnery, talking to some of the nuns. But I don't see you as a nun. You don't pray often, do you?"

Sheona shook her head. "Mama did, but I do not view the church in the same way she did."

"I don't either. I pray, but not as often as I should. Please tell me more about Taskill and marriage. Why is it you don't wish to marry? Is it Taskill or any man? And if so, why?"

"I don't think I'm a good match with Taskill."

"But I remember you having fun with him when you were younger. He would tease you and chase you and toss you in the sound like you were a feather. And you paired up for the obstacle courses. You always laughed with him, didn't you?"

"I did, but we were kids. He also rejected me. He told Da he wouldn't marry me, so why would

I wish to pursue him? I don't know him at all now. All I know is what I hear about him …"

Marta lifted Margret and held her against her shoulder, patting her back to try to get her to burp. "You mean that he is a flirt? I don't think he is. Taskill is one of those people who loves life. He enjoys talking with everyone. Just because he jests with a lass or teases her doesn't mean he's bedding her. I don't know …" Margret fussed after letting out a loud belch, one that made Sheona giggle, but then the lassie began to whimper. "I have more, lassie. Calm down." Then she tried to put her back to the breast.

While Marta fussed with her daughter, Sheona considered something she never had before. Perhaps she should disclose her reason for rejecting marriage; the notion unsettled her to the point of dizziness. Was it time to tell her sister the truth?

Why she knew she could never marry.

Explain what had happened that taught her so much.

Why no Grant—Hagen or Jowell—would suit her. She would die of embarrassment before she'd tell her sire, but Marta would listen and understand. Wouldn't she?

Margret cried and swung her wee fists. "She just won't latch on this side. I tell her she gets too impatient and then it doesn't work." The bairn hollered louder and Marta got more upset and the babe cried harder and …

"I'll come back later, Marta."

She couldn't tell anyone the truth, so Sheona left.

She was destined to become a nun.

CHAPTER SIX

TASKILL

———— ❧ ————

"I HEAR YOU'RE GETTING married, Taskill," one of the serving maids teased when he came in to grab a loaf of bread to take to the men at the gates.

Taskill sauntered over to the pretty maid. "And where did you hear that, Florie?"

Jasper entered behind him for an ale. "What say you, T?" Then he laughed.

That was Jasper's latest entertainment, asking Taskill if he would marry this one or that one. Didn't matter if they were married, a serving maid, or a wench who traveled the road.

"Nay, Jasper," he shouted, refusing to look at the man.

Florie shrugged her shoulders and giggled. "I don't remember. Is it true?" Her eyes were wide as saucers as she waited for his answer.

"I'm sorry to tell you that it's not true. I have not chosen a bride yet."

"Oh, surely you have your eye on someone," she whispered, fanning her eyelashes just so. "Who would you choose?"

Taskill noticed she gave him her best smile, stuck her chest out, then settled her hands on her curvaceous hips. He'd said nothing to encourage her, yet here she was, aiming to strike him with her feminine wiles. "I don't have anyone in mind. Now about that bread?"

"But would you ever marry a serving lass?" The innocent look on her face nearly made him jest with her, but he decided it was time to stop his teasing.

"I would marry the one who stole my heart. That's all I can say."

"But what would it take …"

"Florie!" His mother's voice carried from the balcony. The serving lass jumped and ran back into the kitchens.

Rut MacVey's voice boomed from the staircase. "Honestly, Taskill. If you would not encourage them, it would be easier to chastise them. Leave them be."

Taskill took the bread handed to him before Florie hurried away, then he spun around. "Mama, did you overhear the entire conversation? Because I'd like to know how I encouraged her. You all think I like to spend my time basking in the admiration of female company, but sometimes I'm just answering questions and trying not to hurt someone's feelings."

His mother approached and her gaze went from his toes to his head before she sighed. "I suppose you cannot help it if you look like your mother. You are a fine specimen of manhood, Taskill, and the lasses are not blind. It certainly is not entirely your fault. I know that to be the truth. They do often fall at your feet."

"Not quite, Mama, but they do ramble on and wiggle quite a bit."

"The lads fell at my feet, so I understand your problem. Now, what to do about Sheona."

Taskill groaned and hung his head. "Mama, truly? Now?"

"Taskill, inside Lennox's solar. Now." She pointed and while Taskill let out a loud groan, he followed her inside.

"What, Mama? I thought this entire situation was over. I'm not marrying Sheona." At least, he thought it had come to an end.

"Apparently, you don't know that old coot the way I do. He's not going to let this go until Sheona is married. Now, you have two choices. You marry her, or you find someone who will marry her willingly."

"But she's not ready to marry either. And she should choose her own husband." When would this torture end? All because of this foolish secret he kept inside. He reached for the rock on his brother's desk and tossed it back and forth from one hand to the other.

"What the hell is in your head?"

"What?" Damn, but his mother was good. Except most of the time, she had her energy focused on Lennox and Eva. She'd always ignored the one in the middle, but now, all of a sudden, she couldn't take her focus away from Taskill. He had to fix this somehow.

"You're hiding something."

"What?" He jumped up from his chair and paced in a circle.

"Oh, that's not an admission of guilt at all, Taskill. Out with it. What is holding you back?"

"Naught. I'm just upset by all this." He took his seat again and set the rock back on his brother's desk. Hellfire, but no one had ever noticed what he did most of the time. Eva had always been Da's wee lassie and Lennox had been heir to the chief.

No one had ever cared what he did all day.

This change since his siblings had married did not suit him one bit. He had to take the attention away from himself. "All right, let's find another for Sheona. Who would we suggest? I'm willing to talk with anyone. Sheona is a beautiful lass. She's smart, and Eva said she's doing well learning axe throwing. She'd make someone a fine wife. Why, her bairns would be lovely."

"Keep going. Mayhap you'll convince yourself. I couldn't have said it better myself."

"She's not for me, Mama!"

His mother's hands rose as a sign of her giving up. "I'll accept that. Let's move on, then. There is a festival at Duart Castle this eve. I was not planning to attend, but Lennox and Eva are going, so I think we should go too. We'll move through the crowd and see who is available. Have you any ideas? Who are all the unmarried men on the isle? And when you think on it, make sure you consider how fussy the bastard Dermot is going to be." She twirled a loose hair as she stared at the wall over Taskill's head.

"Mama. Since when do you curse like a Norseman?"

"Since Eva moved to Rankin land."

He chuckled over that comment, but then considered all the men on the isle. "There's Brian MacQuarie. And there's also Broc MacNicol."

"Broc is betrothed to Merryn."

"Not officially. They handfasted, I think."

"He's not a choice. But Brian is definitely a reasonable candidate. Keep going."

He leaned back in his chair and steepled his fingers. This was important. "Brian would be an excellent candidate. He's always said he wanted bairns."

"Fine. Speak with him this eve. Who else?"

"Tristan MacClane."

His mother scowled. "I suppose. He's a busy man. I doubt he's ready to commit to anyone yet."

"You don't know that."

"True. Fine. We have Brian and Tristan. Who else?"

A knock interrupted them, and Meg stuck her head in. "May I join you? What's going on with Taskill and Sheona?"

Taskill sighed. "Aye, please join us. I'm running out of names." And he needed someone to support his stance against his mother. Anyone to draw his mother's attention away from him.

"Meg just moved here. How is she going to know anyone, Taskill?" His mother shook her head but waved for Meg to join them.

Meg asked, "What do I not know?"

Taskill explained, "Mama has come up with

the brilliant idea to find another man for Sheona, so that I can be let out of this arrangement. She thinks Dermot won't change his mind, so we are trying to create a list of alternative potential husbands."

His mother stared at the wall. "I'll fix that old goat. He'll not be bossing my bairns around." A quick smirk passed over her face before she covered it, brought her attention back to Taskill, and said, "We need more names. More prospective husbands for Sheona. They shouldn't be too far away. Dermot won't like his daughter going too far away."

"You must know him well, Rut," Meg said with a smile, casting a sideways glance at Taskill. "Who do you have so far?"

Taskill sighed and said, "Brian MacQuarie and Tristan MacClane. That's all. Can you add to the list? We're going to the festival at Duart Castle and hope others will be there this eve. Know you any single Grants or Ramsays?"

"Aye, they'll have to have noble blood. Dermot will insist upon it." Rut pursed her lips and leaned back in her chair.

Meg frowned. "I'm not noble blood."

Rut gave an unladylike snort. "I'm not Dermot Rankin now, am I? I'm much more accepting than he is." His mother lifted her chin a notch, and Taskill had to stop from smiling. Was there something between his mother and Dermot? "Go ahead, Meg. I'm hoping for at least one more."

Meg laughed. "One? There are plenty of Grants and Ramsays."

Taskill had to admit that her answer shocked him. He had no idea, and he'd lived here much longer than Meg had, so how did she know? "Names, please. Any male who is unmarried."

"There's Broc's brother, Paden. And Alaric has a brother named Jowell. He's really cute. And Hagen has that golden-blond hair like a Norse god, all bronze-skinned from the sun. He would be a splendid choice. Oh! And the Ramsays. I heard Connor say his cousin Brigid had two lads who were driving all the lasses daft. One was here. I think they called him Hawk, and he has a brother named Merek. Oh, and Eli's only brother named Errol, but I don't know how old he is."

Taskill and his mother both stared at Meg. He was shocked that Meg spoke the way she did.

"How do you know all these men, my dear?" his mother asked.

"At the battle. There were so many Grants there that I was fascinated. And it's easy to see who goes together. All the blonds go with Dyna, Connor, and Sela. And the handsomest ones go with Alaric. And then Broc's family has the reddish coloring from their father. And Alasdair. It's too bad he didn't have any brothers. He looks just like Connor, who looks just like his father, so they say. And John looks exactly like Alasdair, so they call him a miniature Alex Grant. Long dark hair and fierce looking. With his blue sword, he was unbelievable for his age. I'd not fight him.

And the Ramsays? They say Errol is just like his grandfather Logan."

That made Rut smile. "Oh, we have to introduce him to Sheona. Dermot and Logan. I would enjoy watching those two together."

Taskill asked Meg, "Has Lennox heard you talk like this about all these men?"

The door opened, and Lennox came in. "Aye, he just did. I'm not worried about my wife. She's only trying to help you, Taskill. So, you have a few to pick from. Brian, Tristan, Jowell, Hagen, Paden, Hawk, Merek, Errol. But when do you plan to do this?"

Rut said, "At the Grantham festival this eve. It's supposed to be a large one. They may not all be there, but we'll have some to speak with."

Lennox kissed Meg's cheek and said, "Add two more. Angus MacKinnis's two lads—Emrys and Madoc. His wife is from Wales."

"Are you going, Lennox?" Taskill asked.

His brother snorted, something he didn't do often. "Of course we're going. I wouldn't miss the food. With all those archers, there will be so much pheasant that I'll surely get my fill. And I heard they now have sheep and a few cows too."

Meg giggled. "I love Grantham festivals. You'll see, Taskill. We'll find someone for Sheona. It will be delightful!"

Taskill didn't say what he thought.

If Dermot Rankin showed up, it was destined to be more like a disaster.

CHAPTER SEVEN

SHEONA

———— ❧ ————

SHEONA'S PALMS SWEAT more than they ever had before, but for good reason. Her father had warned her that if she couldn't find an acceptable man to marry this eve that he would be taking her to the Iona nunnery soon.

She did not wish to go to a nunnery.

The group arrived outside the gates of Duart Castle late in the afternoon. Sloan rode with Eva, while Sheona rode next to her father, the familiar guard Clyde with two others behind them for safety reasons. Sloan had brought Ingelram along to keep an eye on their father and his wanderings. She'd overheard Sloan tell Ingelram that if his father became unruly or belligerent that he was to get Sloan immediately and he'd send Dermot home. Sheona prayed her father would keep quiet.

By the looks of the paths coming to the castle, it would be a large festival. Most festivals started when the sun was still up, but there was no promise as to when the festivities would end. There was a line of horses ahead of them.

The ones closest were the MacQuaries; Thane and Tamsin, Brian, and Mora, with two guards. Simone and Artan were ahead of them. And Tristan MacClane approached on the opposite path from the far coast with two men, probably guards who worked for him.

Mora looked back over her shoulder. "Greetings to you, Rankins. Eva, you look so happy. Married life suits you. And Sheona, how is the new bairn of Marta's? And what did she name the wee lassie? Does she sleep at night yet?"

As usual, Sheona knew enough to wait until Mora finished asking all her questions before she answered. It suited her fine because then she could choose which question and conversation to have. "She named her Margret Ailis."

"After your mother? Is that not the sweetest ever? I cannot wait to meet the lass. Brian, will you take me to Rankin land so we can pay our respects to the lass soon? I'll make her something new to wear."

Dermot ignored Mora and shouted, "Brian, are you betrothed yet?"

Brian swung his head around to face Dermot, a slight scowl on his face. "Nay, I'm not. Have you a suggestion? Is there a reason you ask?"

Sheona blushed the shade of the darkest apple in autumn. "Da, please."

"Sheona isn't betrothed yet either. Mayhap you should have a chat with her tonight."

Brian nearly smirked when he looked at Sheona, but she mouthed the word, "Sorry."

"I'll make sure to come and find Sheona later,

Chief." Then he smiled and urged his mount forward since the line had moved along.

That gave Sheona time to turn around and glare at her sire. "Da, could you please not be so obvious? Don't ask them. I'll make a point of talking to them this eve. And promise me you won't follow me around. Sloan, may I please walk around on my own? Or with Mora?"

"Aye, I trust you inside the castle walls, Sheona. Not outside," he said with a smile. "Please enjoy yourself."

"I will. My thanks to you."

"But in order for the lass to do that, Da, you have to leave her be. You'll not be bothering Sheona this eve. We'll chat on the morrow," Sloan said.

Their father didn't look at her brother but stared straight ahead. Sheona noticed he'd dressed up in his finest leine and plaid this eve, even trimmed his beard and combed his hair. Her father had been a handsome man in his day. "Fine. I'll find my own entertainment."

Sheona wore her favorite gown, the dark blue one with green ribbons that matched the ones in her hair. She wore trews under her gown, though she made sure her sire never saw them. He'd forbidden her long ago to wear them, though she still snuck into them when she could.

Sloan wore his nicer plaid too. Eva was, of course, beautiful and wore a dark purple gown. The two together made a striking couple. "They'll probably need you to check their brew, Da. I'm sure there will be many samples. You know Logan and Connor will have them and so will Drew, if he's still here."

"You're right. And I brought my own wee sample for later."

Sheona sighed with relief. Sloan always knew how to distract their father. After all that had happened with their brother Rinaldo, she had to give Sloan credit. Their father had always favored Rinaldo, but he'd turned out to be a lying, conniving man, and their father had disowned him before killing him with his own sword.

Sheona hated Rinaldo.

She'd always wished to ask Sloan if their father had ever apologized to him over favoring Rinaldo, but she never had the courage.

As they approached the gates, her father moved his horse ahead of theirs, announcing himself at the gate. "Chief Rankin. I'm coming in. I have a new cask of my brew for Logan Ramsay."

Broc waved him inside, standing next to another guard who looked like him, but with lighter hair. "Hagen, help Lady Rankin down and take her horse for her."

The place was busy, but the blond, blue-eyed guard came forward, leading her horse away from the crowd. "Here, I'll take you over here, my lady. Then I'll help you."

"My thanks," she replied, noticing that her father was already inside the keep and Sloan was helping Eva down while chatting with Derric over their earlier hunt.

"I don't recognize you. Who are you related to?" she asked, surprised at her own boldness.

"I'm Hagen. First son to Connor and Sela Grant. Dyna is my sister. And you are Lady Rankin, but I didn't hear your given name."

"Sheona."

"Married to?"

"Not married," she said, amazed at her own shyness. "You?"

"Nay. I'm still looking." He hooked her horse on a post, then helped her down, his hands slipping around her waist as he lifted her as though she weighed no more than a handful of beach sand.

She landed without the least bit of grace, and he grimaced. "Sorry, I'm a bit new at this. There aren't many Grant lasses who would allow me to help them down. If I tried to help my sister, she'd put a boot in my teeth." He wiggled one tooth and said, "She did once, but my tooth recovered."

Sheona laughed, gripping his arm until she steadied herself on the uneven ground. Her gaze locked on his, and the blue in his eyes was so deep that it mesmerized her, the silver flecks dancing in the newly lit torchlights as darkness began to fall. "My thanks to you. You did a fine job, Hagen."

"I hope to see you inside, Sheona Rankin."

She smiled and said, "I would like that."

Eva appeared at her side, "Greetings to you, Hagen. It looks to be a lovely gathering. The night is accommodating."

Hagen said, "It is. At your service, ladies. Anything else I can do for you?"

Sheona shook her head and Eva said, "Not at the moment. Mayhap later."

Sheona pushed her elbow into Eva's side.

"Then I'll take care of your horse. Enjoy the party!"

And Hagen was off.

Eva said, "Sheona, you like him?"

She shrugged. "I guess. As much as anyone, but I hardly know him. However, he is cute."

"True. We'll have to find him later. Come, your brother is hungry."

Sheona said, "Sloan, you don't have to stick next to me all night. I'll make my way around the hall. I know many who I can chat with."

"Fair enough. If you change your mind, we won't be far."

Sheona made her way inside, looking at all the people, hoping to see someone to chat with. The hall looked magnificent with autumn colors everywhere. Red and purple flowers decorated the tables, and boughs with orange and red leaves hung over the hearth. The first thing she did was move over to the hearth to greet Meg, who was chatting with Merryn. But as soon as she turned, she nearly ran into someone.

A man with Shealee on his shoulders nearly knocked her down, but she was caught by another man who came up from behind her. "Paden, do be careful. You nearly knocked this beautiful lass on her sweet … I mean, knocked her down."

Shealee giggled as Paden lifted her, then swung her like he was about to settle her in a tall tree before he set her on the ground. "Go see Mama. I must apologize for my rudeness, lassie."

Sheona said, "Nay, it was my fault. I wasn't

paying attention. I was too busy looking to see who was here."

The other person came from behind, his hands still at her waist, and said, "I saved you from my cousin. He'll knock anyone down. I'm Jowell and this is Paden." He dropped his hands as he moved to one side, knocking his cousin out of the way.

Sheona stared at the two men, her gaze going from one handsome face to the other. What did they feed the lads on Grant land? "And which Grants do you belong to? I'm trying to learn all the names, but there are many of you."

Jowell laughed. "I'm Alaric's brother. Jamie and Gracie are our parents. And this is Paden, brother to Broc, whose parents are Kyla Grant and Finlay MacNicol."

And the two then had their fun with her.

Jowell said, "I'm the best-looking. We often argue between the three of us—me, Hagen, or Paden."

Paden offered, "I'm the one with the bit of red in my hair, like my sire. That makes me unique and thus the most handsome."

Jowell glared at his cousin before he spoke. "But I look almost exactly like Alaric, and our mother Gracie was known as the most beautiful lass in all the land. And my hair is much lighter than Alaric's, more like my mother's golden-white hair."

Hagen came up from behind them. "Do not listen to them, Sheona. I'm the best-looking. My mother Sela had the reputation as the queen of Inverness because of her beauty. And my sire, well, everyone knows he looks just like our grandfather, Alex Grant."

"Is Alex grandfather to all of you?" she asked.

"Aye," the three barked in unison.

She giggled, watching the young lads try to outdo each other.

"He did like me best."

"I was his favorite. Surely you all know that."

"Is that why he always came to me first?"

Sheona was thoroughly entertained by their banter.

"And he thought me the best swordsman."

"Nay, I was the best back then. Connor is my sire, after all."

"But Grandda said my swing was most like his."

What Sheona enjoyed most was that there was no ill will in the banter. It was all done for fun and, if she were to guess, mostly for her entertainment.

Jowell finally turned to her. "Sheona, are you betrothed or married?"

"Nay, she's not. But she's already spoken for because I'm going to take her for a stroll in a few moments," Hagen said. "I already asked her."

"If you're taking her in a *few* moments, then I'm taking her in *one* moment," Jowell declared.

"They're always trying to outdo each other. I'll let them argue it between them." Paden held out his arm. "Then that means we can go right now."

She stared from one face to the next, not knowing what to do, so she said, "I promised Hagen first, I think."

"Too bad, laddies. Off we go." Hagen set his arm around her shoulders.

Sheona glanced over at her father, but he was busy talking about his brew. Eva gave her the wave and Sloan smiled.

So off she went with Hagen, who began talking as soon as they exited the keep. "It's too hot in there with so many people. I was surprised at how large Duart Castle was, and how finely built, but with all the people on the isle, I think they will need to build more. Is your castle as large as this one?"

"Nay, but our hall is large," Sheona said. "I've heard all about your grandsire, but not your grandmama. What was your grandmother's name?"

"Madeline, though she was called Maddie."

"Why is Alexander Grant so well known?"

"Because he was quite a swordsman. It started after he met my grandmother. Her stepbrother abused her, so my grandfather rescued her from him, but her stepbrother had betrothed her to another evil one, so Alexander fought him in front of Grant Castle. Everyone heard about it, and my grandfather was unbelievable, so I've heard many times. Fierce, but always tender with my grandmother."

"Tender?" *Tender* is not a word she would use to describe her father with her mother. Although he treated his wife better than anyone else, he still was not what Sheona would consider tender-hearted.

"The Grants believed differently about many things," he said as he made his way over to a bench under a tree. "My great-grandmother was a healer and so are two of my aunts and several of my cousins now. My great-grandmother believed in two things that she wouldn't allow any argument on. First, keep yourself and your house clean, and second, choose your own spouse. She made my grandfather promise to allow all his bairns to choose their spouses. So here we are. My father believes the same."

Sheona sighed. "I wish my sire believed in that. He's in a sudden rush to get me married."

"You're beautiful, so I'm sure you'll find someone easily."

"Hagen!" someone from the gates bellowed.

"Just a moment," he said, taking Sheona's hand and squeezing it for a second. He got up and headed toward the gates. "What is it, Broc?"

"I need you. The MacQuaries are here."

"I'll be right there as soon as I escort this lovely lass back inside." Then Hagen turned to her. "Sorry. I can return later."

"I would like that." Hagen had definitely given her something to think on. She'd never heard of someone being kind to their wives. Could it be so? Her father hadn't been that kind to her mother. Though he'd never hit her, he was often angry about ridiculous things. Her brother Rinaldo had not been nice with any of his romantic interests. She'd thought at one time it was because he was simple-minded, but he'd proven that to be false.

So, what was her lot in life to be? A mistreated wife who had to jump at everything her husband told her to do, or life as a nun who prayed to God every day? Was a nunnery the only option she had if she didn't wish to become slave to one man, ordered about and treated poorly?

Though watching Sloan and Eva had shown her that things could be better. They truly adored each other and enjoyed each other's company, something she'd never seen in her brother.

Hagen held the door for Sheona, and she stepped inside the hall, only to see her father coming straight for them.

"Did you touch her?" His voice echoed across the entire hall. "You touch her, you marry her!"

Hagen quickly said, "Forgive me. I didn't know I needed to ask permission to take your daughter out for a stroll in the courtyard. There were many others about, Chief. I acted like a gentleman. I'm sure she'll tell you so."

"Da, please don't make a scene. He was verra proper and respectful. It was fine." Sheona kneaded her hands together, praying he would let this go.

Her father moved up to Hagen. "Since I didn't give you permission, it seems you wish to marry her in the morn."

Connor came over and said, "That's my son you are yelling at, Rankin. Care to explain yourself?"

Dermot stood back. "Grant took her out without asking my permission. It's dark. Who knows what he tried to do with my lass? I'll have him in front of a priest by the morrow."

Sloan yelled, "Da, enough!"

Connor moved his son aside and stood toe-to-toe with Dermot. "That's not how we do things on Grant land, Rankin."

"That's how it's done on Rankin land, Grant."

"You're on Grant land now. My rules."

"I'll drag him to the kirk even if you don't like it, Grant. Your son or not, he'll not make a mockery of my daughter."

CHAPTER EIGHT

RUT

———— ❧ ————

RUT MACVEY HAD never been more excited. She'd heard Dermot's bellows from the far end of the crowded hall and made her way over to the battleground as quickly as she could.

She did her best to hide her delight. If the two finest specimens of older men weren't standing in front of her, then the Lord should strike her down right now.

Connor Grant stood with his eyes narrowed, at least a head taller than Dermot, but Dermot was not backing down.

She had to wonder which one she'd rather have sneak into her bed.

Connor, with his long dark waves slightly streaked with gray, carried himself with a dignity that was unmatched in the hall. His broad shoulders were wider than any man here, his chiseled jaw clenched.

Rut had something grinding inside that was nearly out of control. She fanned her face with a book she found nearby.

Dermot stood strong, his gray hair also to his collar with that way of looking messy, but not unruly. His hair had once been the color of chestnuts but was still full and thick, similar to Connor's. The muscles in his upper arm flexed with every sentence, his green eyes set on Connor Grant, and he was not going to back down, even though he had to know that Connor could deliver a knock-out blow with one swing.

Dermot had always been a fine-looking man, but the swagger he had was almost untouchable—not unlike the swagger of Logan Ramsay, the man who commanded attention wherever he went.

Connor's blue eyes widened as he listened to something else Dermot said, but Rut never heard it. She was too busy studying the fine-looking male bodies on display in front of her, imagining them in ways she'd never admit to anyone. She'd apologize to dear Douglas for her thoughts, but he knew how long it had been for her.

And what happened next nearly did her in.

Logan Ramsay came tearing down the stairs, shouting, "What the hell is all the bellowing down here?"

If Rut were the fainting type, she would have dropped to the floor that instant. Logan flew by her, all the maleness dripping from his pores, the scent of the magnificent man hitting her like nothing else had in many years.

There they stood, three big bulls battling over a woman, so close Rut could nearly touch them, and she practically cried tears of joy just to be able to watch them.

And they had an attentive audience. No one in the hall dared speak or move, including the serving lasses who were peeking wide-eyed out of the kitchens.

Dermot yelled, "His son is marrying my daughter, Ramsay. No one asked your thoughts on the matter, so stay out of this. It is not your affair at all. He took advantage of her innocence."

Connor didn't let up either. "By a stroll outside? That doesn't constitute taking advantage. He'll marry his choice, not yours."

"He'll marry her on the morrow as soon as I bring a priest here."

"The hell he will. We don't force marriages on our land. Hagen will choose his own wife."

"Rankin, calm down. You've had too much of your own brew." Logan touched his shoulder, but the man shrugged him off.

"Stay out of this, Ramsay. This is not your concern."

But Logan wouldn't be pushed aside, something else Rut admired in the man. "I thought your daughter was betrothed to another, to MacVey's brother, Taskill. Where the hell is he? MacVey, are you going to claim your bride or what?" Logan's gaze scanned the area, but Taskill was nowhere to be found.

Taskill? Now they were after her son?

That comment gave Rut the gift she needed. She shoved people out of her way and pushed herself between the three stallions to stand up to Dermot. Fortunately, her temper kept her from smiling, though the scent of maleness was nearly too much for her. "Don't you dare make this about my son. Taskill has naught to do with this. This is Dermot being an arse. You can't force people to do your bidding, you wiry old hedgehog. Your poor daughter. I feel sorry for the lass."

"Silence, Rut. No one invited you into this conversation." Dermot's green eyes found hers and sparkled.

The hairs on her neck bristled. "You invited me when you involved my son, who is clearly not here to defend himself. You love to fling accusations around, Rankin, and I'll not stand for it."

"Stay out of this, Rut. This is men's business. Women have no say in this."

And that did it for her. How she hated that ancient, outdated, foolish belief. Women had more value than he would ever guess.

Rut hauled her hand back and slapped Dermot hard in the face, right against his cheek. "I've had enough of your antiquated, narrow-minded thoughts that since I don't have a piece of meat dangling between my legs that I have no brain. My mind is quicker than yours, Dermot. I've known that for a long time, so don't ever tell me to shut up again."

"You hit me." His voice came out in such a low tone that Rut was unsure whether he would retaliate.

She dared him to try.

"Insult me again, and I'll hit you again, you bullheaded ram." The two stared at each other, and a moment later, Sloan reached for his father and pulled him back. "Eva, go find Ingelram for me. You're going home, Da, and you'll apologize to the Grants, both of them."

Lennox took his mother's shoulders, pulling her back. "I think you've done enough, Mother. Time for you to go home too."

"Not until I kick him where he deserves," she said, swinging her leg out at Dermot. "He's had it coming for a long time, Lennox, and I'm going to be the one to set him straight. I'll teach him the true value of a woman. He belongs in a pigsty."

"Nay. I'm taking you home. Meg, I'll be back within the hour. Enjoy yourself." Lennox dragged his mother outside, but she eventually went willingly.

She shook her son's hands from her shoulders. "I'm sorry, Lennox, but that poor girl. Now I know why she doesn't want to marry. I'd rather become a nun to get the hell away from the old goat."

Lennox called for their two horses from the lads, and they waited. "Why? I know you're not thinking straight, but please tell me why you say that."

"Because Dermot will kill her husband, and she'll feel responsible. He's a miserable old man ever since he lost Ailis."

Lennox said, "I can't argue that. But next time, don't slug him, Mama."

"Oh, horse bollocks. It was just a wee slap."

Lennox snorted. "I doubt Dermot looked at it that way."

She chuckled. "But it felt so good."

CHAPTER NINE

DYNA

DYNA CHATTED WITH Avelina and Maeve while they watched the bairns in the bedchamber. She'd decided that with the festival going on, she'd keep her three in one place and guard them herself with Derric's help. Lia and Magni were not coming, and neither was Rowan, so she was hoping to have a quiet night for the bairns. Grant was sitting in his bouncy chair built by his sire, watching the other three play battle on the sea with their animals and carved wooden boats.

Derric stood guard outside the door of the bairns' bedchamber, watching the show below. Dyna could hear Connor and Dermot arguing over something, but she wasn't sure what. Sylvi stopped and moved over to the window, pulling the fur back to peek outside.

"What is it, Sylvi? You're letting all the chilly night air in."

Sylvi shook her head and mumbled, "Mama, there's a storm coming."

Sandor got up and began to run in circles, so she

guessed Jake was chasing him again, something that happened on occasion, even though Alasdair and his family had returned to Clan Grant.

Derric opened the door and said, "Diamond, get out here."

Tora tugged on her legging and said, "Mama."

"Just a moment, lass. I must see Da about something." Tora scowled but went back to playing with Grant.

Dyna stuck her head out and asked, "What is it, Derric?"

"Hagen. He took Sheona Rankin out for a stroll, and her father is telling him that he has to marry her on the morrow."

Dyna's head nearly burst open. "What?" She pushed past him and moved over to the balcony railing so she could watch the action in the hall.

Dermot bellowed, then her father got out of his chair and pushed Hagen behind him. "Go, Da," she whispered.

Tora opened the door and said, "Mama."

"Just a moment. Derric. Go see what she wants. I have to watch this." Derric ushered Tora back inside, so Dyna's attention went back to the show in the hall.

Everyone was watching. She could have fired three arrows into the tapestry on the opposite wall and no one would have noticed.

Logan came out of his chamber and raced down the stairs, bellowing this way and that. It was no surprise that he would get involved, but her father had to convince Dermot to leave Hagen alone.

Logan bellowed.

Dermot shouted and waved his arms.

Her father hollered.

Then someone mentioned Taskill, so Rut shoved past Logan and her father, her finger in Dermot's face.

A rumble of thunder echoed, and the bairns shouted a bit, Sandor and Grant laughing at the brewing storm. There were three adults with them, so Dyna wasn't worried.

She couldn't hear the words, but Rut swung her arm back so fast that Dermot never saw the slap coming. Her hand struck his cheek hard enough that Dermot's head jerked to one side. But that wasn't as quick as the fire that lit his eyes at the assault.

The argument grew louder.

Tora opened the door and said, "Mama!"

Sylvi was behind her sister. "Mama!"

Dyna waved her hand and said, "I heard the thunder. Go sit with Da. I'll be right there."

The door closed again. Another bolt of lightning and a louder rumble of thunder, then Sloan grabbed his father, Lennox grabbed his mother, and Rut tried to kick Dermot.

The door opened, and Derric shouted, "Diamond. I need you in here."

She stepped inside and Sylvi had both hands covering her ears, screaming, "Nay, nay, nay!" She ran in a circle, so Dyna tried to stop her.

Then Grant began to cry.

Sandor fell and screamed.

Tora yelled, "Mama!"

Dyna grabbed Sylvi and clutched her close while Maeve picked up Grant. Avelina reached for Sandor at the same time as Derric.

And Tora disappeared out the door.

"Derric!" Avelina had grabbed Sandor, so she shoved Sylvi into her husband's hands and ran after their youngest daughter.

Tora raced down the staircase as fast as her wee legs would carry her, chanting to herself. "Gwandda, Gwandda, Gwandda …"

"Tora, come back. Please!" There were too many people down there. Lennox was shouting, Rut was fussing, Dermot was pushing and arguing with Sloan. Her father stood to the side.

Tora headed straight for her grandfather. She wove in between this person and that until she finally stood in front of him.

Dyna breathed a sigh of relief when Tora made it to her father because Dyna couldn't move among the adults as easily as her daughter had. What the hell was wrong with Tora? And why was Sylvi shouting and covering her ears?

Tora tugged on her grandfather's plaid. He looked down and swooped her up into his arms so fast that Dyna nearly sobbed with relief.

When she reached them, her father said, "What is it, Tora?"

Tora cupped his face with both tiny hands and said, "I don't like him."

"Who?"

"Him. He's here, and he's mean." Then she pushed against him and headed back upstairs.

Dyna caught and picked her up, carrying her

over to the side, her sire following. "Who, Tora? Who?"

"I don't know." Then she smiled. "I want to play again."

Dyna stared at her father.

What the hell did that mean?

CHAPTER TEN

TASKILL

———— ∾ ————

TASKILL, NEAR THE stables, conversed with two lasses as distant thunder rumbled. He'd taken his time going inside because he feared a confrontation with Dermot again. The last thing he wished for was to be a spectacle in front of everyone at the festival. If Dermot got enough amber liquid inside him, he'd definitely be calmer.

One said, "Why have you not chosen a bride yet, my lord MacVey? You surely are a handsome one."

"You know my name, but I don't know you. Where are you from?"

"We came along with Chief Rankin. We helped in the kitchens all day, but they no longer require our assistance."

"I like the color of your hair," one said.

"But I like your strong shoulders. You must work hard in the lists."

"I do. It's been lovely chatting with you, but I'm going to head inside. I heard the food is wonderful. It probably is if you both made the tarts."

The two giggled and blushed. "We did. I hope you like them."

One serving girl's hand lingered on his arm. "You could escort us home, Taskill MacVey. I've a warm hearth waiting."

Once, he might have accepted. Anything to forget the ache in his chest, the loneliness that followed him like a shadow.

But that was before Dermot's announcement. Before he'd seen Sheona's face go white. Before he'd remembered what it felt like to want something—*someone*—he could never have.

"Not tonight, lass." He gently removed her hand. "But I thank you for the offer."

Someone flew out of the keep. Brian MacQuarie came directly to him. "Taskill, they're looking for you inside."

"Who is?" Taskill asked, stepping away from the lasses and moving Brian from their prying ears.

"Logan. Hagen took a stroll with Sheona, and when they came back inside, Dermot demanded he marry her. Then Connor got involved, and then Logan. It is a wild melee, and I just saw your mother going over to argue with Dermot. It's kind of entertaining to watch them all battle so."

"Shite." He moved toward the door, and though he hated confrontations of any kind, he needed to be inside. "My thanks, Brian. I'll go see."

Brian grabbed his arm. "Wait. Are you betrothed to Sheona?"

"Nay. Dermot is trying to force it, but neither of us is ready for marriage."

Brian lowered his voice. "So, Sheona is available? She's surely a pretty thing."

"Sheona is a wonderful person. I've known her all my life, and I guess that's why we aren't interested at the moment. Too familiar, I think. We played together when we were younger."

"Well, you'd have to be able to tolerate her sire, but he won't be around forever. And besides, she'd move out of Dun Ara, would she not?"

"She probably would. If you're interested, Brian, then make sure you visit with her this eve." The two headed toward the door just as his brother exited, his mother's voice louder than the others.

"He deserved it, Lennox. Taskill, there you are. Where the hell have you been?" Then she stared up at the sky. "Is it going to rain, because I'll not go home in the rain."

"Mama, we'll go to the stables and see. I think this is going to pass right over. The thunder is in the distance."

The two lasses giggled as they passed them.

"Taskill, I know where you've been, or should I say with whom." His mother gave him that look of derision he knew so well as she tossed her head toward the two serving girls.

"I chatted with many people, Mama. I just finished a conversation with Brian. Now what happened?"

Lennox said, "I'm taking her home as soon as this storm passes. Go find Sheona, and once Dermot is gone, find a private place to calm her down. It was not pretty, but it gave everyone much to talk about for a while. She can tell you all."

Taskill scratched the bit of scruff that was his beard but then moved along, glad to get away from his mother's accusations. Once inside, he saw Sloan and Ingelram leading Dermot out the door, so he held it for them. Sloan said, "Da, not a word to him."

"He could have stopped it all if he'd done what he was supposed to do," Dermot said, glaring at Taskill.

"I'm sorry, Chief, but I don't know what I could have stopped."

"Ignore him. Go in the keep, Taskill."

Taskill went in and headed for the table with a tray of fragrant meat pies, but his ears couldn't ignore all that was being whispered as he passed.

"Did you see her hit him?"

"I thought he was going to punch her."

"I thought Connor was about to put his fist in his face."

"Logan was about to hang him by his bollocks."

Taskill turned around to listen, but his gaze caught Connor escorting Sheona into the solar, so he followed.

"Sheona?" he asked as soon as he stepped inside. "What happened?" He looked at Connor, who answered him.

"Dermot got excited and did some bellowing. Sheona's going to sit in here for a bit. All the excitement will settle down shortly."

Taskill looked at her, noticed the tears misting

her eyes, the clench in her fist held up to her mouth, the tremble in her lower lip. "Was it about me? Did I do something wrong?"

"Nay," Connor replied. "I'm going to speak with Logan. I'll be right back. Sheona, do you mind if Taskill stays for a bit? You can update him on what happened."

She nodded. "As long as Da is gone."

"He's gone. I'll return soon." Connor left and closed the door.

"What happened?"

Sheona stared up at him, her eyes glazed with tears that were about to fall, and all he wished to do was hold her.

"Da." Her voice hitched. "Hagen. He invited me for a stroll in the courtyard, and when we returned, Da demanded he marry me on the morrow."

"What? Why?" He moved closer and massaged her shoulder a bit, hoping to comfort her. Honestly, he'd never had such a powerful gut reaction to someone. All he wished to do was wrap his arms around her and hold her until her tears were spent.

What the hell was wrong with him?

"Because Hagen didn't ask for his permission. Da was yelling and screaming and hollering. Told Hagen he had to marry me, so Connor jumped up and defended him. Said that all Grants chose their own spouses, and Hagen wouldn't be forced. Then Logan came down and bellowed too. All three of them were hollering …"

"And that's when my name got into it."

"Aye, Logan said he thought you and I … were … betrothed."

Then her tears fell hard, and Taskill did what he was compelled to do, wrapping his arms around her and holding her tight. Hell, but he'd always wished to protect Sheona, and the instinct was still there.

She stepped back enough to finish. "And then your mother heard your name and pushed Connor and Logan out of the way and started yelling at my sire, who told her to be quiet because she was a woman … or to stay out of men's business. Something like that."

"Oh, that wouldn't go over well." Then Taskill grinned because Sheona smirked. "What happened? Tell me, please."

"Your mother slapped my father." She began to giggle, and Taskill chuckled. "And she said something like just because she didn't have a piece of meat dangling between her legs didn't mean she didn't have a brain."

Taskill guffawed. "How did I miss that? What the hell! And what did your father do? I doubt he took it lightly."

She swiped the tears away with a linen square Connor had given her. "He was stunned. He stared at her and said, 'You hit me.'"

"Oh, I can only guess what my mother's response to that was." Taskill berated himself for staying outside. "Let me guess. Did she hit him again?" He wished he'd seen the situation as it unfolded. They'd be talking about this for many moons.

Sheona shook her head. "She said she'd hit him again if he didn't stop. That was when Sloan pulled him back, and Lennox came over and pulled your mother away, but not before she tried to kick my father."

Taskill closed his eyes. "Hellfire. No wonder everyone was whispering. I'm sorry, lass."

"I don't know what I'm going to do. Da says I have two days to decide, or he'll take me to Iona Abbey and the nunnery."

"Truly? The nunnery? Do you wish to be a nun?"

"Taskill, I'm so confused. I liked Hagen, but I'm sure he'll not come near me again. I have no idea what I should do with my life."

Taskill pulled a second dry linen square out of the desk and said, "Here. We'll get your tears cleaned up, and we'll go back out there and enjoy the festival. There's no reason for you to hide. It sounds like you did naught wrong. Go out with your head held high. I'm sure everyone understands the awkward position you were put in. I'll go with you, and we can present a united front. It sounds like Meg is probably still here, and Eva too. I'll lead you over to the hearth, and you can sit for a moment. I'll find you a fruit tart and a goblet of wine. Then you can relax and forget about it. With both of our parents gone, there will be no more trouble. I'm certain of it."

He dried the tears on her cheeks the best he could, then smiled.

She whispered, "I've soaked two linen squares."

"That's naught to be embarrassed about. I should

be embarrassed over my mother's behavior, but she's been like that for a long time. Everything she does is out of love. She's as protective of her bairns as a wild boar. Your da is the same. You'll be laughing about it on the morrow."

She nodded and smiled. "You're probably right."

The door opened, and Connor stepped inside. "They're both gone, so you can come out and mingle. The meat is being served. Come enjoy yourselves."

"I'll escort her, Chief."

Connor nodded and the two left, stepping into the crowd. A few stared but then everyone turned back to the food and the other guests.

Taskill said, "I see Eva and Meg over there and an open seat next to them."

"I would love to sit with them." He escorted Sheona to a chair next to Eva, then turned about, hoping to get other opinions on what had happened. He saw Tristan first, so he approached, though he had two of his men with him.

"Greetings, Tristan."

"Taskill. I brought two of my best guards with me, Percival and Roger. They've been with Clan MacLean for many years. They're heading back outside once they get themselves a meat pie. You know the Grant pies are the best."

"Greetings to you," Taskill offered the two. Percival appeared much older than Roger. "You have quite a few men working with you now, do you not?"

"Aye, after all the trouble here, my uncle sent another ten, so we are around twenty now. We are nearly done with the tower in time for winter. The stable is completed for the horses, and the wall is nearly finished."

"You'll be glad for the protection being so close to the sea there. Tell me, Tristan. I was outside and missed the excitement. What actually happened?" He wished to hear it from another perspective. Percival and Roger made their way over to the sideboard and then headed out the door, chuckling along the way.

Tristan said, "Do you mean the battle of the elders?"

Taskill nodded, moving his hand to encourage Tristan to tell all.

"Dermot is a curmudgeon in his old age, but he wishes Sheona to marry quickly, apparently. Hagen was innocent, but he was nearly forced into marrying Sheona on the morrow. But …" He glanced over both shoulders before continuing. "No one is going to make a Grant or a Ramsay do anything without Connor or Logan's support." Then he grinned like a stable lad. "And your mother was the best of all."

Taskill groaned but waited.

"Dermot insulted her for being female, and she slapped him so hard that it was nearly like she punched him. And then I thought she was going to belt him again, but Lennox got to her before she was able to."

"I think I'm glad I wasn't here."

"Probably good that you weren't. I was honestly hiding in the corner because I didn't wish to get pulled into the 'who's eligible to marry Sheona' battle. She's a beauty, but I'm not ready yet. Too much work to do first."

"I should have been here." And all Taskill could wonder was why the hell had he stayed outside instead of coming in? Was it truly because he wished to avoid confrontation or was he seeking something else? Once he saw the lasses staring, he didn't move away, and he could have. Had he avoided coming inside just because two lasses had fallen over him? Why did he persist in basking in all the compliments?

Tristan said, "I'm going for some food, Taskill. Relax." He clasped his shoulder and disappeared.

Taskill scanned the hall, taking in all the people he knew and loved, while noticing all the unfamiliar faces. Brian was with someone he didn't recognize. Alaric and Eli were with people he didn't recognize but he guessed they were probably Grant men. Maitland chatted with two others Taskill had never met.

Perhaps it was time for Taskill to stop listening to all the lasses and spend his time chatting with men. Though he heard it repeatedly, he still found it perplexing when someone praised his appearance. His vanity, he guessed. He loved hearing the kind words.

When he was younger, everyone fussed over Lennox. Everywhere they went people would fuss over the next chieftain, and their father's chest would puff out, throwing all the compliments Lennox's way.

And if Eva was around, their father fussed over her endlessly. Spoiled her, even.

In an odd way, Taskill guessed he was always waiting for someone to throw him a compliment, but it never happened. It was as if no one saw him. Not until he turned twenty summers did everything change and then all the lasses noticed him. That's when the compliments began.

He'd been so shocked the first time that he thought they were teasing him. But the flattery never stopped, so neither did he. It wasn't what everyone thought. He hadn't bedded them all or even kissed them.

He just enjoyed the accolades.

CHAPTER ELEVEN

SHEONA

———⚭———

TWO DAYS LATER, Sheona bolted up in bed, wide-eyed. What had awakened her?

"Get up, Sheona. We're leaving soon." Her father stood in the doorway, his arms crossed as he stared at her. "Pack a bag. You won't be back for a while."

"What?" She rubbed the sleep from her eyes, moving her legs over the side of the bed at the same time. "Da. Where are we going?"

"To the abbey. I told you the other day."

"What abbey?" Icy tendrils raced up her spine, gripping her like the fear of standing alone in the dark and witnessing something you knew you shouldn't, yet you can't pull your eyes away. As if for some reason, you're supposed to see what's in front of you, even though every part of you rages against it.

She forced the images in her mind back into their hiding place. "Da, what is happening?"

"Did you find a man who will marry you?"

"In two days? Nay, Da. No one would agree that quickly."

"Then we're going to the abbey."

"I don't wish to go to the abbey. Which abbey?"

"Iona. We're going to the MacClanes, then using their boat to go to the Isle of Iona. You wish to be a nun? Then you must visit to see what their life is like. You need to know what you are choosing."

"But I didn't choose it yet." She grabbed a gown from her chest and shook it out, doing her best to straighten the errant hairs on her head before she plaited it.

"We're visiting. There will be no arguing, lass. We're leaving in half the hour. Move along." Then he was gone, slamming the door.

She donned her gown, straightened the wrinkles the best she could, then grabbed a bag to pack another outfit and her leggings that Dyna had given her. Then she put two axes inside, just in case. Sloan. She had to find Sloan. He would talk their father out of this daft endeavor. Collecting anything else she might need, she rinsed her teeth and washed her face, glad she'd taken a tub bath the night before. She'd not have time now. It would take half the hour to warm the water.

Hurrying out of her chamber, she grabbed her bag and stopped at Marta's chamber, knocking on the door. "Marta?"

Silence. Marta usually awakened at dawn with the bairn, so she was probably below stairs with the wee lassie. Sheona raced down and out the door, grabbing her mantle at the last minute. "Sloan!"

She didn't see him, only some of his men. "Miles, where is my brother?"

"He and Eva went to MacQuarie Castle for a visit."

"Damn it," she muttered, waiting for Miles to chastise her for cursing, but he just arched a brow at her. "Have you seen Marta or Gideon?"

"Aye, they left for a quick boat ride. They took the wee Margret with them."

"Nay …" Sheona closed her eyes and said a quick prayer. "Miles, please don't let him take me to the abbey." Her voice came out in a whisper. "Not until my brother or sister is here. Please?"

"Sorry, lass. He's already chosen his guards for the journey."

"You? Ingelram?"

"Nay, Fitz is leading. He said it was just for a visit. Don't panic. I'll let Sloan know when he returns. He said it's for a sennight, possibly. It might be good for you to take some time away after all that has happened between you and Taskill."

"Naught has happened between Taskill and me! I wish people would stop talking about us. Da wished to order him to marry me. Taskill refused, as I did. End of story. We are not betrothed."

Miles gave her a weak grin and said, "It might be good for you to visit Iona. It's a lovely isle so they say. It's said to be full of sandy beaches and grassy knolls. Artan lives there with his wife, Simone. Have you met her? She's an archer. Look for her. She'll help you if you ever need it."

"Who is Simone?"

"Logan   Ramsay's   adopted   daughter. An

exceptional archer who only wears the leggings like Dyna does." He leaned forward to whisper, "They say she killed Glenna of Buchan with an arrow in the middle of her eye. Dropped the wicked bitch to the ground so fast that some never saw her hit until she landed on her back, the arrow sticking straight out of the center of one glowing orb."

Sheona shook her head to rid the image from her mind but considered that perhaps the woman could assist her if she needed it. Asking Marta was impossible. "What is her name again?"

"Simone. Married to Artan, Thane's second."

Her father appeared out of the stable door. "Sheona, I'm ready. Get over here or I'll have Miles carry you over his shoulder."

"Can you not stop him, Miles?" she begged, grabbing his hand.

"Nay, he's the old chieftain. We must do as he says. I promise to tell Sloan and Marta when they return. Enjoy your journey. The isle is beautiful, as you know."

Sheona let out a deep sigh and trudged forward, knowing her path was now set.

She didn't speak to her father, instead bringing out her horse, attaching her bag to the saddle, and retrieving another axe from the stable and hiding it in the bag. She needed all the weapons she could find.

Fitz hurried over to her side. "May I assist you, lass?" He gave her a wide smile and held out his hands as an offer, but she shook her head as she climbed onto the mounting block.

"I can manage." She was in no mood to speak with anyone.

Her father had already mounted and headed past her, pausing for a moment. "Move out, lass. Time is short, as you know, and we have much land to cover."

She moved her horse, four guards surrounding her as they headed across Mull to the opposite side where the MacLean holding was.

Fitz asked, "Did you have a good time at the festival the other day, lass?"

Her father said, "Do not talk to my daughter. She's a lass and not worthy of your time. You should be thinking about battle tactics, Fitz. You have much to learn."

Sheona wished to throw an apple and hit her father in the face.

But she didn't.

She always did what she was told.

CHAPTER TWELVE

TASKILL

<hr />

"JUST GO WITH them," Lennox said, standing by the gates of Dounarwyse Castle. "You need to relax a bit."

It was two days after the festival and the big argument that everyone was still talking about. Jasper said, "Come with me, T. I hear they have a slab of venison all smoked and lots of ale."

Taskill thought for a moment. The day was beautiful, nice and crisp, yet too early for snow. In the summer, they swam at the guard festivities, but this time it was all about food.

"There's brew for the biggest fish."

Lennox chuckled. "Now you've tempted him. He thinks he has the best lure of any fisherman."

"I do," Taskill said with a sneer. "Don't believe me? Then you'll see." Still hesitant, he knew what was not far from there.

As if reading his mind, Lennox said, "Sheona will not be around, and Dermot won't bother you."

"You don't know that."

Jasper glanced over at Lennox, who gave him a subtle nod.

"What?"

Jasper swung his weapon over his shoulder before he resheathed it. "They're not there."

Shocked by this, he didn't even try to hide his surprise. "What is going on?"

Lennox sighed. "Ingelram told us that Dermot got up and took Sheona to the Iona nunnery early this morn."

"Nunnery? Sheona? She doesn't belong in a nunnery." Nothing could have shocked him more. Sheona was too vibrant, too full of life, too much fun to be a nun. All those times they raced in the water, skiffed about in boats, laughed under the waterfalls. She was as much a nun as he was a priest.

"You don't know that," Lennox said. "Mayhap she's changed her mind."

"Nay, sitting in prayer all day long? Sheona? Absolutely not."

Jasper said, "That's not what they do all day. The ones on Iona work with bairns."

"But only with other women," Taskill said, his hands fisting at his sides. "What the hell is wrong with Dermot? I'm going after her."

"Nay, you are not," Lennox said, grabbing his arm. "Let it go for now. If it's not for her, she'll tell her father that and she'll return. If you wish to see her, you'll have to wait. This could be good for Sheona. Miles said Dermot wished to show her what her life would be like as a nun. He's hoping it will force her into marriage."

"Shite!" Taskill blurted without thinking. Both men stared at him.

Lennox crossed his arms and tapped his foot. "You're cursing over Sheona. What does that mean?"

"That he's probably trying to force her into marrying me. That's not what I want either."

Lennox blew out a breath through pursed lips. "Do you even know what the hell you want? You confuse me, Taskill. Make up your mind. Do you want Sheona or not?"

Taskill ran his hand down his face and paced a large circle. He honestly wasn't sure how to answer his brother. He didn't wish to marry Sheona or anyone, but he also didn't want to see Sheona married to anyone else.

That confused him. The thought of Sheona with another man caused his fists to clench. What the hell was wrong with him?

Lennox said, "You're going to fish. Neither one is on Rankin land, and the place they fish is far enough away that you'll not know when they return. Go and get in your cups for a change. Forget about Dermot and have a good time. Catch some fish. Bring me a few good ones for a fine fish stew. Catch a few cod."

"I'll bring pollack and mayhap a few mackerel."

"Then go to the loch and catch a few trout. They make the best stew."

Taskill finally nodded. "I'll go. I need some brew. You're right. How many others will be there, Jasper?"

"Homer is going with me. Clyde and Miles will be there. Brian MacQuarie is coming, and he'll probably bring a few along. Does it matter?"

"Nay. I'll be right back." Taskill headed into the hall, hoping to slip past his mother so he could change into his favorite pair of trews for fishing. The bugs were bad by the water, so he preferred to keep his skin covered. He stepped inside and scanned the area, not seeing her, but she heard him.

"Taskill, where are you going?"

"Fishing, Mama. I don't have time to chat."

"Fine. Go ahead. If you see that fool Dermot along the way, stick a hook in his backside, would you, please? And tell him it's from me."

"Sure, Mama." He wasn't about to tell her where Dermot was because that would set her off too. He raced up the stairs, grabbed his best lures that he kept hidden in his chamber, changed his clothes, then headed back out, stopping for his fishing nets in the stable.

"I'm ready, Jasper. Where's Homer?

"Right here. I'm ready."

They mounted up and headed toward Rankin land, taking the last fork to the left, since the right led to the castle. The left led to the coastline where most loved to drop their nets—it's where many launched their boats. Taskill enjoyed fishing on the coast but hadn't been in a while. Dusk was nearly upon them, the best time for biting fish.

Jasper led the way and dismounted, shouting out to the others, "Three more for your contest. Don't start without us."

"No need to worry," Miles said. "No one has caught anything yet."

Miles handed Taskill a skin of brew. "You are my best friend, Miles, and I thank you. Dermot makes the best. I hope you've learned his ways."

"I have. I know his secrets, though he doesn't know it." Miles laughed and headed back to the shoreline.

Taskill found his spot and settled down, his empty bucket by his side, ready to fill. Eight men were fishing—Brian, Miles, Jasper, Clyde, Homer, and Brian's two guards, Ewing and Bearnard—all quiet at the moment, hoping to catch the biggest prize for the bragging rights.

It gave Taskill time to think. He knew Sheona as well as anyone, and there was no manner of thinking that made him believe the lass should become a nun. When they were younger, Sheona could keep up with the three of them: Lennox, Sloan, and Taskill. Once in a while, Dermot would force her to stay home and Ingelram would go in place of her, but he preferred Sheona. She could ride a horse better than anyone. The only thing she wasn't skilled at was using a sword.

But she'd never tried.

She could control her mare better than any of them, always whispering sweet words to the beast, and it would respond by doing the highest leaps of any horse he'd ever seen. She could fish with the best, run obstacle courses, swim across the sound, roast hazelnuts, and carve her own daggers out of wood.

Then something happened. Something that had changed everything.

Sheona's chest blossomed.

Her hips began to curve, she grew breasts, and she grew taller so fast that she became uncoordinated, which led her mother to insist she stay at home.

Once, he'd seen her tears when her father had announced there would be no more playing with the lads. That she was to act like a lady and learn how to do needlework.

Taskill's heart had ached terribly that day. He hadn't recognized it back then for what it was. What ended up in his heart probably hadn't developed yet. Instead, the feeling had only sprouted, every sighting of the lass watering it a wee bit more. He replayed every conversation over and over again until several moons ago when the truth had finally come to him.

Taskill missed Sheona. He'd always wished to protect her, and as she grew older, his feelings for her had only expanded, but was it strong enough to be considered love? Nay. And he also knew he could never offer for her because he'd make a lousy husband. He and Sheona would not make a good couple.

Sheona deserved better than someone like him.

After Taskill had caught half a bucket of fish, Clyde, a newer Rankin guard who no one seemed to like, meandered closer to him.

Clyde started the conversation exactly where Taskill didn't wish to start. "So, you heard that Sheona is off to Iona to the nunnery?"

"I did. A visit I was told."

Clyde snorted. "That's what Dermot told her, but I don't think that's his intent. He plans to leave her there. I think he hopes it will scare her into becoming betrothed. Mayhap to you. What say you?"

"I say it's none of your concern."

Clyde arched a brow. "Fair enough. I was just hoping to get your blessing."

"Blessing for what?"

"I'd like to court Sheona, but if you plan to offer for her, I won't."

Taskill nearly choked on the ale he'd just swallowed. "You're a guard. Think you Dermot will accept you? Don't get your hopes up. You aren't good enough for her."

"But you are?"

"I'm noble blood. Second to a chieftain. Dermot will accept me." He cast a sideways glare at the fool, hoping to convince him to stay away from Sheona.

"But I heard you were not interested. Are you or are you not?"

"Not your concern."

"But it is." Clyde wasn't a bad-looking man, but he was arrogant and boisterous, always thinking he was the best at everything. He was not.

"He'll not accept you."

"But Sheona likes me. If she wants me, Dermot will accept my suit, I think."

Taskill snorted. "Get the hell away from me, arsehole. You're a fool. She is not interested in you. If you ever hurt her, I'll kill you."

Clyde chuckled and picked up his bucket to take his leave. "The way I understand it, she's not interested in you either. So I think I have a chance. You don't know what's in her mind. Mayhap we'll make a perfect couple."

But Taskill was certain that Sheona was not interested in that fool.

Or was she?

CHAPTER THIRTEEN

SHEONA

———◆———

SHEONA CLIMBED OUT of the boat and stared, taking in the beauty of the Isle of Iona. They made their way across the beach, watching for the rocks and stepping carefully.

"Da, it's beautiful. There's a view of the sea in almost every direction."

"It is. I'm sorry I never brought your mother here. She would have loved it."

Sheona turned to their guide. "That building. Is it the nunnery?"

"Aye, the abbey is beyond the nunnery. Also a stunning building."

"And the nuns sleep there?" Sheona asked.

"Aye," their guide said. "The prioress is Mother Mary, and she is who you must visit first. They say there are around ten nuns housed here. And there's an orphanage nearby. That grouping of cottages we passed along the way is where the orphans are kept by four women. I'll give you an hour to visit, then I must take off. If you wish to go back to Mull, meet me here in that time.

Otherwise, I'll not return for two days when I bring supplies."

Dermot handed the man a coin and said, "I'll return by then." He picked up Sheona's bag, and they strolled down the path to the stone building, made with arches around the outside of the main building in the center. There were benches everywhere, a garden that had been overturned as the season ended, and a small orchard of fruit trees not far away. There were two nuns busy picking what apples they could.

"Greetings to you," one called out. "Are you here for a visit?"

Dermot said, "Old Chieftain Dermot Rankin of Clan Rankin and my daughter Sheona. We'd like to tour the nunnery, if you please."

"Of course," one said. "My name is Ada, and we'd be happy to give you a small tour. Ilene can take you about while I stay and finish our work for the day."

"Welcome," Ilene said before Ada returned to her work. Both wore long black robes that swept along when they walked. The slight breeze was a bit cool, but not too bad.

Ilene led them down the path and asked, "Are you considering taking your vows, Sheona?"

Her father said, "Nay."

Sheona answered, "Aye."

Her father was more surprised than she was at her quick reply. His brow furrowed, and he tipped his head at her, but she ignored him. It was the stillness, the calm beating of the waves against the rocks echoing across the area, the scent of the sea that called to her. A flurry of terns flew over them, their frantic chirping putting a smile on her face.

"The birds welcome you," Ilene said.

Ilene had beautiful brown eyes, her wimple covering the color of her hair, but her smile was as warm as any Sheona had ever seen. She led them into an extensive building and stood at the doorway. "This is where the sisters eat. The kitchen is at the far end, and many help with the food."

Then she led them out the door and into a second building. "This is where we sleep." The nun opened the door to one large chamber and stood off to the side, holding the door while they perused the sleeping chamber meant for six or less. "There are three large chambers with shared quarters. The prioress has her own chamber. The chapel is at the far end. I can show that to you, then we'll look for Mother Mary in her office. Please follow me."

Sheona and her father followed. Sheona took in everything along the way. It was a simple beauty, the colors of autumn giving way to the coldness of winter, though no snowflakes had flown yet. There were a few squashes in the garden yet to be harvested.

"Have you any questions?" Ilene asked.

"Are there any men here?" her father asked.

"Nay, none. We have the few who bring supplies. There are several monks on the other side of the abbey that is down that way, but they rarely bother us. On occasion, we are invited to mass there and we enjoy it. But not often. We keep to ourselves, using our chapel except on special occasions."

Separate from men. Never to be stared at as if she had gold coins pinned to her chest. No more lustful glances. And no worry of *that* ever happening to her. That shameful act she'd learned about. The act that sent a chill down her spine whenever she thought of it.

How did women survive marriage?

She would never have to worry on it if she lived here. Perhaps she did belong at the nunnery.

They continued down the path toward the chapel when the sounds of heavy work caught her.

Ilene pointed to an area up ahead. "Oh, you can hear Brynja and Hildi practicing. Come watch for a bit."

Sheona stepped off the path and froze at the action taking place in front of her. Two women threw spears at a target at the end of the clearing. Each had a unique grunt that could be heard whenever they launched the long weapon. But that wasn't what caught her attention the most.

It was their dress.

Ilene waved her hand at the two women. "I just love their clothing. They honor their Norse heritage with the garments they wear and the braids in their hair. Come, let's greet Mother Mary."

But Sheona couldn't tear her gaze from the lasses throwing spears. They both wore leggings like Dyna and Gwyneth did, but with long tunics and boots, more colorful than the Granthams wore. They had spots where daggers clung to their clothing, as if they sewed an extra layer for their weaponry. And their braids were so striking that Sheona wished to plait her hair in the same way. Brynja had three braids on each side of her head, pinned out of her face. Somehow, the six braids were woven together into a large plait at the back of her head.

Striking, mysterious, and a bit sinister looking.

Exactly what Sheona wished to become. Convinced this was the place for her, she thought on what she would miss if she chose to stay.

Her sister, her brother, and her wee niece were the only things she would miss. Her father had become more of a nuisance, so the idea of getting away from his constant insistence on wedding quickly was most welcome indeed.

She'd miss Marta, Margret, and Sloan. Eva too. Was there anyone else she would miss?

She briefly thought of Taskill but rejected that because she knew he would be relieved to find that she was no longer available. Her father would no longer pester Taskill into something he didn't want.

And she could live in peace and forget about a man with golden hair and a smile that could melt any lass's heart.

They'd arrived at the office, and the nun knocked on the prioress's door.

"Come in, if you please."

Ilene opened the door and said, "Greetings to you, Mother Mary. We have visitors. This is

Chieftain Dermot Rankin and his daughter Sheona, who is considering taking her vows."

"Please come in. Chief, I recognize your name from the Isle of Mull." The woman also wore dark robes, her hair covered. But she looked to be younger than Sheona would have expected. She had a warm smile and welcoming eyes, a pretty shade of blue.

"Old chieftain. My son is the present chieftain."

"And your daughter wishes to take her vows?"

Her father looked more confused than she'd ever seen him. "I'm not certain." He glanced over at Sheona, but she said nothing. "She's considering it." Then he waved his arms over his head. "What the hell do I know?"

The prioress arched a brow at him and her father quickly apologized. "Forgive me. I forgot where I am. What I'm doing. Why I'm here." Then he shrugged his shoulders. "I don't know what I'm doing. Talk to her." Then he stepped outside.

"Your father doesn't wish for you to take your vows, lass?"

"He suggested it. I didn't think I was interested, but I would like to stay for a while and consider it. If you don't mind. May I stay and think on it?" Sheona couldn't stop the tears from forming in the corners of her eyes. She blinked hard to stop them but failed.

"I will allow it, but please allow me to speak to your sire alone, lass. Did you bring your things with you?"

She nodded, the lump in her throat expanding.

"Ilene!"

The door opened, and the prioress said, "Please show Sheona to the chamber with Hildi and Brynja. She will be staying for a bit. Do you agree, Sheona?"

Sheona nodded, excited to be with Brynja and Hildi. She left, casting a quick glance at her father before he was called into the prioress's office.

She was glad to be staying, to get some time away from her father.

Time to think.

CHAPTER FOURTEEN

DERMOT

DERMOT STEPPED INSIDE after watching his youngest daughter depart, the tears in her eyes visible, though she did her best to hide them. He didn't know what to say to her. The truth was he'd never been more surprised to hear that Sheona wished to stay.

Why, he had no idea.

"Chief Rankin, please sit down. I can see you're unsettled, and I think I can help you with this a wee bit."

Dermot had never felt so lost, his insides churning from the tears he saw in his daughter's eyes. His wee lassie. "How can you possibly help me with my daughter? She was my wee bairn who sat on my lap for so many years. I fixed every skinned elbow, every tear, every fall, no matter what. Now I have no idea how to help her. If my wife hadn't died, there'd be no problem. But I know not what to do for her. She doesn't wish to stay here, so why did she change her mind all of a sudden?"

"Chief, please allow me to explain what I see." The prioress waved him toward a chair, so he flopped into it. Then she continued, "Many times, when young women come to me, it's not because of the reason you think it is. In other words, it's not because they wish to become nuns."

"Why else would someone wish to come here and be shut off from everything and everyone who loves her?"

The prioress moved her chair back and folded her hands in her lap, thinking for a bit. Too long, in Dermot's mind.

He blurted out, "Why? Why the hell would a beautiful lass wish to be here when she should be getting married and having bairns?"

"Some do love God enough to stay, but many have other reasons behind their actions. In my experience, it's usually because she's running away from something. Is there anything you can think of that would cause her to wish to hide from everyone? Has something happened to her that you're not thinking on? Or …"

"Nay. I wished to help her get married, find a man to betroth her to, but that shouldn't be enough to make her hide. I didn't expect her to wish to stay. I was just trying to scare her into marrying the lad who lives nearby." And keep her away from the fool he'd overheard talking about his sweet lass. He'd still been unable to determine who the bastard was, but he would. Until then, Sheona would be safer here, though he couldn't tell her why.

The prioress nodded, continuing to think.

"I will add that she lost her mother a year ago and that's been hard. But then why now?"

The prioress still didn't speak.

"And she lost a brother, though I try not to think on that. He betrayed me in the end. But that wouldn't force her to run away. He's gone now."

The prioress smiled but remained quiet.

"Her sister just had a bairn and her brother married, but that's no reason to take her vows. Is it?" He scratched his head. "Nay, why would she leave our castle when she has such a beautiful new niece? It took poor Marta many moons to have that bairn. Years, even."

"Chief, I'll try to mention this as delicately as I can. It sounds as though you've had much going on in your clan. And may I add that we've heard of recent troubles on Mull. Rowan and the other bairns being kidnapped. Cruel men coming over curtain walls to steal some away. Was there not a woman stolen from Duart Castle? Sometimes, when so much is going on, some people are overlooked in the excitement and things happen, things we wish would not happen, but they do. Especially to young lasses …"

Dermot stood up. "What the hell are you saying? What the … You mean … Nay, not my lassie. Nay. I'm telling you nay. I forbid anyone to touch my lass. She was never kidnapped." A fury flew through him at the thought of someone mishandling his beautiful, innocent lassie. His wee lass. "I brought her here to protect her from that. It hasn't happened yet. I would know. She would tell me, would she not?"

"Chief, allow her to stay for a few days. I'll speak with her. See what I can learn. I'll agree with you. She is not the usual type I see who wish to devote their time to prayer and Our Lord, but if she wishes to find time alone to understand herself, I'm willing to give her that."

"Are there men here?"

"Nay, none. There are monks at the abbey, but none at the nunnery."

Dermot nodded, the sudden urge to run away, hide his head, deny her suggestion to the world overpowering his thoughts. Perhaps it was best to leave Sheona here, to allow her time to think.

The prioress whispered, "Did something happen that might have precipitated this sudden awareness or sudden fear in her?"

"Nay, naught." But then he thought, his face betraying his true feelings. He'd done it to her.

"What is it, Chief? I will keep your confidence."

"I tried to force her to marry a neighbor …" His voice trailed off. "I'm sorry. I must take my leave. I will return within a sennight for my daughter."

Dermot nodded to the prioress and left her office, hurrying down the path toward the dock. He had to get on that boat, no matter what. But he had to find Sheona first. The very thought of what the prioress suggested nearly ate his insides raw. He had to consult with his daughter about this issue.

"Sheona!" he yelled, catching her not far from one building.

His beautiful daughter turned to him. He approached, took both her hands in his, and nodded to Ilene, who stepped away to give them time alone.

"Sheona, you may stay. I'll return in a sennight. And please know that I'll not force you to marry Taskill. Or anyone. You decide what you wish to do."

"My thanks, Da."

"I love you, lassie. And I'm sorry." He bent down and kissed her cheek, then ran to the shoreline, calling over his shoulder. "You'll be safe here." Why the hell had he said that? He didn't want her to know that someone was after her. He always mucked things up. Where was Ailis?

He had to catch that boat.

Chapter Fifteen

Taskill

———❦———

WHAT THE HELL was wrong with him? What exactly did he want from Sheona? Since when had these new feelings emerged?

"Can't seem to make up your own mind, can you, fool?" Taskill muttered to himself. "You want to protect her, then you don't care. You don't want her for yourself, but you don't want anyone else to have her. Which is it?"

He pulled his net in and found two nice-sized pollacks among the smaller fish and tossed both in the bucket. His insides were reacting to Clyde's bold suggestion of pursuing the lass. He was certain that was all it was.

He didn't love Sheona. The thought had never occurred to him before. It didn't fit. They'd been friends forever. Playmates long ago. Jumped in the same lake, played warriors against the pirates on the coastline.

He recalled that day vividly. The weather finally had been warm enough to allow them to swim. He'd been paddling about in the sound with

Sloan and Lennox. Sloan had said that Marta didn't wish to swim anymore because of the fish. Eva had stayed home. And Sheona came running down the path in a new swimming outfit.

Sloan and Lennox jumped off the boulder into the water, bellowing about making the biggest splash, just as Sheona came along.

Taskill had been swimming when Sheona called his name, her voice bright with laughter as she always was back then. He turned, treading water, ready to splash her the moment she dove in—

And froze.

She stood on the bank, unlacing her overdress, the afternoon sun turning her damp hair to copper fire. When had she grown curves like that? When had the gangly girl he'd known since childhood become... this?

Heat flooded through him, swift and unwelcome. *No. Not Sheona. Anyone but her.*

"Are you coming in or not?" she called, oblivious.

He couldn't answer. Couldn't breathe. Couldn't stop staring at the way her wet chemise clung—

"Sheona Rankin!" Her mother's voice rang out like a thunderclap. "Get out of that water this instant! You're too old for this foolishness."

The joy drained from Sheona's face. She looked at him, pleading silently for him to argue, to defend their tradition, to tell her mother she was wrong.

But Taskill said nothing. Because her mother was right. Sheona *was* too old to swim with him now. Too beautiful. Too dangerous to his peace of mind.

And he was too broken to deserve her.

When she climbed out, shivering and hurt, she'd looked back once. He'd forced himself to turn away.

He'd been turning away ever since.

And now Dermot wanted him to marry her? To take the one pure, bright thing in his life and destroy it with his damaged soul? Nay, he couldn't do it. She deserved better. He'd hid his feelings for her for five years, so much that they changed.

He'd become protective. That's how he felt toward Sheona. He'd not allow anyone to touch her, of that much he was certain. He would always protect Sheona.

Sloan approached, pulling him out of his memories. Glancing into his full bucket, he chuckled. "You going to keep fishing, Taskill, until there are no more in the sound? Your net has proven its worth."

Taskill frowned and peered into the bucket. "I guess I have enough. Want a few for stew?"

"I'll take a few, if you don't mind. I'll leave the two cod with you. I'm happy with pollack." He grabbed an empty bucket and chose a few fish and dropped them inside. "You must be preoccupied. Something you wish to talk about?"

"I feel bad for Sheona. What a show your father put on for everyone. She was so embarrassed."

"She was. Unfortunately, there's been too much going on in our clan, so our father ignored her for a long time. The truth is that with Mama passing,

then Rinaldo, my wedding, Marta's new bairn, all
the battles, he's had no time for Sheona. Now he's
found the time. When my father gets an idea in
his head, he doesn't let it go, as you know."

"I do. If I were ready, I'd accept his proposal."

"Taskill, I'm all right with my sister not being a
good suit for you. But it's time for you to think on
marriage. It's the best thing that's ever happened
to me. Lennox feels the same. Consider it."

"Do you have someone in mind besides your
sister?"

"Nay, I don't. Choose your own."

Taskill decided to ask the question foremost in
his mind. "Clyde said your sire took her to the
nunnery. 'Struth?"

"I'm afraid so. Da has returned, said he'd leave
her there for a sennight, then go back later for
her. But he's more upset than I've ever seen him.
I don't know exactly what happened, but he's not
the same."

That caught Taskill's attention. "What do you
mean?" If anything happened to Sheona, he'd not
be happy, no matter what it was.

Sloan glanced over his shoulder to make sure
no one else could hear their conversation. "I'm
not sure, but he went straight to his chamber,
then came out, grabbed a big goblet of his brew,
and went up to the parapets. I thought I'd give
him some time before I approached him for an
explanation."

"Probably guilt for picking on poor Sheona so
much."

"Could be so. I'll find out. Da doesn't hide

much, as you know. My thanks for the fish. I'll take it to Cook. I can't wait."

Taskill pulled his net out of the water, set his fresh catch in the bucket, and packed up. Perhaps Sloan was right. He'd never seen Sloan or Lennox so happy. Was it his time?

But he had the sudden urge to go to the Isle of Iona and rescue a lass who shouldn't be a nun.

CHAPTER SIXTEEN

SHEONA

SHEONA WATCHED BRYNJA and Hildi as they sent their spears into the target they'd made. She couldn't believe how far the two lasses were able to throw their weapons. She surely would not be able to throw one that far.

"Would you like to try?" Brynja asked, her light hair wound with various colored ribbons, giving her a mysterious flair. Hildi's dark hair was wound with the same ribbons but arranged differently. Both had blue eyes, Brynja's alert and striking.

"Nay, not yet. Mayhap later. I'm Sheona, and Ilene sent me here. Said I'm to sleep in your chamber because you have two empty beds. Does it matter which I choose?"

"Nay." Brynja waved to her friend. "This is Hildi and I'm Brynja. We're both Norse, though our fathers were Scots. We prefer our mother's heritage. And you?"

"Scottish. Both parents. And I'm Sheona."

"You taking your vows?"

"I'm not sure yet. Are you both taking your vows?"

"We aren't sure either. Come, we'll show you to our chamber." They set their spears in a wooden crate near the target, then led her down the path.

"How long have you been here?" Sheona asked.

"Two moons."

"And they let you stay without taking your vows?" she asked, wondering if she could do such a thing.

"We were abducted when a group of evil men came and killed our mothers. Used the women first, then killed them. Took us, but kind souls rescued us and brought us here. We were too old for Ionaland, so here we stay. If you've never been, Ionaland is a short walk, and it's much more fun than living here."

"Ionaland? I've not heard of it."

"It's where they take the bairns with no parents. Lots of wee ones running about and playing. I like it there."

Hildi made a face. "Not my favorite place, but I go along when she goes. We help work the garden here and at Ionaland. It's not so bad at the nunnery. What brings you to Iona? We saw you with a man. Your sire?"

"Aye, he wishes for me to find a man and marry soon. Said if not, I had to become a nun. He said he'll return for me in a sennight. I must decide by then."

They made their way across the grounds without any more discussion, the harsh realities the three of them had in their young lives more than they should have had to deal with. Sheona vowed to come out stronger, whether she married or not.

They approached one of the buildings and Brynja opened the door for her before stepping in behind her. "Here we are. I sleep in that bed." She pointed to the one at the end of the row. "And Hildi is in the next one. I wouldn't take the one on this end because it's the coldest one. When the nights are cool, it is truly freezing near the door. Take the next one."

"You don't snore, do you?" Hildi asked with a giggle. "I wouldn't care. I'd probably have a laugh or two."

"I don't snore." Sheona chose the bed next to Hildi and set her bag on the chest at the end, arranging the furs on the bed for later. There was little furniture in the chamber: four beds, a table with four stools around it, and a chest at the end of each bed. There was a small hearth on one side, but there was no wood to be seen. "No fires for warmth?"

"Not yet. We're used to Norse cold, anyway. We go once a year. When it gets colder, we'll be given some wood, so they told us. We have plenty of furs."

Sheona sat down on the bed, pleased that it was pleasantly soft. Not quite sure what to say next, she didn't have to wait long.

Brynja sat down on a stool not far away. "So, were you abused like many who come here just to run away from men?"

Sheona reacted quickly, shaking her head, but then she stared at her hands, thinking about her past and how to explain it to a stranger. What exactly had happened to her? How should she explain it to someone? That somehow she feared one act more than any other besides death?

Brynja waited but then nodded. "I think I understand. You weren't abused, but almost. Enough to make you hate men. I hate men. Hildi hates men. Our fathers were only around enough to make us, then they disappeared. Climbed back into their galley ships, leaving us to our mothers' care. And how do women protect themselves from other men?" She arched a brow. "They don't. That is the harsh reality of life. The only way it happens."

Sheona sat up. "Nay. That's not the only way. My brother just married, and he adores his wife. And the other clans near us have taught me that there are better ways to live. Why, the newest clan has women trained as archers. They travel with their finest warriors. In fact, they just defeated one of the cruelest men around, one who stole bairns from their mothers. He was horrible. But they found him and tied him, giving all the people he harmed the right to just due. They did whatever they wished to him. He was dead by the end, but he'd killed his own wife and her parents. A truly evil man."

Hildi said, "Magni told us all about that. Said he was first and kicked him twice for stealing him away."

"You know Magni? He is so sweet. Where is he?"

"He's living at Ionaland with his parents. Poor lad is afraid to leave Iona, so Beatris told us." Hildi fiddled with the clothes in the chest at the end of her bed.

"Did you witness the just due?" Brynja asked. "Every evil person should be forced to experience the same."

"I didn't, but I heard about it. My brother's new wife threw an axe and hit one man in his heart just before the battle broke out. And another lass hit one between his eyes. She ran away from home because her father was going to make her marry an evil baron." Then she leaned forward. "Said the baron touched her once and told her she'd have to do whatever he said, so she ran away."

"Did he catch her?" Hildi asked.

"Nay, she got away and met one of the chieftains. Married him. She's verra happy." Sheona then said the one thing she clung to. "It is possible to be happily married. I know many who are, but one thing I've noticed."

"What?" Hildi and Brynja asked.

"They're strong women." That's what she had to do. Become strong like Eva and Meg and Dyna and Gwyneth and Eli. "My brother's wife was teaching me how to throw an axe. I brought a couple along with me to practice with, should I get the chance."

"An axe? Magni did mention that. We'll learn with you," Hildi said.

"I'm not verra good, but I need to learn a skill. Learn how to hurt a man who is chasing after me." Sheona stared at the floor, not wishing to explain any more. The two girls nodded, so she said the only thing she could think of. "Please teach me how to throw the spear."

CHAPTER SEVENTEEN

DERMOT

D ERMOT SAT ON his favorite stool on the parapets, in his favorite location where he could look across the water to the mainland. Bloody Bay, Mingary, Ardnamurchan, Morvern, even Kinlochaline was visible in the distance. Listening to the waves, whether crashing or calm, helped settle things in his mind.

And he had much to settle.

Sheona, his sweet bairn who used to sit on his knees, was troubled. But from what?

"Da, where are you?" Sloan called out, closing the door behind him. "Are you out here?"

"Aye, I'm here." Perhaps it was time to ask Sloan. He seemed to know everything that happened on Rankin land. How aware was he of his sister and her activities? "Bring a stool, Sloan."

They kept a few stools about because the parapets held such a beautiful view. Sloan came around the corner carrying one, then set it down. "Da, what's wrong? I can tell when you're upset."

Dermot shrugged, wondering how to explain what he'd learned, though it had all been subtle suggestions about what may or may not have happened. Where to start? He kneaded his hands in his lap, staring across the landscape beneath them.

"Da? What happened at the nunnery? Did Sheona say something that upset you?"

That gave him a start. "Sheona? Nay. She said naught. Just that she wished to stay for a sennight."

"Then someone else said something?"

Dermot mulled over all that had been said by the prioress, thinking to hide everything, but then decided that Sloan deserved to know. Sheona was his sister. Was it possible Sloan knew something about what had happened to her and never shared it with his own father?

Dermot let out a deep sigh, then said, "The prioress asked me if Sheona has been, um … if she had something in her past, umm …" He couldn't even bring himself to say the words. His eyes watered at the thought.

"Did she ask you if Sheona had been abused?"

"Aye. Exactly that. She said it's common in lasses who wish to become nuns. They come to the nunnery to escape. She wondered if something had happened in Sheona's past to make her run away. And I couldn't answer her because I don't know. She's my wee lassie. Sloan, if I found out anyone touched my wee lassie, I'll have him held down so I can cut off his bollocks. I'll do it myself, and mayhap I'll …"

Sloan reached for his father's forearm, gripping him lightly. "Da, I don't know of anything. Do you?"

"Nay. But I want to know." Then he thought again. "Mayhap I don't wish to know. I don't know. But I want my daughter to be happy. She should be having bairns and staring into their eyes with love like Marta does. I don't want her hiding in a nunnery because some fool accosted her or …" His lower lip quivered, and he couldn't stop what happened next.

His tears burst out as though he'd kept them inside for decades. He couldn't handle the thought of some fool touching his wee lassie without her approval. And if it happened, how long ago? Where? Who?

"Who, Sloan? Who would dare to touch …" He couldn't handle it. He leaned his elbow on the edge of the parapet and sobbed.

"Da, I promise you that I will find out. Mayhap nothing happened. Let me see what I can learn first."

It was a good thing Sloan offered to help. Offered to find out the truth.

Dermot couldn't bear it.

CHAPTER EIGHTEEN

RUT

———— ✦ ————

TASKILL STRODE INTO the kitchens carrying his bucket full of fish.

Rut brought her hand up to cover her nose. "Oh, Taskill. Take those smelly things in through the back door. Why must you bring such rank objects through my great hall?"

Taskill ignored her, walking straight toward the kitchens as if his ears were shut off.

"Taskill!"

Nothing. She crossed her arms, knowing enough to wait for him to return. She surely did not think grabbing his arm was the right thing to do since he could spill fish guts everywhere. Rut covered her nose again, then grabbed a nearby book to fan it in front of her face to dispel the odor.

She tapped her foot impatiently, waiting for her son's return. As soon as he entered, she asked, "Taskill. What is going on with you? Why did you ignore me before?"

"Ignore you? I would never ignore you, Mama."

"But you just did." The foot tapped again, a

bit quicker this time, until Taskill stared at it. "All right, young man. What the hell is going on in that head of yours?"

"Naught, Mama. I don't know of what you speak." He lifted his chin and finally looked into her eyes, the first time that day.

"And I call bull. Not just bull, but the shite of the bull will hit your skull for lying to me."

He grinned, that sheepish grin her second-born did so well. The one that from his tenth summer had told her he was lying. Or had it been six summers?

"All right. I'll tell you, but not here. It would not be appropriate."

"In your brother's solar." She waved her hand toward the door, then swished her skirts and headed in that direction, fixing a few errant strands of hair that had loosed themselves from her bun.

Taskill dragged his heels but followed her in. She closed the door, and her hand went straight to her nose. "From here you go back to the sound. You reek of fish. Now, tell me quickly what's bothering you so."

He shrugged, staring at the floor, transfixed by his thoughts. Her son so resembled her dear Douglas whenever he got that look on his face. "Taskill." She reached for his chin and tipped his face back to hers. "What happened?"

"Dermot took Sheona to the nunnery." He lifted his gaze to hers, and the pain she saw there shocked her.

"Why?"

"He said she had to marry or become a nun. I don't know why he chose to leave that quickly."

"How did you hear of this? I'm sure Lennox or Meg would have told me of this atrocious act." She crossed her arms, her mind filling with visions of slapping Dermot for doing such an awful thing to his daughter.

"One of their guards who was fishing with us. Said he wished to marry her, so he was upset when he found out their old chieftain was taking her to Iona. And Sloan confirmed it. The guard's name is Clyde. Know you of him?"

Rut spun away to pace a bit, the swirl of her skirts around her ankles giving her strength. She loved the feel of it, using it as a substitute for a good, hard slap when it was necessary. "I don't know any guards' names, Taskill. I do not bother with them. They'll be here one day and gone the next, especially at a neighboring clan." She paused for a moment to gather her thoughts. "Dermot will not accept a guard for his daughter. You just gave me evidence of how foolish this Clyde is." She shook her head, trying to figure out how to handle this situation. The important piece was how Taskill reacted to this event. "And this upsets you terribly, I see. I thought you had no feelings for Sheona."

A fury lit her son's eyes so fast she had to hide her smile. Oh, how she loved to see him upset over a girl, especially Sheona. Was he finally figuring out that they would suit?

"Of course, it upsets me, Mama. I was supposed

to propose to her. If I had, she'd be on Rankin land where she belongs."

"Mayhap the lass wishes to be a nun." God only knows why anyone would wish to do such a thing, but some did. Rut couldn't imagine not knowing how it felt to be taken to another world with the right man.

Fools didn't know what they were missing.

Taskill sat taller, his indignity telling her he had more feelings for the lass than he would admit. Or perhaps he hadn't figured it out yet.

He said, "She doesn't wish to be a nun, now or ever. How can you say such a thing? She should be home. Mayhap I need to go to her and propose. Mayhap she'll come back with me."

"And what if she refuses? I was under the impression that she has no more interest in marrying you than you do in proposing to her. True or not?"

"She's not interested. But she might be if it allowed her to escape the Isle of Iona. Why would someone wish to live there forever? Such a foolish thought. Mayhap I'll go to her." He knew he had to do something, but what exactly he didn't know. And the biggest problem was he didn't know who to ask. Perhaps he needed to talk with his brother.

"You will not go to her. I forbid it, Taskill. And I'm sure Lennox would agree with me."

Lennox popped his head in the door. "What would I agree with?"

Rut turned to her eldest son. "That Taskill

should not travel to the Isle of Iona to retrieve Sheona. It's no longer his affair."

"I just heard from Jasper. Said one of the Rankin guards is telling everyone about Dermot taking her there. Poor Sheona was not happy about it."

"So, I should go," Taskill said.

"Nay, not until we give this some consideration and discuss it." Rut crossed her arms.

"Why wait?" Taskill said. "I'll leave now, and I can make it to MacLean land by nightfall."

"Because …" Lennox paused when the door opened, and Meg stuck her head around the corner. "He's here already?" Lennox asked her.

"Who?" Rut asked, stepping forward.

Lennox said, "Dermot. I could see him coming up the path, Ingelram behind him."

Meg nodded. "He's here."

"I'll send Taskill out, but I'm going with him," Lennox said.

"Nay, he wishes to speak with Rut." Meg waggled her brow at everyone.

Taskill, Meg, and Lennox all gave their full attention to Rut to see her reaction.

"Oh, bring him in," Rut said. "Taskill, get out. We'll talk later."

Taskill disappeared so quickly that Rut frowned. "Lennox, check on him. I don't like his actions right now. He's not acting stable, nor do I trust him."

"Fine, I'll follow Taskill, see how he is. Meg, bring Dermot to my mother."

Meg left, Lennox behind her. Within moments,

the door swung open, and Dermot stood in the doorway.

"Dermot? What is it?" Rut asked, not liking the expression on his face any more than she liked Taskill's expression.

"Rut, you have to help me."

"Why?"

"Because Ailis is gone and this is women's business. I don't know what to do."

Rut closed the door, but Dermot couldn't have surprised her any more than he did with his actions. She wished to yell and chastise him for all he did, for taking his beautiful daughter to a nunnery, but she had to stop herself.

Dermot Rankin fell into a chair and sobbed.

CHAPTER NINETEEN

SHEONA

~~

SHEONA STOOD IN the clearing, lifting her spear and holding it over her shoulder again.

Brynja said, "Try shooting it higher in the air. Sometimes you send it to get someone's attention. If that's the situation, then you wish to send it as high as you can and have it land in the center of the group of people. I always do that before I aim to kill."

Sheona held her weapon down. "You've killed before?"

Brynja looked at Hildi, who gave her a subtle nod. "Aye. We'll tell you some other time."

Sheona tossed her spear high in the air, but it fell to the ground, hitting and falling flat. Two more attempts did the same thing.

"How do I make it stick in the ground?" she asked Brynja.

"Here, I'll show you." The lass picked up her own spear and fired it so hard that Sheona was certain it would stick in something.

She needed more power, more strength, but her hands shook. "I can't. I need to rest for a moment." Setting her weapon down, she flopped onto a flat boulder.

Hildi said, "Not everyone can throw a spear. Mayhap you should consider archery. Or how about practicing with a dagger?"

But Sheona knew that wasn't what she wanted. She admired Merryn and Dyna and Eli for their archery, the way they climbed into the trees and shot at the enemy, but she admired Meg and Eva more. The axes did much more damage.

She had the impression that throwing an axe with both hands, much like a spear, would be far more satisfying than letting an arrow go. Both acts, the spear and the axe, represented more power in her eyes.

But perhaps a dagger would work. She could carry it easier than the axes she brought with her. In fact, it was foolish to bring them along since she had no accuracy with them at all yet. But she had to learn to fire a weapon in case she was ever given the opportunity to retaliate.

She wished she had been given the chance to fire with power at that person who had ruined her life.

"Who was it?" Brynja asked.

Sheona, surprised by her friend's insightfulness, shook her head and said naught.

"I know you cannot talk about it, but no man has the right to force himself on you. If you learn to punch or kick him in just the right way, he'll never be able to hurt you."

Curious, she tipped her head. "What do you mean?"

"If you kick a man in his bollocks, he'll be powerless to do anything for several moments. It's a protection that not enough lasses know. I consider it my duty to inform anyone of its purpose."

"Why?"

"Nature's protection for the weaker person. Most men are larger and taller than a lass. Size is in their favor, but one tweak to a bollock makes them powerless. Use it if you must. It will give you time to get away before their strength returns." Brynja observed her. "Do you not wish you'd known that?"

"Nay, it would not have helped me in my particular situation."

Brynja scowled. "That would help in any situation."

"Not mine. I think I'll go rest, if you don't mind." Sheona wished to get away from her new friends. While she appreciated their companionship and the way they had trained her with the spears, she didn't know them well enough to discuss her problem. "Is there a place where we can bathe?"

Hildi said, "At the beach!"

"But it's cold now."

"Still feels good."

"Go to the waterfall and wash your hair," Brynja said. "Then we'll braid it with ribbons if you like."

"Like yours?" Sheona asked, wide-eyed. She loved both of their stylings.

"Aye. Just like ours. What color ribbon would you like?"

She thought for a moment, then said, "Green, if you please."

"Green it is."

Sheona headed to their building, gathered her things, and made her way to the waterfall. She'd taken a walk in the morning with another nun who showed her where they bathed. It was a private spot where a burn flowed into a waterfall, several rocks nearby to set her things on.

She stuck her foot under the water first and let out a squeal because it was so cold, but she needed to wash. Her hair needed it too. She played this game of putting another part of her body in before pulling back out, getting used to the temperature slowly. Marta would put her whole body in at once, but Sheona couldn't tolerate the cold as well as her sister did.

Once she was finally immersed in the cool spray, she tipped her head back and sighed, allowing the water to slide over her body, using the sliver of soap she'd brought along to lather up as she stood under the stream. This is what she needed—time away from her father, her brother, everyone.

Sheona needed to think on exactly what she wanted. But there was only one problem.

She had no idea what she wanted.

Weighing her choices, she came up with nothing. Nothing pulled to her, nothing reached for her soul as Eva had said to her once, describing how she knew Sloan was the right man for her. Sloan had tugged at her soul, though Eva had admitted to hating him at one point. Meg had said the same thing about Lennox. She said she hated him so much that they argued before she climbed into a boat on MacVey land. That the two had shouted at each other, arguing for quite a while before she'd left, Lennox following her.

Sheona didn't hate Taskill, she'd thought he was the one for her. Until that day—the day he'd said he'd never marry her. Her interest in the man had flown away as quickly as an eagle after its prey.

Eva had said it took her awhile, but once her heart had changed, she knew it could never be any other way. She loved Sloan with all of her being.

That was what Sheona wished for herself, but her heart was empty.

Not just empty, but cold, and filled with hatred toward one particular man. Not Sloan or her father or even Taskill.

Certain that she'd uncovered nothing, she stepped out of the water and grabbed the linen to dry herself with, then dressed with care, using her fingers to straighten her long locks.

Perhaps if she changed herself, she'd feel differently. Gathering her things, she strolled back to her chamber, stepping inside and jumping. She hadn't expected Brynja and Hildi to be there, but they were.

They had ribbons and a thick comb all set out.

"Come. Sit down. We'll both do your hair. That way it goes much faster, especially when it's still damp. Sit down and be prepared to fall in love with your new hairstyle."

Sheona sat down, a wee bit unsettled about this change, but she was also excited. She knew no one here from her clan, so they could not report anything to her father. Why not try something different?

She sat down and let the two braid her hair, amazed at how skilled and quick they were with their hands. By the time they were done, she touched the long braids carefully, amazed at how tightly the strands were bound together.

"Many thanks to you. I wish I could see myself," she said wistfully.

"Here," Hildi said, producing a metallic bowl from her chest. "You can nearly see yourself in this." She held it up in front of Sheona, who looked in the shiny bowl, her reflection visible enough to get a peek at her new hairstyle.

Sheona loved it.

But she surprised herself even more with the first thought that popped into her mind; she couldn't help but wonder what Taskill would think of her hair.

CHAPTER TWENTY

DERMOT

———— ❧ ————

WHAT THE HELL did he know of women's issues? Naught. Absolutely naught. He only knew that when Ailis was younger, she made him stay away from her once a moon for her womanly issues. That was it.

Oh, she had her odd moments in her last moon of carrying her bairns. Dermot never thought that was so unusual since her belly had been enormous. It had to be exhausting for Ailis to carry that monstrous burden around with her for so many moons. He never bothered her when she neared her time.

He understood those issues.

But this … what the abbess had mentioned … the possibility …

Nay. He couldn't even think on it. Yet he had to. He truly did not wish to send his daughter to a nunnery. He loved Sheona. She looked more like his Ailis than Marta did. He wished for her to marry a good man and have many bairns.

He thought taking her to a nunnery would

scare her into accepting Taskill, but what would he do if she stayed?

"Dermot," Rut barked. "Stop your carrying on and tell me what is bothering you. Please. I cannot help you if I don't know what is happening."

"My wee lassie …"

"She's not wee anymore. Now what's wrong with Sheona? She was fine when she was here."

"The abbess. What she said. What she suggested was just …"

"Dermot. Stop your crying," Rut demanded. "Now. Stop crying and tell me what happened." She crossed her arms and waited for him to finish, but he kept going. She reached over and slapped his hand away from his face. "Stop it, I said."

That crossed the line. "You're pishing me off, Rut."

"Good. Now get mad and explain everything that happened. Stop acting like a girl."

He gritted his teeth and narrowed his gaze, doing his best to give her his most intimidating stare, the one that scared every guard he ever had.

"Your glares don't frighten me, Dermot. Tell me exactly what the abbess said."

Damn it all, but he'd have to work on his glare. "The abbess said many lasses who wish to join the nunnery—"

"Sheona doesn't wish to join."

"She might now. Stop interrupting me, Rut."

"Fine. Continue." She took a seat and waved at him to go on.

"Many lasses who come to her have been abused by someone."

"That does not surprise me one bit. But apparently, it surprises you."

"Hellfire, aye, it did. Who would dare assault my daughter? I was the chieftain of the clan." His head ached every time he thought of the possibility of Sheona being wronged.

"Dermot, surely it does not surprise you that many of your maids are misused. Men are bigger and stronger than lasses. They can hold them down, they can—"

"Not. My. Daughter!" He stood up and bellowed at Rut, not caring who heard them. Rut stood too, surprised at his anger. "Not Sheona!"

Rut nodded and stepped closer, setting her hand on his shoulder. "I'm sure you are correct, Dermot. Why don't you tell me exactly what happened when you went to Iona? Tell me everything. I promise to listen."

Dermot thought on what she said, deciding it was what he needed. He needed to repeat all that had happened and what the abbess said. Just because she said it didn't mean that anything had happened to Sheona. Did it? "When we arrived, we were given a small tour of the nunnery. I only had one hour to move about before the boat left. I had to use my time wisely because I was given none to spare. I saw where Sheona would sleep. I noticed other women moving about, some in robes, some in regular clothing. We met the abbess, and the first thing she asked was whether Sheona wished to take her vows. I said nay, Sheona said aye. That surprised me. I was only trying to frighten her into accepting Taskill's suit. That's all. But then she said she would stay. I didn't know what to make of that. But we all decided it would be best for her to visit for a sennight, then she could make up her mind."

"That makes perfect sense, but I don't understand what upset you so. Is it the fact that she said that she wished to take her vows?"

"Aye. I mean, nay. I don't know." He rubbed his eyes with both hands, frustrated because he couldn't explain himself very well.

"Tell me about the abbess."

"The abbess said she would talk with me privately. She suggested that many of the lasses she sees are there because they've been misused. That someone has taken advantage of them. She didn't use the term *rape* but instead talked about abuse. What exactly does that mean, Rut? What happened to my wee lassie?"

"Did you ask Sheona?"

"Nay!" The word came out in such a long note that it seemed more like a sentence or a paragraph. "Nay, I didn't ask her. How could I? I'm her sire. Men don't talk about such things with their daughters. I need Ailis here. Why did she leave me? She is the one who should talk with Sheona, not me."

"What can I do to help?"

"Talk with her. You ask her if someone abused her."

"Oh, Dermot. I don't know if she'll answer me. Why not ask Marta to talk with her? Or Sloan? Don't they get along well enough? Or what about Eva? They are of similar ages. I'm sure she would talk to Eva or Marta."

Dermot sat down, thinking on this suggestion. Perhaps Rut had the right idea. Sheona would surely talk with Marta, but he couldn't ask Marta to leave her bairns behind to go to the abbey. After all, wee Margret was still at the breast. He didn't know much about it, but who would feed Margret if Marta left?

What about Eva? That idea held more merit since Eva was free to do as she wished. Then another idea popped into his head.

Eva and Sloan.

He bolted up from his chair. "Many thanks to you, Rut. I know exactly what I'm going to do."

"What?" Rut asked, folding her hands in front of her.

Dermot didn't have time to explain it, so he waved her off. "I'll tell you later. I have something I must do."

"Dermot. Stop where you are." Rut's voice told him she was not jesting.

He didn't have time for Rut.

He had to get back on Rankin land, and he had to send Sloan and Eva to Iona to speak with Sheona.

And he'd go along, only to listen at the door.

It was the best way for him to learn the truth.

No one had dared to abuse his daughter.

CHAPTER TWENTY-ONE

TASKILL

TASKILL STEPPED INTO the great hall at Duart Castle, pleased to see Connor was still inside the solar, just as Hagen had told him. He knocked on the door and Connor waved him inside, so Taskill made his way to the desk in the corner. "A moment of your time, Chief?" As the past chief of Clan Grant, Connor deserved the respect of being addressed by his former title.

"Taskill, come on in. Hope your life has calmed down after the night of the festival."

Taskill let out a deep sigh, something he wished he'd held in, but it was too late, so he shrugged his shoulders. "It's the reason I'm here. I came to apologize for my mother's actions. It was rude of her to cause trouble in the middle of your great hall on a night like that. And I'll also admit that my mother is too … full of conviction, I'll call it, for her to come and apologize on her own."

"My uncles used to wish for entertainment like that at every Grant festival. They said it would make each festival distinguishable from the others. And when I look back over the years, they were right. Dermot helped to make it memorable, though I am deeply concerned about how it affected you and Sheona. How are you, Taskill?" Connor sat down behind the desk and motioned the lad to sit in a nearby chair.

"I'm fine. Confused. Dermot claimed my father agreed to the betrothal years ago. No one in my clan knows anything about it. I'm not surprised I wouldn't have been told of such, but for my mother, Lennox, and Jasper all to say they never heard of any agreement makes me suspicious."

"Are you at all interested in Sheona?"

Taskill hadn't expected that question, and he honestly didn't know how to answer it. He liked Sheona well enough. She was certainly beautiful and smart, but she didn't … "I hadn't thought on it until Dermot brought it up." Sheona wasn't … She didn't … She … What the hell was he trying to say about Sheona?

"Have you thought about what you're looking for in a wife?"

"Not sure what you mean, Chief."

"What characteristics are you looking for? Someone strong? Funny? Someone who likes to swim? To fish? To boat? Who likes to travel or stay home? Someone who loves bairns or who doesn't want any bairns at all?"

Befuddled by all his questions, Taskill replied, "I guess I haven't thought much about it." He had considered it, but what he'd reflected on wasn't something he was ready to share with Connor Grant.

"What is it about Sheona that makes you reject the offer? I heard you did right away."

He gave the most honest answer he could. "Sheona isn't interested in me, so it isn't a question that needs an answer."

"Have you spoken with her again? Is her sire being obnoxiously persistent about the issue as I guess he would be?"

Taskill shrugged again, then explained, "He took her to Iona Abbey. She's staying there for a sennight to see if she wishes to become a nun."

Connor arched a brow at him, clearly from surprise. "A nun? I've known several, but she doesn't seem the type. If there is one. My wife spent some time at an abbey once. She speaks of it as quite a unique experience. Not one she wished to do for long."

Taskill stood, wishing to end this conversation before Connor pushed him a little more. "I guess we'll find out in a sennight what Sheona thinks. My thanks for the festival, and again, Lennox and I both apologize for our mother's behavior."

"Think naught more about it. All is forgiven. Best of luck to Sheona and to you, Taskill. It wouldn't be the way to start a relationship, in my opinion."

Taskill took his leave, holding the smirk from the comment Connor had made.

He recalled when he and his siblings had questioned their parents about the day they'd met. Images of three bairns questioning the two popped into his head:

"How did you and Papa meet?"

Their father had replied quickly, "We met when your grandfather came screaming at me that I had to marry your mother within a day."

Their mother had added, "And your father refused to marry me. As I refused his offer."

"Aye, it wasn't until we were at sword point in the chapel that we married. We've been happily married ever since." Their father had grinned and kissed their mother's cheek, and she blushed more than he'd ever seen her before.

Hellfire, but his mind was a bit too active sometimes. He needed to force himself to stop thinking about Sheona in a nunnery.

Taskill headed for the stables, surprised to see a group of lasses surrounding three guards: Jowell, Paden, and Hagen. The flirting was so obvious that he had to smile, though he held his chuckling inside. He knew how it felt to have lasses do what they could to beg for a kiss.

Or more.

The three men kindly sent the lasses giggling off into the distance toward the kitchens. "You dispensed of them quickly," he said to Jowell as he passed.

"I tire of them. On Grant land, they ignored us because there were so many guards. Here, they fall at our feet," Hagen said. "I don't like it. How would I know if they're interested in me instead of how I look?"

"Exactly," Jowell said. "We send them off usually. You can't trust their words."

"Nice to see you, Taskill. We have work to do." The three headed toward the lists of Clan

Grantham. Taskill found his horse, mounted up, and headed back toward Clan MacVey. He rode for a quarter hour before stopping at his favorite spot, a place where he could take his horse to a ledge that overlooked both the sound and the firth at the same time.

It was a magnificent place to settle his thoughts. Connor had given him much to think on. What did he want in a wife? He had been aching for something different but what exactly it was, he wasn't sure.

He thought back on everything, realizing that the arrival of the Granthams had changed so much on the isle, and since then, a great deal had transpired. He thought about Lennox, Sloan, as well as Thane and even Broc. Four of them had married so quickly that it had surprised him.

And three of them had been the kind of marriage he'd often thought would be his own circumstances.

He thought of Thane, rescuing Tamsin from the rocks when her husband had tried to kill her.

Or of Broc who'd saved Merryn from the cruel bastard who'd killed her sister and parents. How he'd lifted her onto his horse and struck down two of her attackers.

Or of his brother who'd found Meg with four rescued bairns, running from two evil men who'd locked them all up. She'd held an axe aimed at his chest when they met. Eventually, he'd saved Meg from the fools who wished to sell the bairns to the highest bidder.

Or of Sloan who'd followed his sister, finding

her locked up, locating the bairns and saving them from the evil men who sent them out in a boat to be taken across the sea to Europe. They'd fought off evil men and even a creature of the sea who'd appeared out of nowhere.

He smiled. Every one of these images was of the husband with his sword bloodied from battle with his arm around his betrothed, exhausted and weak from all they'd endured. True love had overtaken them.

And Dermot wanted him to show up at the kirk and marry Sheona without getting to know her well.

Taskill needed his own adventure. It was supposed to happen when he traveled the isle and came upon a lass who was in desperate need of his help.

"Taskill? What the hell are you doing here?" His brother approached on horseback. "Have you apologized to the Grants yet?"

"I did speak with Connor, Lennox. He said not to worry. He thought it made the festival memorable. I think that's what he called it."

Lennox's eyes narrowed. "Why are you here?"

"I love the view. I like to come up here once in a while."

Lennox nodded, then said, "Enough. We need to talk. Follow me home."

"About what?"

"Sheona. Dermot just left and Mama filled me in on some of their discussion. And this is not to be repeated, but he told Mother that the abbess suggested that mayhap Sheona had been abused by someone. I hope you haven't been near her."

"Nay. Abused her? Lennox, I would never do such a thing. How could you ask me so?"

Lennox chewed on his lower lip. "I shouldn't have asked. I know you wouldn't. Have you any idea who might be capable of such an atrocious act?"

"Oh, there are many among the guards, but a chieftain's sister? Dermot's daughter? They aren't foolish enough to commit such a vile deed." He turned his horse around and they headed away from the view and back toward their castle.

"Why does the abbess ask that type of question?"

"Because Sheona said she might wish to take her vows. Shocked Dermot, but the abbess said many who take their vows have been misused. She was asking for information from Dermot, but he got upset and came right to Mother. He wants her to ask Sheona about it."

"Mama? Nay, do not allow her to go after Sheona. That would be horrible for her. Nay. There has to be someone else."

And he knew exactly who that someone else would be.

Him. He'd heard enough.

He was going to Iona Abbey on the morrow.

CHAPTER TWENTY-TWO

SHEONA

———— ❧ ————

TWO DAYS HAD passed, and Sheona was beginning to feel comfortable at the nunnery. Brynja and Hildi were wonderful friends and extremely patient with her. She'd learned to throw the spear farther each day.

And she loved her new hairstyle. It gave her confidence—it made her feel like a different person.

She wondered what her sire would think of her hair.

She wasn't particularly fond of their time in the chapel as she found it boring. And she hadn't quite decided how she felt about God. She believed in God, but she didn't believe He was paying much attention to her. So then, why pray if He ignored her prayers?

But she decided to make the most of the sennight she was here.

When they exited morning prayer, Hildi said, "Come. We're going to visit Ionaland. Ada said we have vegetables for them, and we'll see what they have to share with us."

"Do you like Ionaland?" Sheona wondered if the two Norse lasses preferred to stay at the nunnery.

Brynja replied quickly, "It's my favorite place of all. I love the bairns. You'll see."

They set off for their destination down the isle a ways, not too far, but enough to give them time to chat.

"Why do you like it there?" Sheona asked.

Brynja said, "I love the wee ones. Magni is my favorite."

"Magni? He is friends with my nephew, Rowan. Do you suppose he'll stay there forever?"

"Aye, they found his parents, and they decided to live there. They adopted Tenney too. He's adorable."

Brynja added, "I like it best when Simone is there. I love to talk with Simone and Beatris. They are both married, and I've learned much from them about men."

"What kind of things?"

Hildi whispered, "The kind of things the nuns won't mention. The things men do to women." Then she giggled. "Do you know of what we speak?"

Sheona nodded. "I've heard of it. I heard it is verra painful for women."

Brynja moved closer to Sheona. "That's what we thought. Our mothers warned us of men who take lasses and force themselves on them. Said it's horrible, but Simone says it shouldn't be. She said it's a crime called *rape* when that happens."

Sheona was more confused than ever from that

explanation. She needed to speak with someone. After all, Marta had bairns and wanted another. Why hadn't she asked her sister about it?

They were nearly there, the sack of vegetables they each carried on their backs growing heavy. She could tell by how their trek slowed compared to how they started, but Sheona was hopeful they would see this woman called Simone. She needed to talk to Simone.

"Brynja!" a lad called out and raced toward them as they approached the small group of cottages near the shoreline. A wee lad toddled along behind the older boy.

"Greetings to you, Magni. We brought a friend, Sheona."

"Greetings, Sheona. I've seen you before. Where?" The lad with the head of dark, tousled curls stared up at her.

"I'm from Clan Rankin. Rowan is my nephew."

"He was kidnapped with me once. When Meg saved us."

"He was, but he's afraid to leave now. He prefers to stay at home."

Magni scowled. "Me too. I stay here on Ionaland where it's safest. God lives over there in the chapel and with the monks, so no evil men will steal us away."

A long-legged woman followed them out, her hair sleekly tied at the crown, hanging like the tail of a pony down her back. "Greetings, Brynja and Hildi. Who have you brought with you?"

Magni moved to pick up Tenney and brought him to the group. "This is my new brother,

Tenney. We stay here now with my mama and papa. I like it here."

"Manners, Magni." Simone nodded to Sheona.

"She's Rowan's auntie. What was your name again?" he asked, tipping his head at her.

"Sheona. It's a pleasure to meet you both." Then she giggled because Tenney reached for her, so she picked him up and he gave her a kiss on her cheek. "Are you not sweet?"

"He's my brother forever."

"Magni, let's help them carry the vegetables. I smell cabbage. And we have treats for you to return to the nuns. A bottle of wine and a hunk of smoked pork sent over from the MacLeans on the mainland. And some carrots from a ship that passed by."

"We have parsnips along with the cabbage," Sheona explained, slipping the sack from her back to her shoulder.

"Come join us for some warm broth," Simone said.

Sheona had a sudden urge to ask questions. "I would love to talk with you a bit, if I may be so forward, Simone." Blushing at her own boldness, she prayed she wouldn't reject her request.

"I'd be happy to get to know you better, Sheona. Come, help us bring the vegetables inside the storage hut, and then we can take a walk down to the beach. It's beautiful this time of year."

Sheona nodded and gulped at her courage. She would not lose it; she would ask Simone what to do in her circumstance. The three days had convinced her of one thing: She was not interested in being forced into a marriage she didn't want. The nuns would not be able to advise her, but perhaps Simone had some ideas.

As Sheona followed her to the storage hut, Simone called out to Beatris, who was surrounded by a group of bairns of various ages in a grassy area where they ran freely. Two other women there waved to them, so Simone returned the wave.

She had no idea they existed on this isle. Brynja said, "We'll wait for you before we return, Sheona. Enjoy the beach."

Simone led her along a path that took them to an isolated stretch of sand that seemed to be from a different world. Once they were far enough away, Simone said, "You are from Clan Rankin. Are you interested in taking your vows as a nun?"

Simone guided Sheona to a large rock and then sat down, pointing for Sheona to sit next to her. "Tell me all. I see you are carrying much on your shoulders. I will keep your confidence. I live on Iona with my husband, and we see verra few people. I love it here. You can trust me, Sheona."

For some reason, Sheona did trust this woman, and it all tumbled out. "I don't know what to do. My sire wished to force me to marry someone from the neighboring clan, but I am not interested in marrying him any more than he wishes to marry me. Papa said if I didn't marry him, then I had to take my vows as a nun, but I have no desire to do that either because it's boring sitting in the chapel for so long, and oh, what shall I do? I—"

"Take a breath, lassie," Simone said, cocooning

her hand in hers. "You'll figure it out. Tell me about the man your sire wishes for you to marry."

She breathed in deeply, the hope inside her ready to burst out simply because the idea of Simone helping her understand everything was more than she could have dreamed of. "His name is Taskill, and I've known him all my life and we get along fine, but I'm not ready to marry. I may never wish to marry. It isn't that I dislike Taskill. I just don't wish to be a wife."

"Don't you have a sister? Rowan's mother?"

She nodded, doing her best to keep the tears locked inside before they drowned out her words. She needed to get them out, try her best to explain what she didn't understand. But how could she if she didn't understand it? "Marta is my sister, and I adore her."

"But you didn't talk to her about this? Or to your mother?"

"Mama passed a year ago. I did try with Marta, but she has the new bairn and she was trying to feed her and the bairn started to cry and Marta is so tired from not sleeping …"

Simone gave a pronounced nod. "Now I understand. New bairns are all-consuming for everyone. And you have one brother or two?"

"Two." Then Sheona stopped abruptly, thinking about how her sire had disowned Rinaldo for all the trouble he'd caused. Did that mean she'd never had him as a brother? "Or one. My sire found out Rinaldo wanted to hurt Sloan and had killed his betrothed a while ago, so he disowned him before he killed him for his crimes."

Simone grew wide-eyed. "I recall something about that. I'm sure that was difficult for your clan." She leaned down, resting her arms on her knees to think. "So, Rinaldo didn't like Sloan, who is chieftain. How did you get along with Rinaldo?"

Sheona's face fell and she stared at her feet, blushing. "All right. He was always different. He had a way of making everyone think he was innocent, yet I saw him for who he truly was."

Simone arched a brow at her.

"He was mean to me when my parents weren't looking. He liked to poke me or my sister, take our things, slap us when no one was aware of what he was doing."

"Sounds like he carried a need to be mean," she said. Simone took her hand again and asked, "Did your brother abuse you? That's not so unusual."

Sheona shook her head furiously.

"Did he touch you in ways you didn't like?"

She denied it vigorously again, wondering how to explain exactly what had happened. "Could you explain something to me? I was told that the act … the marriage act … is verra painful. Why do women marry, then?"

"Because they told you wrong. With the right person, the marriage bed is an act of love. It's an act where each participant shows the other one how much they love them, and from that love comes pleasure, not pain. Now, when forced onto someone who doesn't want it, it's extremely painful. It's called rape."

She scowled, trying to fit Simone's words into

what she'd learned about the act, but she couldn't. "I think I should go." She stood and turned away from Simone.

"Wait, Sheona, please. Why don't you tell me exactly what you were told and by whom? Or tell me how you learned what you did."

Stopping to think, Sheona played with the hairs that had come loose from her braid, wondering how to explain exactly what had happened, but then she rejected it.

It would be easier if she said nothing at all.

"My thanks, but I have to go."

CHAPTER TWENTY-THREE

RUT

———❧———

LATER THAT DAY, Rut went up to the parapets to think on all she'd learned. Something was going on, but she didn't know exactly what it was. After watching Dermot Rankin sob like a wee bairn, she knew there were more things taking place on the Isle of Mull than she was aware of. The question was how to find out exactly what had happened.

The isle had been in turmoil for most of autumn. So much had happened that it was hard to keep track of everything. Tamsin had been left on an island to die by her evil husband. Thane had saved her and married her. Then some twisted, diabolical person had tried to have bairns stolen away to be sold to more sick souls in Europe. All for coin. The bairns of the clans had been tortured too much: Magni, Rowan, Sylvi, Tora, Sandor, Alana, Astra, John, and the poor lad from Aoineadh Mòr.

Then there was Meg, who'd been kidnapped and forced to care for stolen bairns; Rinaldo, who had killed Sloan's first betrothed and wished to kill his own brother; and wee Grant, abducted only to prove he had strange powers that even his parents didn't understand.

But Rut thought the evil force had finally been silenced once Merryn and Tristan MacClane put an arrow through the bastard's heart. Everyone on the Isle of Mull deserved a rest.

But they weren't resting at all. Dermot was unsettled, and it was about more than he was admitting. And what the hell did Sheona have going on that she preferred a nunnery to her own clan?

Rut thought to take her usual stool, but she decided to walk the parapets instead. The light breeze made it a lovely day. The sun was out, something they hadn't seen much of lately. She strolled to the front of the curtain wall, glancing about, seeing nothing of interest until she heard her second-born son.

Rut stopped and sat on a ledge to listen, trying not to be seen.

"Taskill, you are looking fine today. Your golden locks are waving just right." One of the serving lasses, the newer one who Meg had hired, followed him.

Taskill ignored her and kept walking.

A lass from the village called out, "Taskill, will you be coming to the festival on the morrow? I'd love to see you."

Taskill ignored that one too and kept walking. Rut had to stop herself from yelling over the edge of the wall, "*What the hell is wrong with you? Answer them.*"

But he didn't, too wrapped up in his thoughts—
or was it intentional? She couldn't answer that.
Her son had always been admired by the lasses
once he'd matured, and he loved it, basking in the
compliments. Rut was grateful he hadn't fathered
five bairns in the area, for none of the serving
lasses had been carrying, even though they were
mostly single.

As she pondered this, she couldn't help but
remind herself of her son's words from the other
day. Hadn't he claimed he never asked for the
compliments? That he never encouraged the
lasses at all?

And here it was happening in front of her. Both
lasses chased after Taskill, still babbling foolishness
at him, but he ignored them.

Yet they didn't stop.

She gave some thought, but before she could
contemplate it, her son bellowed, "Leave me be. I
didn't ask you to follow me. Go away!"

Had she been wrong all along?

Jasper appeared out of the stables, and Taskill
called out to him, "Where's Lennox? I need to
speak with him."

That made Rut stand right up.

Hellfire, she was too old to run down the stairs
and eavesdrop on their conversation.

But she wasn't too old to try.

CHAPTER TWENTY-FOUR

TASKILL

TASKILL IGNORED THE constant blabbering of the lasses following him because he was tired of the same old thing. He needed to find Lennox and speak with him. All that had happened mulled over and over in his mind and gave him no answers and no relief. Sheona was at a nunnery, Dermot feared she would take her vows, and the abbess thought Sheona may have been abused by someone.

There had to be a way to find out who that person was. He'd thought of a possibility but wished to ask his brother first.

"Jasper, where is my brother? I need to speak with him."

Jasper spun around and pointed toward Duart Castle. "You just missed him, T. He's headed back to Clan Grantham. They're trading seed for next year. You can still catch him."

"Good." Taskill nodded to the guard and said, "I'm going after him." Once the stable lad helped him with his horse, he mounted and took off, straight on the path to Duart. This was a perfect time to ask Lennox for his opinion before he decided his next move.

He also had a pervasive thought that he couldn't get rid of. Since they'd all discovered that Dyna and her bairns had skills that allowed them to see what was going to happen, did that mean that they could see in the past too? Could Dyna look into Sheona's past and see who had abused her?

Somehow, if he could discover who had hurt Sheona, mayhap she'd be willing to come back from Iona. If he had to marry her, he would. It wasn't that he didn't care for Sheona, because he did. He had strong feelings for the lass; he always had. He just knew that he would not be a good husband for her.

There was a failing in his blood that no one knew about. He'd make a lousy husband, but that didn't mean Sheona should be a nun.

That brought up a different thought. Was it finally time to tell Lennox what he'd learned about their father? Nay, he couldn't do it. He couldn't destroy the image of his father that Lennox had. Everyone thought Douglas was the finest chieftain, the best father and husband, the fiercest swordsman on the isle in his time. Surely, many of the Granthams would have bettered him on the battlefield or the lists, but when he was strong and alive, Douglas MacVey could send a weapon flying out of the hands of the strongest men in battle.

It was the truth that in his day, Douglas MacVey had been the hero of the isle.

To everyone else. Taskill knew better.

But he wasn't ready to destroy his father's memory. Not yet. There was no reason to do so.

"Lennox, wait for me!" he shouted when he was close.

His brother glanced over his shoulder, motioned to the two guards riding with him, then slowed his horse. "What the hell are you doing? I left you home to protect Mama and Meg."

Taskill snorted. "You think Meg needs protecting with an axe in her hand? Every man on the isle fears raising her ire after seeing her in battle."

Lennox laughed and motioned for them to continue toward Duart. "And I love to hear it."

"Shite, she planted an axe in the middle of a man's forehead, Lennox. How far away was she?"

"Quite a ways away." Lennox laughed again. "That's my wife. Don't forget it."

Taskill muttered, "The only one I'm more afraid of is that Simone. When she said she was going to put an arrow in Glenna's eye, I nearly laughed at the boast. But then she did. Right in her eye. I don't know which kill was faster. And she was in a tree, hidden from everyone. Makes you want to take up archery."

Lennox grinned. "Or axe throwing. I might try it. What brings you along, Taskill?"

"Sheona. All that Dermot said about her. I know he wants Mama to talk with her, but mayhap she would talk with someone else."

"Mama told me he was upset, but I didn't know he was sobbing. Dermot Rankin? I had no idea he had such a soft spot inside him once Ailis was gone."

Lennox sent the guards on ahead so they couldn't listen in on their conversation.

"Sobbing so hard he could barely speak. I'm really bothered by what he said, Lennox. I think I should go to her. Mayhap she would tell me if someone misused her. We were friends when we were younger. But then I had another thought. Do you think Dyna would be able to see who hurt Sheona? Considering that she knows what's about to happen, could she know what *did* happen to someone? Is it possible?"

"You pose too many questions. I have no idea what Dyna's abilities are. If you wish to ask her, then feel free to travel with me and consult with her. She's more than willing to talk with anyone."

"It's surely possible, is it not?"

"Aye, but then are you prepared to deal with whatever you hear?"

"I don't understand. Of course, I can deal with it. It's probably one of their guards."

"And what do you plan to do about it?"

"I don't know. Take them to the sheriff."

Lennox snorted. "Do you think the sheriff will do something about someone touching her inappropriately? And the sheriff could force a marriage. Do you want her married to Fitz or someone else?"

Taskill hadn't considered that possibility. He scratched the beard he hadn't the time to trim. Lennox stared at his brother, uncertain of how to answer his question.

Lennox barked, "Who would dare touch her? I can't get past that. Dermot would kill whoever abused his lass. And Sloan would beat him for sport. String him up in the courtyard."

"I'd kill anyone who touched Eva. Lennox, is it wrong that I wish to do the same to whomever hurt Sheona?"

"Nay. I know exactly how you feel."

"But what is Dermot going to do? And what about Mama? I wonder if she offered to help him. I couldn't hear everything that was said."

"Nay. I don't know what either one is going to do. Dermot asked Mama for advice, I believe. But I have no idea what she told him. I wished to speak with you before I approached her. What are your plans?"

They arrived at Duart Castle and found Hagen at the gates with Jowell. Taskill didn't miss the change in Hagen's composure, but he asked the best question he could. "Welcome, MacVeys. Any Rankins coming along behind you?"

"Nay," Lennox said. "You're safe. Dermot has gone home."

Hagen visibly relaxed. "I hope Sheona is doing well."

"Maitland or Dyna around?"

"Aye, both just entered the hall for a brief repast. Please join them. Jowell and I will take care of your mounts."

Lennox and Taskill headed into the great hall, greeting anyone they met along the way. Taskill entered behind Lennox, pleased to see that

Connor was also inside. He waved them over to the area in front of the hearth. "Come on in. Winter is coming to Duart. This will be our first full winter here. I'm interested to watch the storms on the seas. Dyna will be right back, and Maitland is grabbing meat pies and ale. Have a seat."

Dyna arrived next with her three bairns in tow: Sylvi, Tora, and Sandor. The three ran to the crate in the corner that held their toys. Sandor grabbed his toy sword while the lasses grabbed miniature bows with small arrows.

Maitland came out of the kitchens taking a bite out of a meat pie, Grant tied to his chest, the lad set to kicking as soon as his gaze fell on the others. "I'll let you down in a moment, Grant." He held the meat pie up to the lad's mouth and he took a bite, hands and feet all swinging. "MacVeys! Nice to see you. What is new on the isle? Pardon my busy hands. It's often easier if I feed the laddie. Otherwise, everything goes flying."

Lennox said, "That's why we come to you. You know more about what happens on the isle than we do, many times. What have you heard since the festival?"

Dyna said, "I heard Dermot took Sheona to Iona, straight to the nunnery. I suspect to scare her into marrying you, Taskill. What is everyone saying about that?" She gave Taskill a pointed look.

"Only that she's decided to take her vows. And Dermot is verra upset about it."

Connor asked, "Does that surprise you? I don't

know the lass well, but she does not seem to be the type to become a nun."

"It surprises me," Lennox said. "I don't know what is going on with Sheona, but I don't see her as a nun. The way she used to dive into the sound when she was younger doesn't strike me as someone who wishes to devote their lives to Our Lord. She was always full of life."

Taskill mumbled, "It surprises me too. Something is wrong. I'm uncertain what, but I intend to find out."

Dyna said, "If you traveled to Ionaland where Simone's sister takes care of all the bairns, you might not think it's so bad. They all love it on Iona. It's a beautiful isle with sandy beaches."

Taskill couldn't explain how he felt. That he needed to go grab Sheona and protect her from whatever, or whomever, hurt her. Keep her away from anything and anyone. "I have to do something. This is gnawing at me, eating up my insides, though I don't know why. And I have no idea what to do to help her. Dyna, may I ask a question?"

"Aye."

"Do you or your daughters have the ability to see what has happened to someone in their past?"

Dyna shook her head, pausing to narrow her gaze at Taskill. "Nay. Why do you ask? Did someone hurt Sheona?"

Taskill looked at Lennox, who nodded to him. "We're not sure. It was suggested by the abbess that it was a possibility."

Dyna sighed. "I'm sorry to hear that. I wish we

could help, but I don't have that ability. I only see what's still to come."

Taskill said, "I was hopeful. Have you any suggestions?"

Dyna said, "Staying with the nuns where she can think on her life may be the best thing for her at the moment, especially if something did happen. Her father is going back in a sennight, is he not?"

Taskill sighed. "He says so, aye."

"Then I would let her stay so she can reflect on everything." Dyna's gaze caught on Tora as she dropped her sword, stared up at the ceiling, then ran over to Connor. Dyna's gaze locked on her daughter and whispered, "Nay, Tora. Nay. Please. No more."

Tora climbed up on Connor's lap, causing everyone to stop what they were doing to watch the lass who had a solid reputation as a seer. They'd all seen it happen multiple times.

She cupped her grandfather's face and said, "Those bad men are after her." Then she pushed against Connor's chest to climb down from his lap.

"Who, Tora?" Connor asked, holding her hand. "They're after who?"

She climbed back up and said, "Sona. At the abbey." Then she climbed down and ran away.

"Who are the men?" Connor asked, but Tora's moment of seeing had passed.

And every face turned to Taskill, who stood so quickly he nearly lost his footing.

"I'm going after her, Lennox."

CHAPTER TWENTY-FIVE

BRYNJA

———~~~———

BRYNJA TIPTOED OUT of her bedchamber in the middle of the night. She'd had one of those dreams that she hated. They always awakened her, so she had to follow whatever she was told.

This time it was a wee lass telling her two evil men were after someone close to her. She climbed out of bed right away and dressed to go to the boat launch area.

Picking up her spear, she grabbed three daggers from her hiding spot and tucked them into the folds in her trews. She vowed to get more leggings from Simone someday, but that could wait.

Heading straight for the sea, she heard oars in the water, and her resolve grew. She had no idea how the dreams came to her, but they did, and they were always right. On one occasion, she'd gone to Simmy and told her to go to MacLean land because there were boats headed that way.

Simmy had thanked her profusely later. She'd been right about her instincts, though she'd not told Simmy how she'd known about the trouble.

Brynja had only confessed to getting an inkling that she couldn't ignore. She didn't know how else to explain it.

She hid behind thick brush to watch, so she knew how many she had to handle. A smile crept across her face when she saw the two men arguing as they approached the shore.

"She's mine. Her brother gave her to me long ago. He swore to it. Promised me. You can have her when I'm done with her."

"Hell nay. Whose boat is it? Mine. Without me, you'd never get here or get anywhere near her. Now shut up so we're not caught."

"For Christ's sake, they're nuns. Who's going to come for us?"

Brynja stepped out of the brush, her spear in her left hand and a dagger in her right. "I will. I'll come for you anytime you come near our isle. Turn your boat around or pay the price."

The two men took one look at her small stature and laughed in unison.

Brynja threw one dagger and caught the closer one in the shoulder, and it sunk deep in the flesh. His bellow echoed through the night. "I have three more daggers and two spears. The big ones go in your chest. One each. The daggers are for other choice places."

They still didn't move, so she launched another dagger, catching the second man not far from the vee between his legs. His shout was louder than the first.

"The next one will hit your bollocks. Gwyneth Ramsay taught me."

The two collapsed in the boat and rowed away, the fear in their faces visible in the light of the moon.

She made it appear like she was leaving, but then she hid behind a tree to listen to the two argue because voices carried so well over the water.

"Now what?"

"What the hell do you think? First, we go to shore and get the bleeding to stop. I don't care to be in the water and draw sharks, do you?"

"I want her badly. I've been waiting a long time."

"Luckily, you met me. You're too stupid to do it alone. We go back and regroup. We'll return in two nights."

"Why two? Can't we return on the morrow?"

"Nay."

"Why not?"

"Because we'll both still be bleeding. Besides, I want that one who got us now. We need more weapons."

Brynja laughed loudly enough for them to hear her. As soon as they did, they rowed faster.

How she wished they'd tip their boat over and become shark food.

CHAPTER TWENTY-SIX

TASKILL

———◆———

TASKILL LED HIS horse out and mounted up, but Lennox stopped him just before he departed. "Taskill, what the hell are you doing?"

"What the hell do you think I'm doing? I'm going after Sheona. You heard Tora." He brought his horse over to the gate. "I don't need you to go with me."

"Taskill, stop for one moment."

He sighed, pursed his lips, and set the reins on his lap while he waited for his brother. "You have a quick moment, Lennox."

"You have no idea if it's Sheona or not. Sona is different from Sheona."

Taskill laughed. "Even you don't believe that, brother. In Tora's words, it was 'Sona at the abbey.' You've been the one who most believed in the lassie's abilities. Something's about to happen, and someone has to be there to stop it. No one at the abbey will save her."

Lennox motioned for the stable lad to bring his horse out, then mounted. "We're stopping home to check on Mama. I wish to know about

Dermot. Then go if you like. But that whole thing about Dermot sobbing and asking Mama to do something for him? I don't like that either. Mayhap she's gone to Iona. I don't know if you've ever noticed before, but Mama is a wee bit headstrong. I wish to see."

Taskill tipped his head with a chuckle. "I'll agree. I was going to get my saddlebag anyway and a bit of food." He led his horse out of the gates, Connor finally catching up to them.

"You are going to Iona, Taskill?" Connor asked.

"Home first, then Iona Abbey. To the nunnery. You believe her, do you not?" Taskill asked.

"I always believe Tora. I don't know who speaks to her, but she hasn't been wrong yet." Then Connor hesitated.

"What?"

"It's unusual for her to speak of someone she doesn't know. And to speak of something that far away." Then he paused and stared at Taskill, something he didn't often do.

"Your thoughts, Chief?" Lennox asked. "Speak your mind, if you please."

Connor looked at Taskill and said, "It's clear you have feelings for the lass, Taskill. Whatever is holding you back, you better get over it before it's too late. You may not get another chance."

Taskill nodded and said, "Good advice if I were the marrying type. But I still have to make sure she's safe."

"Then go," Connor said, heading back toward the keep. "Godspeed. And think on my words along the way."

Lennox led the way off Grantham land and they headed back to Clan MacVey, not slowing to chat.

When they neared Dounarwyse Castle, Taskill said, "You're worried about Mama."

"I am. Dermot is unstable. I would wager she's not here, and we are headed to Rankin land next. Although looking at the activity near the gates, something is going on."

They approached the castle and Lennox shouted to Jasper on the curtain wall. "Where's Mama?"

"She's not here, Chief. Sloan came looking for Dermot, and he's inside with Eva. Your mother's horse is here, but she's not. I don't know how she got past us."

Lennox and Taskill entered just as Eva came out of the keep, frantic, Sloan directly behind her. "Where the hell is Mama, Lennox? She and Dermot are both missing. I don't like this."

Lennox dismounted and said, "Calm down. We'll figure this out. Neither of them is young. If they've gone anywhere, they can't be far. She doesn't even have her horse. How far can she go on foot?"

Sloan shook his head. "Don't discount the craftiness of the two. My sire is capable of many things when he sets his mind to do it. But the last I knew, the two were not getting along, so that part bothers me most."

Taskill gave Eva a hug and said, "I'm worried too. Dermot was here."

"When?" Sloan asked, now holding Eva's hand.

Taskill lowered his voice and explained, "Early this morn. Dermot was crying about Sheona, asking for Mama's help. I did my best to overhear what I could, and these are my thoughts on it. The abbess asked Dermot if Sheona had been abused, and now he fears something happened because Sheona told the abbess she wished to take her vows."

Sloan cursed. "Sheona said what? Are you sure you heard that correctly? Hell nay. She's not going to be a nun. She doesn't have the constitution."

Lennox said, "Let's go into my solar."

The group moved inside, but Taskill couldn't sit. This was too much to absorb. Sheona was in trouble, and his mother and Dermot were both missing.

Taskill repeated all he'd heard from Dermot and his mother. "Dermot was more upset than I've ever seen him. Did he speak with you at all, Sloan?"

"When he returned from the abbey two days ago, he seemed fine, but he headed straight to the parapets. I asked him questions, but all he would tell me was that he would go back for her in one sennight. That she'd agreed to stay, and he'd spoken with the abbess. Damn it all!"

"What?" Lennox asked.

"I can always tell when the man is lying. I knew something was not right with him. We need to send a search party out for them."

"They're not at Duart. We were just there," Lennox said. "I'm not that worried. Without her horse, Mother would not have gone far."

"That's shortsighted of you," Sloan said.

Eva said, "Mama is craftier than you think, Lennox. I'm worried now."

"How far could she get on foot?"

The others all stared at Lennox, but it was Taskill who said, "Boat, Lennox! She snuck around back and climbed into a vessel with someone."

"Oh, shite. I never thought of that. Mama doesn't like boats."

"Doesn't matter," Eva said, looking from one brother to the next. "But I don't like the look on your faces. What else aren't you telling me?"

Meg came flying in. "What's happened?"

After Eva filled her in, she said to Lennox, "Out with it. You're holding back."

Lennox ran a hand down his face, then nodded to Taskill.

He closed his eyes and tipped his head. "When we were in the great hall at Duart, Tora ran over to her grandfather in her usual way and told him that bad men were after 'Sona' at the abbey."

"Sona?" Meg asked.

"Sheona!" Sloan bellowed. "Shite!"

Taskill announced, "I'm going to Iona Abbey right now. Lennox, you find Mama. You all decide what you wish to do about Mama and Dermot, but you'll not deter me from helping Sheona."

And he left, waving over his shoulder. "Find them and I'll make sure Sheona is safe."

Sloan bellowed, "Hold up! I'll take Eva home and join you."

"Nay, I'm going now. The clouds are dark north of here."

Lennox shouted, "You better hurry. There is a storm brewing. I can feel it."

Taskill had already sensed it. Exactly why he wouldn't stop for anything.

He'd get to Iona if he had to swim across.

CHAPTER TWENTY-SEVEN

DERMOT

D ERMOT CURSED, HIS shoulders feeling the strain of rowing against the current.

"Dermot, we're going backward. And that's a thunder cloud over there. I don't care to be on the water in a thunderstorm. We'll be the quickest path for a lightning bolt to find its way to the ground."

"Don't yell at me, woman. I can see what's going on around us."

"You know I'm not fond of small boats. I prefer big ones."

Dermot chuckled to himself and raised a brow at her as he aimed for the nearest beach on Mull. "What else do you like big, lassie?"

"Now I know you don't have your mind functioning. It's been many a day since I've been a lassie."

"Not to me. You're still as beautiful as you were the day you married Douglas."

She couldn't help but smile. "There are a few things that I prefer big, Chief Rankin." But nearly giggled, but she managed to control it. It was a good thing she kept herself busy staring at the clouds so she wouldn't notice his growing cock. He had to admit he hadn't been this excited in a long time. Rut MacVey had always been one fine specimen of womanhood, her curvy hips able to swish her skirts unlike any other. He'd love to get a taste of everything under those skirts.

He'd dreamed of sinking his teeth into one of those hips once. Or perhaps he'd prefer a bite of her well-rounded bottom.

"Where are we? You know I have no sense of direction."

He glanced over his shoulder, the beach not far. If he was correct, the MacClane holding was close to the beach. Tristan's cottage would be fine until they could move over to Iona. And if he was lucky, they'd have to share a bedchamber.

"Is Duart Castle nearby? Can we not wait out the storm there?" Rut's hood blew off as she turned toward the shore, looking for any nearby building.

The air carried a chill to him that he didn't like. There was definitely a storm headed their way. That would delay them for a short bit.

And he had his mind on exactly what he could do to keep himself busy until then. Rut sat across from him, acting innocent. But he knew her well enough to know there was nothing innocent about Rut MacVey.

The waves were getting rougher by the minute, rocking the boat more than he or Rut liked.

"Make up your mind, Rankin. Get us on shore and stop dreaming about whatever the hell you're doing. I'll probably have a grandbairn in less than a year, and I plan to be here to see it. Or them. It could be one Rankin and one MacVey."

"A Rankin lad and a MacVey lass," he drawled.

"Always has to be your way, does it?"

He chuckled, ignoring her intent to prick his temper.

Dermot rowed for all he was worth, ignoring the woman to pay attention to the current and the wind. He aimed for the cove he thought was the best place to land. When he was close enough, he pulled in the oars and jumped out to pull the boat up onto the sand.

Rut shrieked as the boat nearly tipped, but he righted it, finally grounding it enough so he could help her out onto the beach. He knew better than to ask her to step into the water as he'd done, his best boots now soaked.

"Where are we? There's no cottage here. And I'm not staying on the beach for a night, Dermot Rankin. You better at least find us a cave. The tide could come up and bury us and we'd be swept out to sea, never to be found—"

"Woman, cease your prattle, will you not?"

"Nay, I will not. I'm verra nervous, if you have not noticed. I don't wish to die." She stopped to face him, her hands now on her lovely hips.

"MacClane has a small cottage just over that ridge, directly next to the castle. I'll carry you over it, if I must. I'll see you safely there."

"You better. I only agreed to come if you promised the trip would be quick and not challenging. I only wanted a nice dinner overlooking the sea. You know how I hate to spend much time in a boat. If I climb up that knoll, I'll ruin my boots for sure. Oh, Dermot. What have you gotten us into? I may never forgive you for this. Lennox will be furious."

She glared at him, her gaze narrowing, her breathing coming faster. "Where exactly was that dinner supposed to be?"

"MacLean Castle."

"We're here then."

"Nay, I meant Neil MacLean's Castle on the mainland. He has a wonderful cook."

"Across that water? Are you out of your mind, Dermon Rankin? I don't care to go that far." Her hands shook at just the thought.

Dermot moved close to her. "You might wish to calm yourself, lassie."

"I'll do what I wish to do."

"I know what *I* wish to do right now."

"What exactly does that mean?"

"I'd like to throw you down on the sand and have my way with you."

"You wouldn't dare," she said, her voice softening, her breathing telling him she was as excited as he was.

He stepped closer, the wind whipping both of their hair around their faces. He reached up and yanked at her pins, letting her long mane loose. He played with her hair, running his fingers through the silky strands until she panted, her hands now on his chest.

"What are you doing?" she whispered.

"What I've wanted to do for a long time."

Dermot's mouth descended on hers, his lips melding with hers until she parted them, allowing his tongue to do what he wished, and she met him with every stroke, just as he would have guessed.

CHAPTER TWENTY-EIGHT

SHEONA

SHEONA SAT INSIDE Mother Mary's office, her hands folded in her lap, waiting to see what the abbess wished to speak to her about. The abbess was a plain-looking woman, a bit sharp in spots. Even her chin was pointed, her elbows nearly cutting through her robe. But her eyes were kind, so Sheona trusted the woman.

"My thanks for joining me, Sheona. How are you enjoying our life here? It is quite beautiful, is it not?"

Sheona thought carefully before she spoke. "It is one of the most beautiful islands I've ever seen." It wasn't much of a lie. While the beaches were lovely here, they didn't appeal more to her than her own castle, her own chamber. People she loved—her sister and brother, nephew. The brand new sweet bairn. Her dear horse. The dogs. She stopped to keep her tears at bay.

At present, Sheona wished to go home. Even though there were things there that frightened her, she knew her brother and father would always protect her.

Though they hadn't protected her when she'd needed them most.

"Sheona, I believe something brought you here. Something that happened to you in your past. What say you?" The abbess leaned back in her chair and kept her eyes on Sheona.

She shook her head, a lump in her throat holding her words inside. When she was able, she said, "I don't understand your question, Mother Mary. My sire brought me here."

"Some lasses who come here have been … how shall I explain this so you'll understand? Many come here to get away from something. Something that makes them uncomfortable."

"Aye, my sire wishes to betroth me to a man I don't wish to marry. And he has insisted we marry in less than a sennight." She swiped at the tear about to slip down one cheek. "My mother never would have allowed such a short betrothal. She would have insisted on time for my dress, time to send messengers out to invite our neighbors. Why did he insist I marry Taskill so quickly? I don't understand him at all." Her father hated her. That was the only conclusion she could draw from what she knew.

"And you do not like this person?"

"I like him, but I don't wish to marry him."

"Is it someone you've known all your life?"

"Aye, forever."

The abbess lifted her arms up so she could settle them down on the desk just so, the bell sleeves of her robe now underneath her forearms. She

folded her hands on the desk and leveled the most
penetrating look anyone had ever given Sheona,
a look that dampened her underarms, though the
abbess's voice came out soft and calm. "Has that
man touched you inappropriately before? Did
he touch your private area? Has he taken your
maidenhead already? Is that why you don't wish
to marry him? Lass, you can tell me. I won't tell
your sire if you don't wish me to do so."

Shocked by such personal questions, Sheona
had the impulse to run. Run away. Far away. How
much farther from home could she go? It was
too much. Her heartbeat sped up and she stood,
her hands covering her ears, stopping the verbal
assault. "Nay, nay, nay! Taskill would never do
such a thing. Taskill? Never."

And she ran.

Out the door, down the passageway, to the
entranceway, and down the steps, shoving at the
handle on the front door so hard that the door
flew open, and she nearly catapulted down the
seven steps in front of the building.

Righting herself, she dashed back to her
chamber, throwing herself onto her bed and
letting the tears erupt.

She hated it here. It was beautiful, and she
enjoyed her new friends, but it wasn't home.
Perhaps she didn't hate it, but she missed her old
life. The uncomplicated one. The one when she
was younger and jumped in the sound with the
lads.

With Taskill. And her mother was on the shore
and her sister was never far away. When they'd

had fun every single day. Now she was in a lovely place, nearly alone.

Her own father had brought her to this horrible place and left her alone. She'd barely been able to carry on without her dear mother. Then Rinaldo had died, and Sloan had married Eva. Marta had miscarried two bairns since their mother passed and then had the one beautiful Margret. Bairns had been kidnapped, battles had taken place, and how could she be seen in all that tragedy? It had been awful for everyone. She knew it. She saw it in the creases in Sloan's forehead, in the tears behind the closed doors of Marta's chamber.

With all that had happened, she had melted into the stone passageways, unseen by everyone. She'd gone through the worst experiences in her life, and yet she had no one to talk with. She'd become invisible.

And no one had time for her.

The guilt of being selfish overwhelmed her, which was why she never spoke to anyone about her problem. Others had enough to deal with. Here she was, alone again in a strange place.

Which place did she feel more alone at—here or Castle Rankin?

When her tears were spent, she huddled into a ball against the cold, staring at the door, her breath hitching still. Where did she belong?

Who did she trust to help her with this?

Her mother? Impossible. Her sister? Too exhausted and busy. Her brother? Too busy as chieftain and with Eva.

Her father? Nay, he hated her.

Mother Mary? Never.

That left Brynja and Hildi.

She shivered and pulled a plaid up over her shoulders. The door opened, and Brynja entered with Hildi directly behind her. Brynja was verra intuitive and rushed over, her countenance giving away her feelings.

"What's wrong, lass?" she asked.

Hildi said, "I saw you going to see Mother Mary. Has she sent you home? Are you leaving us already? We hope not."

"Nay," Sheona said, pushing herself to a sitting position. "She asked me if the man my father wishes to force me to marry has abused me. She thinks he forced himself on me."

"Has he?" Hildi asked. "We have no one to tell. You can tell us."

"He didn't. But I just don't wish to marry. No one understands me." She'd never told anyone exactly what had happened, instead trying to force it all from her mind.

"It might help to talk about it."

"I don't see how that could help. Besides, I've had odd feelings that someone has been watching me," Sheona explained. "I woke up last night and had this feeling. The same feeling I had over the last fortnight at home. And once in the middle of summer, I felt like someone was following me. I'm too afraid to go home."

How could she explain that the person she hated more than any other had told her that he promised her to someone? Not to marry, but for another purpose.

She should say something.

Nay, she couldn't. They'd think her foolish.

But then again, how could she say anything when she had no idea what her brother had promised? What exactly had he meant that one of his friends would "teach" her something?

What exactly?

Brynja got up and paced, then stopped at the end of Sheona's bed, crossing her arms. "I didn't wish to tell you this, but there was a boat here last eve. They were looking for someone."

"Who?"

"I don't know exactly. They never said. Can you tell me more about who you think is following or watching you?"

"Nay, I have no idea. I never saw anyone. I just felt it. It was like a chill on the back of my neck whenever I thought someone was hiding near me. Watching. Just watching."

"Well, you need to think on it. It's important that we uncover who they were looking for. I hit them each with a dagger, so they left, but I also heard them say they planned to return in two nights."

"On the morrow?"

"Aye, but there's a storm coming, so mayhap they will be delayed by another day."

Her father would be here in four more days. She had to get away. But where? How? With whom? "I don't know what to do," she whispered.

Hildi came over and gave her a warm hug. "Don't worry. We do. We'll take you to the angel at Ionaland. She'll know exactly what to do."

"An angel?"

"Aye, that's what she calls herself. Her name is Lia, and she knows things that are going to happen before they do. She mostly spends her time with Magni."

"I've heard about Lia, but I've not spoken with her before. I didn't see anyone with Magni when we were there the other day."

"She must have gone somewhere for a short visit."

"What does she look like?"

"She's six."

"An angel who is only six? I heard she was a lass, but I didn't realize she was so young. And how can she help me?"

Hildi giggled. "She looks six, but she talks as if she's older than Mother Mary. She knows everything."

Brynja said, "Hildi's right. We need to speak with Lia. If she doesn't already know who came here and who is after you, she'll be able to find out. Are you willing to listen to her?"

"You truly believe she'll know who those men were?"

"If not, she'll find out."

Sheona sighed. She had to trust someone.

"Let's go."

CHAPTER TWENTY-NINE

TASKILL

ASKILL HEADED BACK toward Duart Castle, then down the beach path, vowing to get to the Isle of Iona before the storm hit. Lennox was correct in sensing that there was a squall somewhere. He'd always had the odd ability to know when the weather was changing. Both clans depended on his inklings for the blizzards.

Though it was autumn, the breezes could still be warm. The nights were cool, which made the water even colder, but Taskill could still jump in for a quick bath. He came down the stretch where he could see the beach, surprised to notice a rowboat where there were usually none, but no one was in it. It was pulled up far enough to be out of the water at this point. Who knew what would happen as the waves continued to beat against the shore?

Glancing up at the gray storm clouds, he pushed his horse farther. "Get to MacClane's, and I promise you a nice stable and a fine dish of oats." Launching from Tristan MacClane's land was the best place because it was the shortest route to the nunnery from Mull. Other isles were closer, but this was the best way from Mull.

Once Taskill came upon MacClane Castle, he slowed his horse, surprised to see Tristan waving from the top of the new section of the curtain wall. He brought his mount close and shouted up to him, "Tristan, may I borrow a boat to go to Iona? I'll be back after the storm. I promise."

Tristan said, "I have two available, same size, but if you wish to make it safely, you better hurry. You going for a special reason?"

"Going to find Sheona."

"I'll be right down. I'm finished."

Taskill waited, staring over the sea, noting that there were no waves. In fact, it was almost the calmest he'd ever seen this part of the sea. It was what Lennox referred to as the quiet storm waiting for the wild. Lennox was often right. Eerie quiet like this was often followed by a wild storm.

Tristan joined him. "There's been more activity on Iona of late, and there are storm clouds headed this way, but I think you can make it. Obviously, living where you do, you must be skilled with the oars, and the size of your upper arms tell me I'm right. Help yourself. Leave your horse at the stable. Someone there will help you. I'm just checking everything before the storm comes. We've been moving in, and I don't wish to lose anything. Checking for leaks and loose stones one last time. Getting all the animals tucked into the fine stable the Granthams helped me build."

"My thanks, MacClane. I'll return on the morrow." He waved to his friend and left his horse with a stable lad.

"Godspeed!" Tristan called out as Taskill took the boat out into the serene waters.

Determined to get to the Isle of Iona, he said a quick prayer and headed across the water.

While he rowed, he gave careful thought as to who the bad men could be that Tora had mentioned. What cruel men would be after Sheona? And why?

They'd taken care of Kelvan and all his men, even escorting K's second-in-command deep into the Highlands to make sure he didn't take over the bastard's operation.

Nay, Taskill had to wager that this was something different. Someone different. He rowed in his favorite rhythm, which he did without much thought, keeping his eye on the target. He would aim for the abbey, and if the current pushed him a bit away, he'd be at Ionaland, still not far from the nunnery. And he'd be on land during the storm either way.

So, he focused on Sheona. There were two issues. Were they separate or one and the same? First, the abbess had suggested Sheona had been abused by someone. But who would do such a heinous crime?

Second, who was Tora seeing as the "bad men"? And they'd specifically said "men," not "man." Multiple men. Who would dare go after Sloan's sister?

Who would dare touch Dermot Rankin's

daughter without his approval? The man was older, but he kept himself in good physical shape, his arms still powerful enough to knock someone on their arse before they ever saw him coming. He had that shifty tendency about him, able to hide his intentions better than anyone. And everyone had witnessed how he'd acted when Hagen had gone for a stroll with Sheona. Dermot had been ready to force marriage on the two that moment.

If not for Connor Grant and Logan Ramsay, Dermot would have pushed harder for a betrothal.

No one had ever been able to predict Dermot's actions, not even Sloan. Who could ever forget that the man had plunged a dagger deep into his own son's chest before anyone could stop him? He'd turned his back on the dead man and never looked back.

Rinaldo had been evil, fooling many, so he did deserve his sire's ire. But Rinaldo was dead, so he was certainly not one of Tora's bad men.

Clyde popped into his head. The way he'd questioned Taskill about Sheona during the fishing competition had bothered him. Hadn't he said he wished to propose marriage to her? Clyde was a distinct possibility for being one or the other.

He went over the name and image of every other guard he knew on Rankin land, coming up with no one, mostly because none of them were daft enough to attack Sheona.

The old chieftain had killed his own son. What the hell would he do to someone who attacked his daughter?

When he came close to shore, Taskill had been right about the current. He was closer to Ionaland than to the nunnery. Dark would fall shortly, so he pulled his boat onto shore as far as he could, then headed toward the row of cottages. If he was lucky, Simone and Artan would be about. He was more than comfortable asking for assistance from them. The others he didn't know.

He strode up the path, the gusts gaining in strength, letting him know there would indeed be a storm soon. To his surprise, a lass sat on a gigantic boulder up ahead.

He swore it was Sheona.

CHAPTER THIRTY

SHEONA

HILDI LED THE three over to Ionaland, taking vegetables with them so the sisters wouldn't question their visit. Sheona had two daggers with her but didn't carry a spear like Hildi and Brynja each had. She'd left her axes back at the nunnery because they were so heavy.

Brynja had said, "I don't trust that those men won't be hiding somewhere. Never go anywhere without a dagger close to your hand."

Sheona nodded, beginning to believe she could use one after practicing with her new friends.

"The wind is coming up," Hildi said. "And look at those clouds. The storm will be here right after the sun drops, I believe. It's getting closer."

Magni saw them first, running over to greet them. "I knew you were coming," he announced proudly, his chest puffed out.

"How could you possibly know?" Hildi asked.

Magni grinned and pointed to the wee lass trailing a distance behind him. "Lia told me. She always knows. She's my sister."

Sheona glanced over at Brynja for confirmation

because she'd never heard that they were brother and sister, especially since Lia was supposed to be an angel. Brynja shook her head, indicating not to ask anything, her wide eyes telling Sheona to keep her questions inside. Brynja whispered, "Later, I'll explain."

Hildi covered quickly by asking Magni, "What else did Lia say? And where has she been?"

"She had to leave for a bit, but I don't know where she went. She said she'll never leave me, so I knew she'd be back. And she returned a wee bit ago. Look. Here she is!" He rushed over and hugged the tiny lass with the prettiest golden hair. "You can ask her how she knew."

"Greetings to you, Lia. We missed you on our last visit. May we deliver our vegetables and then chat with you?" Brynja asked.

"Of course, and I do believe we have some bread for you. Follow me, and we'll find your bread after you leave the cabbage and other goods."

Once they completed their task, Hildi led the small group out to a bench near the shore. Lia glanced up and said, "A storm is coming, but it is much needed." Her gaze fell back and landed directly on Sheona. "Greetings to you, my dear. Ask me all your questions. I hear you have many."

Puzzled, Sheona glanced over at Hildi, who nodded. "Go ahead."

"It is lovely to meet you, but my first question is about you. Are you truly an angel? I've never met one before."

A wee lad came toward them giggling, and Lia

said, "Magni, why don't you play with Tenney? He's missing his dearest brother."

Magni took off toward the boy and swung him in circles, then began a game of tag.

Lia folded her hands in her lap after straightening her skirts and said, "To your first genuine question, I'm not really Magni's sister, but it makes for a good explanation of our relationship. I am what's called a guiding angel. I can guide people in certain directions, but I can't force anyone to do anything. I was sent here to protect the many bairns who were being stolen away, and I think we were successful in ending that evil threat against our sweet isles. But there is always danger lurking where you least expect it." She smiled, and if not for her size, the lass gave off the aura of a woman of many decades. Lia lifted her head to the breeze and smiled. "The air is sweet this eve, is it not?"

"Are you able to answer my other questions?" Sheona asked.

"I will do my best." Then she nodded to the three. "Ask me. I'm here for you."

Brynja cleared her throat. "The two men I saw approaching the isle last night. Did you see them?"

"I did."

"Who were they? And who are they after?"

Lia shook her head slowly with a *tsk* of her jaw. "They are men with evil souls. They search for someone to satisfy their pleasures."

"Someone they know?" Sheona asked.

"Aye." Lia got up and approached Sheona. She

reached for her hands and cocooned them inside her own small hands, which nearly made Sheona giggle until she looked into Lia's eyes.

What she saw there gripped her and didn't let go. A fierceness and an essence flowed from her soul, even through her hands, warming Sheona's in the cold. "Sheona, I was on a mission, but I was called back for you. Someone is here to speak with you. She wishes to send you a message through me."

Sheona jerked her hands away from Lia. "Who? Who could send me a message? No one I know is here."

"Her name is Ailis, though you called her something different." Lia hesitated and tried to take Sheona's hand again.

"Nay," Sheona ground out, taking two steps back, fighting the tears threatening to spill over.

Hildi said, "Listen to her, Sheona. Trust us. Do you know someone named Ailis?"

Brynja said, "It won't hurt you to listen. You're troubled, and someone wishes to help you. Are you familiar with Ailis?"

Sheona's eyes misted, the threat of tears overpowering her though she squeezed them tight. She knew Ailis, the only one—her dear mother who had passed on over a year ago.

Brynja whispered, "Sheona? Trust her. Who is Ailis? She could tell us about the men."

She took four rapid breaths and paused. "My mother was named Ailis."

"It's her," Lia said. "This woman is your mother."

"Is Rinaldo there too?" Sheona would run

back to the nunnery if she said he was with her mother.

Lia strode forward and took both of her elbows. "Nay. Rinaldo is not here, and your mother said he will never hurt you again. And that she is sorry she was not there to stop him before. That he deserved the sword in his belly from your father because his soul had turned evil. It is not your fault. And she wishes she could make you a batch of apple tarts covered with cinnamon."

Sheona nearly collapsed, her tears now flowing freely. "Mama, I miss you so."

"She said her heart misses you every single day, but she is always watching over you. And she said the next time, she'd stop you from eating three tarts at once. You wouldn't have gotten sick if she'd stopped you at two."

Sheona openly cried, unable to stop the tears at the memory of baking with her dear mother, of the possibility that she was standing nearby. Her heart ached for her dear mother.

Lia said, "Sit, please. Your mother has an important message for you."

Sheona sat, swiping her tears away, her gaze locked on this odd lass in front of her. She had to listen. Who else would know that when she'd first tasted cinnamon, she declared it was her favorite flavor ever, and that her sire had sent to London for a small flask just for her? "I'm listening," she whispered.

"Ailis says you must trust Taskill. She said he is coming for you and that you need to go with him. There is an evil friend of your brother who is searching for you. And what he wants from you is meant for your husband, so you must stay away from him."

"I'll go with Taskill. Who is it? Who is after me, Mama?"

"One man you don't know. The other one is Clyde. Promise me you will stay away from Clyde."

"I promise. Tell me, Mama. Should I marry Taskill? Or what do I do? Da is being unreasonable."

"Da will no longer trouble you, daughter. He is in his own trouble now. Trust your heart and you will find the one for you. Ailis says she loves you, but she must go."

"Wait, Mama. Is Taskill the one I should marry? Mama? Please tell me. I don't know what to do. And what trouble is Papa in?"

Lia said, "She's gone, lass. I'm sorry. They only have short times to pass on their messages."

"Mama, I miss you so."

Lia reached up and cupped Sheona's cheek, "She misses you too. I could feel it in her heart. Do you know who Clyde is?"

"I do. He was a friend of my brother Rinaldo's."

Hildi ran toward shore and pointed. "There's a boat coming. One man is in it, not two."

Lia said, "It's not Clyde. Go see for yourself. Godspeed with you, Sheona. Trust in your angels and in God."

"My angels?"

"Aye. Your mother is one of your guardian

angels. She will always protect you, if she can. Go. You have a wonderful life ahead of you once you find your way through this confusing episode your sire started. But sometimes the greatest pleasures come after the worst pain, my dear." Lia waved goodbye and went after the two lads.

Sheona wiped her tears and asked Brynja and Hildi, "Do you believe her? Should I believe all she said?"

Hildi giggled and asked, "Do you like cinnamon?"

Sheona laughed and nodded at the same time.

"Who else knows you love cinnamon?"

"My mama and papa and my siblings. Sloan, Rinaldo, and Marta." Then she scowled as she reviewed the conversation in her mind. Could it have been Rinaldo leading her in the wrong direction?

Brynja asked, "Were your siblings there when you were sickened from eating three tarts?"

Sheona stared at Brynja wide-eyed. "Nay. Only Mama. Even Da doesn't know I ate three. She made me promise not to tell him." She broke into a wide grin. "My thanks to you, Mama."

Hildi said, "That boat is almost here. Will you go with him?"

And the oddest thing happened. Sheona knew exactly what to do.

No quandaries, no doubts, no questions. Unlike how the last few days of her life had been, she was certain this time.

She would go with Taskill.

She raced to shore and found a boulder to sit on after hugging her friends. "I promise to visit again. Take care of my axes."

The two hugged her. Brynja held out her hand with a proffered treat. "Here. Take some bread and Godspeed with you. Do what the angels tell you to. Beware the storm. I hope you'll come back when your wonderful life has started. Then mayhap you can ask your mother about our lives."

Hildi whispered, "I would like to know if we'll find happiness someday." Her voice was so quiet, it nearly broke Sheona's heart. They'd helped her in so many ways.

Sheona gave Hildi and Brynja each a hug. "I will. I promise. I appreciate all you've done for me, but I must go."

Sheona sat on the boulder and waited for Taskill.

CHAPTER THIRTY-ONE

LENNOX

L ENNOX AND SLOAN headed straight toward Duart Castle at the first flash of lightning. He had a great respect for the powerful bolts that he'd seen kill a guard and his horse in one quick flash. He'd been a suitable distance away but was tossed off his horse like a fabric animal thrown by a one-year-old angry at the world.

"Duart Castle is closer, so I agree with you," Sloan said. "Move along. This storm is blowing in like a bastard."

The gate opened as they approached, Hagen coming down from the parapets to help a few guards close it after. "Welcome. Get inside before the squall, MacVey. I'll take your horses. Jowell is inside." He collected the reins of both beasts after closing the gates. "No more parapets in this thunderstorm. I'll be in soon. Do they need feeding?"

"Aye, if you please. We came from MacQuarie's."

Lennox grabbed his saddlebag and headed toward the keep, Sloan behind him. He had no idea where his mother had gone, and Sloan had no more thoughts than he had. He pushed the door open, the wind blowing it out of his hands once it finally moved, banging against the wall.

Logan Ramsay and Connor Grant sat inside near the fire, the rest of the clan eating their evening meal at the tables. Gwyneth sat closest to the hearth, working on a pair of leggings.

"Hellfire, close the door, MacVey. That's a stiff wind brewing," Logan bellowed.

"My apologies. I did my best." He hung his mantle on the wall, then stomped the dirt from his boots in a box by the door.

Connor moved over to a side table and grabbed two goblets of ale. "Ale or food first?"

"I'll take the ale and the fireplace first," Sloan said, accepting the ale and settling in the chair. "It's a hell of a gale brewing out there. We were halfway here when it started and hoped we could make it home first, but decided the lightning had a mind of its own. Hope you don't mind."

"You're welcome any time, you know that," Dyna said from the table.

Logan asked, "Why were you at MacQuarie's?"

Lennox let out a long sigh. "We still haven't located our parents."

Connor nearly spit out his drink. "Rut and Dermot are both still missing? For how long?"

"Nearly a day. Dermot came to see my mother this morn. Taskill overheard them talking about Sheona. We thought they may have gone to Iona, but we came from Thane's. He hasn't seen any boats going that way. Artan would know. He said they were not on Iona or Ulva. We have no idea where they could be," Lennox said, taking a long swig of his drink.

Sloan continued, "We're headed to MacClane's once the storm ends. I doubt they would go there, but we have to check. Taskill has gone to Iona to talk with Sheona, see if they are there."

Connor said, "I thought Dermot and Rut hated each other. I've seen the two have words before. We all have."

Logan let out a sneaky guffaw. "There's a fine line between love and hate. If you think those two don't have any needs they need seen to, you're not seeing clearly."

Sloan shouted, "Ramsay, nay. Please do not put that idea in my head."

Lennox stared at Sloan. "What's wrong with my mother?"

"You know what I mean, MacVey," he said. "The two together? At their age? Nay. Just nay. Your mother is too old. And so is my sire."

Logan looked at Connor, and the two broke into laughter.

Connor said, "Weren't you both here when Dermot tried to force Hagen to marry Sheona? When Taskill's name came up and Rut shoved her way between the three of us?"

"What three?" Dyna asked. "I was upstairs. I want all the details—every look, every sigh."

"Dermot, Connor, and me. Rut was in the middle of us, and I've never seen her happier. That woman likes men," Logan said. "My apologies,

MacVey, but your mother had to be something when she was young. She's still a fine woman."

"Och, nay." Lennox bolted out of his seat and walked away. "Now you've gone too far, Ramsay. I need something to eat."

Maitland laughed so hard that Grant began kicking at his chest. "Have a meat pie. It will calm your belly."

Tora left the trestle table and ran over to her grandfather, causing the group to quiet instantly, waiting.

She cupped Connor's face and said, "They are together." Then she hopped back down.

"Who?" Connor asked his granddaughter. "Dermot and Rut?"

And she ran off without answering.

Sloan whispered, "I'm not sure if that is good or not."

Tora ran back to her grandfather, climbing on his lap again to gaze into his eyes. She always made sure she had his full attention before she spoke. "And they are together too. In the storm."

"Who, Tora?"

And she jumped down again.

Lennox said, "Dyna, interpret, please? I have a brother and a mother out there."

Maitland looked at Dyna and shrugged. "I know what I think, but I'll let you answer first before everyone else."

"Same with me," Logan answered. "Your thoughts, Dyna?"

Lennox paced in front of the fireplace as he waited for their replies.

Dyna said, "Rut and Dermot are together. Taskill and Sheona are together somewhere else, probably Iona. I've no idea about the elders' location."

Sloan got up and stood by the table. "What if it's Rut and Taskill, Sheona and my sire?"

Logan said, "I'm telling you that Rut and Dermot are safe somewhere. You may think your sire is careless and doesn't always think straight, but he's been around a long time. He has Rut somewhere safe. And I won't guess what they're doing because of all the tender sensibilities in the hall."

Sloan nearly spit his drink out, and Lennox just said, "Nay, nay," as he continued to pace.

Logan added, "Sheona and Taskill are in the storm together. In a cave or on Iona."

Maitland's grin vanished. "Agreed. Both conjectures are my thoughts exactly."

Connor nodded. "Same."

Tora ran back to her grandsire and climbed again. "Bad men still after Sona."

Sloan closed his eyes and said, "What do I do? Where shall I go to find her?"

Lennox dragged both hands through his long locks. How he prayed that Taskill could protect Sheona. "We stay here until the storm is over. Taskill will protect her. We all know he will. Then when the wind stops, we head to Iona."

"And our parents?"

"I have no idea where they are," Lennox muttered, closing his eyes. "I just pray they are all safe, wherever they are."

CHAPTER THIRTY-TWO

TASKILL

TASKILL BROUGHT THE boat ashore, surprised to see he had been correct. Sheona sat on a nearby boulder, a smile on her face. "Sheona? Are you hale?"

"I'm fine, Taskill. But why are you here? I'm glad to see you, but I'm confused. Were you headed to Ionaland or the nunnery?"

"I came for you, Sheona. I headed to the nunnery, but the sea current brought me here. A storm is brewing, and I just wished to get on land."

"Is there a problem somewhere? Why did you come?"

He settled the boat, then strode over to where she sat, taking a seat next to her. He'd forgotten how beautiful she was. Her hair was plaited, but the wind had pulled a good many of the silky strands out of their binding and they formed a halo around her face. Her green eyes glittered with hope instead of the fear he'd seen there so often.

"I came to see you. I was worried about you. Do you like it here?"

"Aye, it's beautiful, and I've made two friends whom I really like."

"So, do you think you wish to be a nun? Will you take your vows?"

She shook her head. "Nay. I am not interested in becoming a nun, but it's been good to be away from home, especially with all that happened, but now I'm ready to go back. My sire will be here in a few days."

Taskill took a deep breath, then took Sheona's hand in his, pleased that she didn't pull away. "That's why I'm here. Your sire and my mother are missing."

She bolted to her feet and stared at him, confusion dancing across her features. "Missing? My sire is missing? What do you mean?"

He stood and placed his hands on her shoulders. "He was last seen at our holding. He headed straight inside and demanded to speak to my mother. The two went into the solar because he was verra upset about you. Said he needed help with you. No one has seen them since. No horses are missing, so we're all a bit confused. We're assuming they are together. Lennox and Sloan were heading out to the MacQuaries to check if they'd visited there, and I headed to Ionaland to make sure you were hale. Have they been to visit you? Either one or both?"

"Nay. I just came from the nunnery. We've had no visits. Taskill, we have to search for them."

Taskill was taken aback. "Search for them? You and me?"

"Aye. We can take the boat back to Mull and search everywhere. My father is missing, and we must find him. Don't you feel the same about your mother?"

"Aye and nay. I'd like to find them, but there's a storm brewing, and I think it best to wait until it has passed. On the morrow would be a better time to search for them. It's too dark, and the winds are coming up now, and you know how they make the seas wild."

She pointed toward Mull. "But look. There are no waves yet. The sea was calm as could be a wee bit ago. I think we have time."

Taskill rubbed his jaw, staring at the small waves, yet something inside him wished to please Sheona. "I don't care to be caught on the water when a thunderstorm breaks, drenching rain pounding down as the thunder rumbles all around us. That could be deadly, Sheona. We'll have to wait it out until the morrow, lass."

"Nay, I cannot wait. Please, Taskill." She grabbed his arm, squeezing it. "Take me away from this isle now. We can beat the storm. It won't be here for a couple of hours. I have to leave here now. You don't understand." The way her breathing increased, he knew this was about more than her sire.

His gaze locked on hers. Something else was afoot, though he couldn't guess what it was. But he had to give her the chance to come to the right conclusion. Even Sheona knew what it was like to be on rough waters. "Sheona, to leave now would be dangerous. You're experienced enough as a boater to know that. The journey back to MacClane's could be treacherous at best."

"But …" She teared up.

And that was like a fist to his gut. He hated when lasses cried. "What's wrong, Sheona?"

She locked her arms across her chest. "Taskill, someone else is after me. Two men came last eve for me, but my friend frightened them away. She heard them discuss returning either this eve or tomorrow eve. I have to get away. I cannot put anyone here at risk. Please help me."

A fury Taskill could not tamp down rose inside him and his words came out with a tougher edge than he intended. "Who? Who came for you?" He thought of Tora saying that bad men were after Sheona. These were the men she referred to. Tora had been right.

Sheona's gaze jumped from her feet to something behind him to the dark sky above and back to her feet.

He took her hand in his and said, "Who, Sheona? I need to know."

Her gaze lifted to his and she whispered a name, "Clyde. Clyde and someone else. He's one of our …"

"I know who the hell that bastard is. He needs a lesson." While he knew she could see him unclenching and clenching his fists repeatedly, he couldn't stop himself. He pictured that fist knocking two of the arse's teeth out. But then reason stopped him. "How do you know it was Clyde? Did you see him? Who is his partner?"

"I didn't see him. My friend did, said there were two of them, but she couldn't identify him as Clyde."

"Then how do you know?"

She glanced back over her shoulder. "Have you met a wee lass named Lia?"

"Aye," he whispered, a bad feeling coming over him like a death shroud. "She's an angel. Can tell what's going to happen. What exactly did she tell you, Sheona? Exactly?"

"She said Clyde was coming for me and that I should go with you when you arrived."

That was good enough for him.

"Get in the boat. We're leaving, rough waves or not."

No one argued with Lia.

CHAPTER THIRTY-THREE

SHEONA

GLAD TO HAVE convinced him, she settled her mantle around her to cover her legs once in the boat. The wind grew sharper as the temperature dropped. "Do you have another set of oars? I can help row."

"Can you get your arms out of your mantle enough?"

"Aye. I can do it. If two of us row, we'll get there faster." She arranged herself the best she could and took a set of oars. "We're heading that way, correct?" she asked, pointing toward what she thought would be MacClane Castle.

"Aye. And once we arrive, we can get inside at Tristan's home. They're in the castle now. Hopefully, we'll be in front of a fire in a little more than an hour. The current is in our favor."

They started across the water without any issues, the only boat as far as they could see. Sheona couldn't help but look over her shoulder, as if Clyde would suddenly appear behind her.

As if reading her mind, Taskill said, "I'll not

let him hurt you, Sheona. You know I'll always protect you."

She nodded, tears misting her eyes. "I know. Many thanks to you. I just hate that I have to deal with him. And I can't understand why my father disappeared. What does Lennox think? And Sloan?"

"They were headed to MacQuarie land to see if Thane or Artan knew anything."

"What?" The wind had picked up, making it hard to hear over the lapping waves. And shortly after that, the rain began, lightly at first.

"Never mind. Just row! It's coming soon. I don't like those black clouds, Sheona. They're coming up on us too quickly."

She matched his pace, pulling her hood up to protect herself from the increasing rain. "Can we go back?"

"Nay, we're about halfway there. We may as well head to MacClane's. It's safer there, and that's the direction the current is going. We'll never be able to go against the current. The wind is making it too strong."

She nodded and pushed ahead, her arms aching from the force she'd used to move through the building waves. Taskill's arms were powerful, his movements graceful compared to the awkward attempts she was making to assist him. He was such a fine-looking man, someone she'd always thought attractive. His looks were even more appealing to her out in the middle of the sea in a storm, though she was uncertain why. It could be the line of his jaw, the stubble of his golden beard, the blue eyes that could be so serious but also glittered when he laughed.

Taskill had everything she could ever want in a husband. So why didn't she? Thoughts of Rinaldo convinced her that she didn't need a husband. And Taskill wasn't interested in her, either. It was as simple as that.

If she did, she'd probably choose someone just like Taskill.

A bolt of lightning lit up the sky, the flash startling her so much that she let out a squeak, glancing over her head.

"Shite," Taskill said. "I'd hoped to make it to land before this started."

The thunder took a while before they heard it, confirmation that they weren't in the worst of the storm yet, but the drenching rain told them it was nearby and coming soon. Sheona's hands gripped the oars so hard that her knuckles had turned white. Another flash, another boom, and another jump warned her of how quickly the weather was changing.

"Don't drop your oars. We need them, Sheona."

"That last one was loud. I won't let them go. I promise." Even if her fear of capsizing increased with every passing moment. Every approaching wave. Every spout of water that landed inside the boat. Every shot of lightning that came closer and closer.

The boat rocked and tipped amid the rain. Sheona again yanked the hood of her mantle up over her head, attempting to protect herself. But it did no good.

"Pull the oars in, Sheona, and hang on to the sides. We're going to have to let the waves take us. I can't fight them any longer. Once the sea calms, we'll find our way." He reached for her once the oars were in, cocooning her against his body to protect her the best he could.

Another flash of lightning lit up the sky, two more bolts following it with ear-piercing thunder.

Another forked flash hit a tree on shore, the leaves on the tree falling to the ground as the bark on one side of it disappeared. Sheona screamed at the instantaneous thunderclap that was so loud, it shook the boat, the wood trembling.

"We're going to die, aren't we?" she shouted.

"Nay, we are not. I won't let you die. If the boat goes over, we swim to the nearest shore. That way." He moved to sit next to her. "Over there. That's where the tree was. It's not that far from us. I can see land and it's closer than you think."

A monstrous wave hit them and sent a deluge of water into the boat, sending Sheona into another scream as the small vessel tipped but then righted itself—this time. "We're going to sink, Taskill!"

"If the boat goes down, we'll swim. Promise me that you'll fight, Sheona. You have much to live for. I know it."

She shivered in the pelting rain, thinking of all that Lia had said. Things would be wonderful, eventually. Not yet. Worse first.

Would she survive?

She thought of Brynja and Hildi and suddenly made the decision to fight. "Help me get this off, Taskill."

"What?"

"My mantle will take me under. I have to get it off if I'm to swim. I need to remove it." She had a small, more valuable sack inside the larger one, so she took that one out and tied it around her waist. It had a necklace her mother had given her and two daggers. She couldn't lose the necklace. Everything else didn't matter.

They managed to remove her mantle and toss it behind her in the small boat. Another lightning bolt, another swell, another loud boom.

"You're right. I'm taking my boots off in case we go over. You should take yours off too." They both fussed, one at a time, but finally set their boots at the far end of the vessel.

A gigantic wave hit the boat and sent it careening onto its side.

"Hang on, Sheona! It will right itself! Hang on!" But unfortunately, that didn't happen.

The boat tipped and exploded into pieces.

The two catapulted into the cold sea.

CHAPTER THIRTY-FOUR

DYNA

~~~

THE STORM CAME on them in a flash, lightning bolts renting the air while thunderclaps blasted quicker and louder. The rain was mild at first but soon came in pounding sheets that rattled everything.

"Diamond!" Derric shouted over the balcony railing into the hall. "I need to put the chest in front of the window to hold the fur against it. The rain is coming straight in. Help me."

"Da, watch the bairns." She raced upstairs, taking two at a time. How she hated a wet floor on the stone of their chamber. "I'm coming, Derric." She opened the door and her eyes widened, listening to the howl of the wind as it came across the sound. "I knew this view would prove to be bad." She'd begged for the chamber facing the sea because she loved the sound of lapping waves. "Bloody hell, this is a mess!"

"I need to get another fur on it as protection after we move the chest."

She hurried to the other side of the solid trunk and helped her husband move it over in front of their one window. It took them a bit to maneuver it with the furs, but they managed. Once it was in place, she breathed a sigh of relief, grabbing one of Derric's tunics to wipe up the rain on the floor. Once she sopped everything up, she let out a low whine, grabbing her head.

"What is it, Diamond? Who is it?" He lifted her up into his arms, cuddling her close.

"Derric, check the bairns. I have a powerful headache. Something is happening."

Derric set her down and helped her out of their chamber and over to the balcony so they could both look into the hall to see that all was well.

Maitland left the chamber, then returned quickly. "Mama's got a sudden headache." He glanced up at the balcony. "Dyna? What's wrong?"

"Headache." She cradled her head with both hands as she let out a low moan.

Derric picked her up in his arms and headed down the stairs.

"The bairns, Derric. Where are they? I can't see right now." Her voice came out in a strained tone they rarely heard from her, but the pain was so outrageous that it hurt to speak.

"All three are in front of the hearth, though I'm moving them back. The flames are dancing from the wind." Her father had already gotten out of his chair and approached the bairns. "Move back. Sylvi and Tora, if you move back, Sandor will move back."

But Sandor got up and ran in circles around the great hall, giggling and slapping at something.

Her father whispered, "Nay, not again." He

glanced up at his daughter to see if she'd noticed Sandor's behavior.

Sloan pushed himself to standing. "What the hell does all this mean?" He spun in a circle, staring at Dyna and Sandor and Connor.

Lennox said, "The two seers have headaches, and Sandor is chasing ghosts again."

"Bloody hell!" Dyna roared. "My head!"

Drew entered with Avelina in his arms. "Dyna? You too? Her headache is horrible."

Her father stood in the middle, looking from one place to the next, uncertain what it all meant. "Dyna?"

"Just make sure the bairns are away from the fire. I don't know what is happening."

Drew set Avelina into a chair near the hearth. "It started so fast that I didn't know what to do."

Avelina moaned as she held her head. "Water. I need water."

Tora ran over and tugged on her grandsire's plaid. "Up, Grandda. Up!"

Dyna whispered, "Nay …" Now it was Tora too. She knew what was coming, sadly.

Her father lifted Tora into his arms and gave the sweet lass all his attention. "What is it, Tora? Tell me everything."

Her hand cupped his cheek and said, "The boat bwoke."

She pushed to get down, but Connor held firm. "Whose boat, Tora? You have to tell me who is in the boat."

"Sona." Then she shoved away and hopped down.

Her father then went after the youngest of the bairns. "Who is chasing you, Sandor?"

"Unca Shakie chaseen me aden. 'Top it, Unca Shakee." Then he paused, grabbing his belly and giggling. "He tickle me."

"Uncle Jake, what is it?" Dyna bellowed. "Help me, please!"

Sandor stopped and stared up at the rafters. "Unca Shakee say bad men chaseen Sona."

"Where are they, Jake?"

"In da boat. Behine her." Sandor took off running, then stopped quickly and began to play on the floor again, Sylvi and Tora joining them.

Then Sloan paced, cursing. "It's this storm. Their boat crashed. But where? And is someone with Sheona or is she alone? Or does Clyde already have her?" He stopped and stared up at the rafters. "What the hell do I do?"

Dyna said, "The parapets, Derric. I need to go up."

Derric replied, "Hell nay, Diamond. It's storming out there. You'll be hit by lightning."

"I have to go up there too," Avelina said. "Or this headache will never stop. Maitland, help me. Drew can't get me up those stairs."

Maitland handed Grant over to Maeve and helped his mother to the stairs, picking her up when she stumbled. Dyna climbed behind him, Derric supporting her.

Sloan shouted, "I'm coming with you!"

Lennox was next. "Aye!"

Dyna waved them up. When they finally landed on the parapets, forcing the heavy door open,

Avelina and Dyna each sat on stools, settling next to each other with everyone's help, linking their hands. Derric covered Dyna with a mantle, doing his best to keep the pelting rain from her face. "Damn storm."

Avelina kept her back to the downpour, Drew behind her.

"What do you see, Dyna?" Avelina whispered.

"The boat. Two people in it. I see the abbey behind it."

Sloan said, "It's Sheona. It has to be. What else? Is it raining?"

Avelina let go of Dyna's hand to massage her forehead. "The rain is pelting Sheona. The waves are beating against the boat. I see a tree falling into the water, sending large, battering waves their way."

"Who?" Sloan bellowed. "You say 'their way?' Who is with her? Taskill? Clyde? My father?"

Dyna screamed, holding her head, tears now pouring down her cheeks. "Nay, nay!"

Sloan moved toward her, but Connor held him back. "Leave her be. Let her do this."

Sloan closed his eyes and stepped aside, waiting, Lennox behind him, clasping his shoulder.

Avelina wailed, "Nay! Look out! The wave is coming! The giant wave will …"

Dyna cried, "The boat! It's Taskill, Sloan. Taskill and Sheona. But …"

"But what?" Lennox and Sloan bellowed in unison.

Dyna dropped her hands and stood, Avelina doing the same, the two turning toward them.

Dyna shouted over the storm. "The waves hit the boat, and the boards exploded. Sheona and Taskill are in the sea."

"Shite!" Sloan bellowed. "Come on, Lennox. We have to find them."

Maitland said, "You'll never find them in this storm, Sloan. You could lose your own life on the way. They could be close to shore. They're both strong swimmers, are they not?"

Lennox said, "Aye, and Taskill won't leave without her, Sloan. Maitland is right. In good weather, we're over an hour away. They have to save themselves. As soon as the storm ebbs, we'll head to MacClane Castle."

Connor said, "Do you see anyone else, Dyna? Anyone on shore? Any boat nearby?"

Dyna shook her head, but Avelina nodded. "I do."

"Who?" Sloan asked. "Who?"

Avelina smiled and whispered, "Lia. She's on the shore watching."

Lennox clasped Sloan's shoulder and said, "That's a good thing, I believe."

Dyna prayed they were right. Her headache had disappeared.

CHAPTER THIRTY-FIVE

TASKILL

❧

TASKILL HURTLED THROUGH the air, landing with a loud splash as the boat shattered from the powerful wave. He gasped at the temperature, even though he'd adjusted to the cold from the waves that had sprayed them along the way. Holding his breath, he opened his eyes in the water, searching for Sheona in the murky depths, kicking as hard as he could to break the surface to fill his lungs.

But he didn't see her anywhere.

When he finally broke through, he gasped, taking in air before he was hit by another violent wave, but he gained enough breath to shout, "Sheona! Where are you?"

He gulped a mouthful of the salty sea water, spit it out, and kicked, his gaze scanning the area for her head among the broken wood. "Sheona!"

He said a quick prayer to get her to the surface. Then he'd help her get to shore. He could see that it wasn't that far away. They were both strong swimmers and could surely make it to safety.

"Here!"

A faint voice called out, or was he imagining what he wished to hear? He pushed the debris aside and swam toward where he thought she was. Her head was above water, battling to stay up in the rough waves.

"Are you hale? Any injury?"

"I think I'm fine, but which way, Taskill? I can't see in the dark."

A bolt of lightning shot through the air, giving him enough light to see how far away they were from shore. "This way." He tipped his head in the direction they were going. "Can you swim?"

"Aye, I'm fine. I don't know if I can make it that far. It's cold."

He grabbed her tunic and tugged her along behind him. "Roll onto your back." Then he did the same, one hand holding her while the other one went over his head rhythmically, his legs propelling them farther.

She fell back and he tugged her along, kicking to assist him. "We have to get away from all the boards first. Once we're free of them, I'll relax. If you see one coming toward us, let me know. We can't get knocked out, either of us, or we'll never make it."

He swam on his back, pulling her along with him without any trouble. Once they cleared the debris, he calmed himself, knowing he would need all the strength he had to get the two of them to shore.

"Don't leave me, Taskill. Promise?"

"I promise. Just try to relax. Save your strength. You'll need it."

He could feel the gasping ache in his lungs and knew he was working extra hard due to the conditions, but they'd both been in the sea all their lives. They had to make it to the edge of the isle. He tipped his head and stared up at the stars that broke through the clouds, switching his kick to one that seemed stronger, the one like a frog used. He held Sheona with one hand to his side, making sure his feet missed her and that her kicks continued to be strong enough to help him. If she fell unconscious, he'd never make it to shore.

They'd both go under.

The rain let up a wee bit, and the length of time between the lightning and the thunder stretched longer and longer, indicating the storm was moving away. He glanced over his shoulder, disappointed to see how far away the coastline was from them, but he powered on.

"Taskill, are we going to die?" she whispered.

"Nay, do not think like that."

"But I'm losing my strength. It's so cold."

"Don't talk. Save your strength." He kicked on, his one arm repeatedly going over his head to pull them along. They'd already traveled down shore from where they started, though as long as they continued toward land, it didn't matter. He thought it was Mull near MacLean land, but he truly had no idea in the dark. If they were pushed much farther than MacLean land, they'd be propelled out to sea toward the mainland.

They'd never get across that. He could pray for a boat to come along to save them, but he doubted there were many foolish enough to be out now.

"I'm losing strength. I can't kick much longer, Taskill."

Sheona shivered underneath his hand, her teeth chattering enough that he could hear it. He had to get her to shore, or they'd both drown. If she could at least stay awake, she could float. If she passed out, she'd be dead weight.

Out of nowhere, an object landed on her belly, and she screamed, pushing it toward him. He stopped swimming for a moment, staring at this odd object that floated in front of him. It was white, a sizable chunk of something. He tried to bat it away, but the odd thing was light as could be and stayed on top of the water, floating back to them.

"What is it?"

"I have no idea, Sheona, but it floats. I want you to hold it close to you. It won't cut you or anything. It's smooth. It must be some type of wood. Mayhap it fell from the tree that was hit by lightning. Hang on to it. It may help you."

She clutched the object to her belly, her hands shivering. "Go ahead. I'll kick when I can."

He moved onto his back again and continued, surprised at how much easier it was to slide through the water.

"Taskill, this is better! I think we'll make it. Is it easier for you?"

"Aye, it is. Much easier. We'll be successful with this help." He glanced over his shoulder, the rain now light, the wind having died down enough for him to see the shore. They were almost there.

They continued, Taskill catching drops of water occasionally to keep his thirst quenched. There was nothing like fresh rain to refresh yourself. He noticed Sheona did the same.

"You made it! Well done!" a youthful voice called to them.

Taskill nearly let go of Sheona, but he held tight, leaning forward to look back over his shoulder. Who the hell had just spoken? To his surprise, his feet touched the bottom. "Sheona! We made it. Touch. You can touch!"

"Welcome!" the voice said. "I've been waiting for you. I have the perfect place for you to warm up. Follow me!"

"What the hell?" Taskill turned around, now holding Sheona's hand to keep her close in the small waves as they made their way to shore.

Sheona asked, "Who was that?" Then she stared around her. "Where did my thing go? The thing that kept me afloat?"

A lass stood on the edge of the beach. "I sent it away. You no longer need it. Follow me."

Lia stood before them with a wide smile.

CHAPTER THIRTY-SIX

SHEONA

SHEONA WAS SO grateful to be on land that she didn't care where they went, as long as she could dry out somewhere. The rain continued, but at a much slower pace. Taskill reached back to take her hand, his gaze asking her permission first. She nodded.

She'd go anywhere with Taskill.

Lia said, "Follow me. There's a lovely cottage up ahead that has a chest with extra clothes and a warm fire. There's dried meat and cheese with some apples. I hope I've thought of everything. Eat your fill and rest up. I'm sure people will be looking for you when morn comes."

"You aren't leaving us, are you?" Sheona asked, still unable to believe a wee lass wielded such power.

"I must. But I've left you all you need. Do not worry. You've been through the worst of your journey." She opened the door to the cottage and held it for them. "You see? The flames are prepared to warm you. There's wine and food aplenty. If you search through the chests, you'll find clothing for both of you. Rest yourselves and promise me you won't leave until after dawn."

Taskill said, "I don't have the strength to leave before then."

"A good eve to you, then," Lia said, closing the door.

"Wait!" Taskill called out.

"Aye?"

"Where are we? Mull? Iona?"

"Nay," she said as she stepped out. "You missed Mull. You're on Erraid. Not far from Iona and Mull. Fear not. Just wait for low tide."

And Lia left.

"Taskill, where is Erraid?"

He shrugged, then yanked at his tunic. "I have no idea. Forgive me, lass, but I wish to get out of these wet clothes. I'll worry about our location after I eat." He tossed his tunic near the fire, then opened a nearby chest. "Find something to fit you. Anything. We have to get dry, then we can eat. I'll sleep on the floor. You may have the bed."

Forcing her gaze away from his handsome chest, she took a breath and looked into the storage trunk. Too exhausted to question anything he said, she knelt next to the furniture, finding a lovely dark blue woolen gown on the top and a warm night rail underneath it. "These will work for me." She had the oddest feeling that both would fit her perfectly. The fine wool of the gown was just what she needed on the morrow, but she'd don the night rail first.

Taskill said, "I'll turn my back. Get dressed, then I'll find clothes for myself." He strode over to the door. "Never mind. I'll step out. Open it when I can return. And if we're lucky, they have boots that fit too!"

Shivering, she removed the tunic and hung it on a peg near the hearth, then peeled off the leggings Brynja had given her, hanging them on another peg. She wished to keep them, though her sire would not like them.

But she didn't care. She moaned as the warmth from the fire spread through her. She removed her undergarments, hanging them under her tunic, then donned the night rail with a sigh. She hugged herself in front of the fire as the flames thawed her all the way to her toes. Why had she never appreciated such a simple thing as heat before?

"Taskill, you may come in."

He opened the door but stopped, staring at her as she unplaited her hair and threaded her fingers through her long locks, trying to dry them. "Sheona, you are lovely, even wet."

She blushed, wishing to touch the hairs on his chest, to lean closer into his embrace. Shocked by her own thoughts, she wondered when the last time was that she'd been interested in a hug from a man.

Never that she could think of.

If he'd just hug her once, she could relax, but that would be improper. She stepped back and said, "I'll go outside while you change."

"Nay. It's still cold and wet. The wind is whipping the branches about, drenching rain in some spots while none in others. Just turn your back and I'll dress quickly. I do not wish for you to get cold again."

She spun around, staring into the flames, thinking on all that had transpired in the last sennight. More confused than ever, she reviewed all that had happened with Taskill, and then something else popped up in her mind, as if put there by someone.

Lia. Obviously, Lia wanted them together. What exactly did that mean? Should she consider marriage to Taskill MacVey?

"I'm finished, lass. Come, have some wine and cheese."

She sat across from him at the small table, nibbling on the cheese before taking several sips of the wine. Taskill reached across and said, "Slow down or you'll lose your head too fast."

She scowled, not understanding his meaning.

"I don't mind if you get in your cups, but we have much to do in the morn. We only have a few hours left of this night, and we're both exhausted from the swim."

"My father didn't allow me to drink wine. Sloan would sneak me a goblet here and there."

Taskill grinned. "Your father is ornery, is he not?"

"He is. But I still love him."

"Of course. Your sire was a fine chieftain for many years. Everyone respects him."

They ate in silence for a few moments, then Taskill said, "After what we just went through together, I feel like I could tell you anything. So, I'm going to tell you this much. It was never you

that I didn't wish to marry. In fact, if I were to
marry, I would be pleased to have a wife as lovely
and smart as you, but I'm not …" He paused for
a moment and took a sip of wine. "I'm not the
kind of person to marry. It's hard to explain, but
I wish for you to know that it has naught to do
with you. It's about me and how I fit into this
world."

"Is it because you have been with so many?"
She'd heard he'd had multiple lasses in love with
him over the years.

Taskill nearly choked, but then said, "I'll tell
you a secret if you promise to keep it. No one
knows this but me. Not even Lennox."

She had no idea what he could mean, so she
said, "I'll promise. I'm verra good at keeping
secrets."

"I've not been with as many women as everyone
thinks I have. For some reason, I attract women,
but it doesn't mean I bed them."

Stunned, she didn't know what to say. Most
men had many relations, at least that's what
Rinaldo had told her. Had he lied to her? She
chewed slowly on a bite of apple and wondered
how many of Rinaldo's words had been lies.

"Sheona, can I ask you something? Were you
abused by someone? The abbess told your sire that
she guessed you had been. That it was probably
the reason you didn't wish to marry."

Her gaze flitted to the fire, hoping to hide the
tears that had popped up. She forced them back
inside, the wine she'd had already loosening her
tongue. Then she made a major decision. After

all, she trusted Taskill completely. She'd rather tell Marta, but her dear sister was overwrought with the new bairn, and Sloan was overworked being chieftain of their clan.

She dropped her gaze. "It was Rinaldo. He locked me in a stall in the stable. Told me he was going to teach me something. I didn't wish to stay, but no one was there to unlock the gate. So, I waited until he brought a lass into the next stall."

She closed her eyes as memories of the poor lass's cries filled her mind. "He forced himself on her, tricked her, then when he hurt her, she begged him to leave her be, that it was too painful, but he persisted, covering her mouth with his hand and berating her. She cried and screamed. Then I screamed for her. When someone finally heard us, they came into the stable and he stopped.

"I couldn't see anything, only hear what happened. He whispered to her and said if she ever told, he'd cut her face, so she promised not to tell. He had two friends covering for him, so he snuck her out the back while they talked with the person who came along asking about the screaming.

"When Rinaldo returned, he finally unlocked the door and told me that I would be next. That it was his job as my brother to take my maidenhead. He promised me it would hurt terribly and that I wouldn't be able to walk. Then he laughed and pinched my breast hard and told me mayhap he'd give me to one of his friends."

Her tears slid down her cheeks, and she swiped them away.

Taskill asked, "And did he do as he promised?"

She shook her head. "Nay, he died two days later. I hated Rinaldo. He was so cruel, but Da seemed to love him. He had everyone fooled, thinking he was a simple person, but he wasn't. He was a conniving, lying bastard. Even when we were young. He would tell Da one thing, then do something completely evil as soon as Da walked away."

"Rinaldo was evil. Sloan discovered the truth and so did your sire. It's why he killed his own son, Sheona. You did naught wrong."

"Nay, but ever since then, I swore I'd never marry. The kitchen lasses say their husbands like to do it every night. I don't want to live like that."

"Did you know the lass?"

"Nay. I heard one of Rinaldo's friends say he would take her back home. She wasn't part of our clan."

"Sheona …" He leaned forward and took her hand, cocooning it in his. "I don't know exactly, but I can tell you the marriage bed is meant to be a pleasant experience. It will hurt the lass the first time, but after that, if the man does it right, it's pleasurable for both."

She sopped up her tears. "That's what Simone said. Rinaldo lied about everything, then?"

"Aye. He lied and he forced himself on that poor lass. That's why it hurt her. Most couples enjoy the marital bed, or so I've been told. Lennox surely does. He and Meg giggle and carry on like lovers on the run."

A weight lifted from her chest in a matter of

moments. She had to admit that Eva and Sloan were both happy. And so were Marta and Gideon now that they'd had a second bairn.

The intense fear she'd held all this time for marrying had been wiped away.

"I'll marry you, Taskill. I know you'd never hurt me."

And she meant it.

Taskill stared at his hands, then said, "But I can't marry you. It's hard to explain, but someday I'll try. Not now."

CHAPTER THIRTY-SEVEN

DERMOT

"COME ALONG, RUT." The morning had turned out to be far better than last eve. "Isn't it a beautiful morn?"

"Aye, it is. But Lennox will be looking for me. I should go home."

"Not yet." He took her hand and led her along behind him.

"Where the hell are you taking me now? Mayhap I might like to go home. And aren't you going after your daughter?" She moved along the coastline of Mull, her skirt billowing lightly in the wind, her hair tied into a bun at the base of her neck.

Rut MacVey had proven to be even finer than he would have guessed. But he'd already made his mind up about Sheona. He wasn't the one his daughter needed right now.

"Nay. I've decided to wait three more days, as promised. Then I'll find her and get the truth. I have to hold to my word. I told her I wouldn't return for a sennight."

"But what about the abuse? Don't you wish to know who or when?"

"Nay. I'll let her discuss it with the abbess. They don't need me involved."

"Then where are we going?" She stopped her forward movement and crossed her arms.

Dermot took two steps back to kiss Rut's cheek, then held his hand out to her. "Come, I'll help you. We have to get past these rocks over here."

"And then where?"

"We're going on a wee journey. Sheona is on an island of women, and if she were abused, then she's in the safest place possible. But you and me? We had a pleasant time together last eve, and I'm not ready for it to end. We have a score to settle, and we're going to settle it now."

"And where the hell are we going to settle this, Dermot?"

"Look, we started something last eve in MacLane's cottage. With all that lightning, it made for a unique time together. Once wasn't enough for me," he said, dropping his voice to a whisper. "And I doubt it was enough for you, either. Good thing we had the thunder to cover your shouts, lassie." He grinned from ear to ear.

"Fine, you big bull. It was an entertaining night, but I'd expect more from a chieftain like you."

"And you'll get more, my sweet, but not here."

She scowled at him. "Then where are we going?"

"On the boat. The one that is awaiting us. If you don't get on, I'll throw you on."

She yanked her hand back as soon as they crossed the rocks onto the sand. "No one tells me what to do."

Dermot picked her up and tossed her over his shoulder, her bottom sticking up in the air.

Rut let out a scream, then bellowed, "Set me down, you old curmudgeon! Now. Right this moment. Let me go, you wicked beast."

Dermot laughed all the way as he carried her onto the large vessel. He then shouted to the captain as soon as they were safely on board, "Move out!"

Dermot set Rut down and she promptly slapped him. "I'm getting off this boat."

"Nay, you aren't, unless you like to swim."

She glanced over the railing of the galley ship at all the oars sticking out of the sides as the vessel glided into the sea. The captain shouted to her, "Is there a problem?"

Rut glared at Dermot and said, "Nay, I'm fine."

Dermot smirked. The woman did love to put on a show, and it was always guaranteed to be one worth watching. He drawled, "Don't want to swim?"

Rut slapped him again.

CHAPTER THIRTY-EIGHT

SLOAN

SLOAN STOOD ON the shore of Iona after the storm the next morning and scanned the area. Lennox paced the beach, Meg and Eva both sitting on rocks nearby. The four had come with Hagen and Jowell, who'd assisted with the rowing. The sea was still ferocious, so they had asked for help.

Lennox asked, "Now what do we do?" They'd arrived an hour ago and gone right to the abbess, who revealed that Sheona had been missing since she'd gone to Ionaland. Dermot and Rut had never appeared.

The abbess had taken them to Sheona's chamber, giving Sloan and Eva the chance to sift through her meager belongings, but there were no clues there. "Mother Mary," Sloan had asked. "Have you seen anyone else looking for my sister? Two men in a boat?"

"Nay, no one has come looking for her. I don't know what has happened, but Simone is looking into it for me. She will return when she knows where Sheona is. I trust Simone."

Sloan nodded, agreeing with her. "Simone is a fierce woman. If anyone can find her, Simone can."

The abbess left, so the group made their way to the shore again, trying to formulate a plan. Lennox stared up at the morning clouds. "The storm is over. I say we travel back to MacClane's and visit with Tristan. Mayhap he's seen some activity. He's directly on the point and can see far from that new curtain wall they built."

Eva said, "That's as good a suggestion as any I can think of. How the hell can four people disappear like that?"

Lennox gave his sister a glare. "You know the answer to that, and I refuse to say it."

Sloan wouldn't say it either. The idea that all four had been in a boat didn't sit well with him because that meant they'd all been on the water when that storm hit. And the thought that Dyna and Avelina had been right, that Taskill and Sheona's boat had been destroyed, didn't sit well with any of them, especially if they never made it to shore.

No one would say the words.

Meg muttered, "It came on so quickly." She hugged herself and shivered, Lennox wrapping his arms around her and kissing her cheek.

"We'll find them. All of them."

Hagen and Jowell readied their boat, swords sheathed, but kept an eye on everything around them.

Two lasses came flying toward them, running as fast as they could. "Wait! Please wait!"

Hagen froze, his gaze locked on the taller of the two. Her hair was a mix of gold and yellow, braided on both sides and plaited to the back of her head. Ice-blue eyes caught him, along with the slight curves of her lithe body. She had powerful shoulders for a lass, and her legs could probably level a man with one kick. She wore brown leggings with a tunic of gold and green. He would wager they came from Simone.

He'd never seen anyone more beautiful in his life. Totally entranced, he had to find out who she was.

Sloan and Lennox moved together to greet the lasses, standing in front of their wives to protect them. Sloan had no idea who the lasses were or what they wanted. "What is it?" Sloan asked.

One lass stopped, the other directly behind her. "We were in the same chamber as Sheona. We know where she went."

"Where?" Sloan asked, stepping closer. He gripped Eva's hand tightly, pulling her next to him.

"She got in a boat with someone named Taskill," the fair-haired girl said. "I'm Brynja and this is Hildi. She went with us to deliver vegetables to Simone at Ionaland. We saw Magni."

"How do you know his name was Taskill?" Lennox asked. Meg moved up next to him and the four circled the two lasses, listening intently.

Hagen and Jowell strolled up behind them, giving the lasses their full attention.

Hildi said, "Because Lia told us he was coming. She said Taskill was coming across the water, and that Sheona needed to go with him because Clyde was coming for her with another man. As soon as Taskill arrived, they left. He didn't wish to go because of the oncoming storm, but when he heard about Clyde, they hopped in the boat and headed toward Mull."

"Do you know where they were going?"

"Back to the direction Taskill came from," Hildi said. She pointed toward MacLean land. "Where you came from."

"Hildi, tell me more about Clyde. Did you see him? And who is the other man with him?" Sloan asked. He had to discover where the bastard was so he could rip out his heart.

"Is he not one of your guards, Rankin?" Lennox asked.

Sloan glared at him. "Probably, but I'd like to hear all she knows. He's capable of it."

Brynja spoke up, "Hildi never saw him. I did. I saw the boat arrive in the middle of the night, so I came out to see who it was. They were looking for a lass and were arguing about who was going to get her first. So, I shut them up."

Lennox asked, "How?"

Hildi giggled. "She hit him with her knife."

Brynja pulled out a dagger and fired it at the nearest tree. It landed deep in the bark with a loud thwack. "I put a stop to them getting off the boat." Her hands settled on her hips. "I would have used my spear, but it was dark. I had to get close to do any damage with my spear so I chose the smaller weapon."

"Did you kill either one?" Sloan asked.

"Nay, just wounded them both."

"Who was the other man with Clyde? Think carefully. Did he use a name? Any identifying characteristics?"

Brynja chuckled. "Nay, no name, but I'm sure the hole I put in his shoulder with my dagger will give him away. It should be full of pus by now. I hit one in his right shoulder and the other in his thigh. They rowed like wee laddies."

Sloan smiled and said, "Many thanks to you. I appreciate you coming to find us. We'll find them, I'm sure."

When Hagen was finally able to move, he followed the lass named Brynja. Jowell grabbed him by the shoulder and asked, "What the hell are you doing?"

He shoved his cousin away and said, "I have to know more."

He followed Brynja but then grabbed the dagger she left in the nearby tree to return it to her. "Lass, you forgot this."

He held it out, hilt toward her, his gaze locked on her face, doing his best to remember every detail. Brynja was the most stunning lass he'd ever seen, and the fact that she could use a weapon like that amazed him.

"My thanks to you," she said, taking the weapon from him. "Are you related to Sheona?"

"Nay, we are Grants. From Duart Castle." He stared at her, enchanted. "Your hair. Where did you learn that?" It was a style exactly like his mother wore.

"My mother. She's Norse. A Scot raped her and left her with me in her womb. Then he left. I prefer to think of myself as a Norsewoman, not a lass." Her eyes carried a pain he didn't like to see.

"I'm Hagen Grant. My mother is also Norse. But she wasn't raped by my father. He married her. Scots can be good."

"The only Norsewoman I know in the area used to be known as the Ice Queen. Her name is Sela. Have you heard of her?"

Hagen smiled. "Aye, I know her well. Sela is my mother."

Brynja smiled, then spun on her heel and strode away.

Hagen felt like he'd been punched in the gut. He took a step toward her, but Jowell grabbed his upper arm. "We're leaving. Let it go. She's going to take her vows. That's why she's here."

"Nay, she's not."

"How the hell do you know?" Jowell asked.

"Because I'm going to marry her."

Hagen strode back to the ship, his steps a bit lighter than usual.

CHAPTER THIRTY-NINE

MERRYN

B ROC AND MERRYN strolled across the recently finished curtain wall of the new MacClane holding on Mull. When they'd made one full rotation, she stopped to yell over the side, "Tristan, it is lovely. I cannot wait to see everything inside."

"Join me for a brief repast. We have cabbage stew simmering on the hearth." Tristan waved at his sister, then stepped back inside the new keep.

Broc kissed Merryn, nuzzling her neck. "I love it when you are so excited. But I'll have to keep my hands to myself for a bit."

She giggled. "I have fond memories of last eve before we left Duart Castle. But I do feel a bit bad about leaving Shealee."

"She looked completely happy to be sleeping with Tora and Sylvi last eve."

Merryn rolled her eyes. "So true. She's adjusted better than I have to everything. The storm didn't bother her one bit."

"Only because she doesn't have the memories you have." He led her down the staircase, taking in the fresh sea air as they descended, the sky cloudy but not totally gray.

Once inside the keep, Merryn's brother called out to her. "Come sit. We have new chairs by the fire and Aunt Alma sent cushions. I have to admit that I treasure them. I believe it will be a cold winter here on the coastline."

Broc offered, "I'll help cut firewood before we go back to Duart Castle."

"I'd appreciate that, though I've had the men cutting wood often once we finished the keep."

"Where are they now?" Merryn asked, surprised to see the great hall so quiet.

"They're modifying the cottage a bit. That's where the men will be sleeping. And they've added some stalls to the stable, making one fit for sleeping with pallets. Broc, you did a great job leading that project. It's a solid structure against the wind. We've got some sheep in a separate stall at the end for the winter months. We've come a long way, and I thank the Granthams for all their assistance. I feel we are well prepared for winter."

"Our pleasure. We love to help our friends." Broc glanced over at his wife and squeezed her hand. "We must ask again over our purpose, Tristan. Many are upset."

"As I said, Taskill was here, but that was before the storm. I have not seen him since then. And it was a horrible thunderstorm. Do you see them often here on Mull, and are they all that horrendous?"

"Nay. That was the worst outburst I've seen anywhere. It shook our rafters, and Duart is soundly built. That thunder frightened all our animals. We had to leave several men in the stables to keep the horses calm when the thunder got so close. But you need to ask the Rankins and MacVeys. They've been here much longer than I have," Broc reminded him.

Tristan kneaded his hands in his lap, shaking his head. "Taskill took a boat to Iona to look for Sheona. That's all I know. I've not seen anything since then," Tristan said, approaching the sideboard and bringing a basket of apples and cheese over to share. "I hope he made it, though the storm was a few hours after he left, so he should have made it across to Iona. They sent you to search for them?"

"There have been patrols before and after the squall. Rut and Dermot are also missing. Lennox and Sloan went to MacQuarie Castle, but they've not seen anyone there. They're not on Iona as you know. This afternoon, Lennox is planning to head to MacKinnis land while Sloan will travel to Mingary Castle, hoping that no one has taken up in Kelvan's place," Broc explained, chewing on a hunk of cheese that he'd broken off to share with Merryn. "They were headed here until we told them we were coming."

Merryn added, "We volunteered to come here and go to the mainland. I'd like to visit Uncle Neil and Aunt Alma to make sure they are hale after all Kelvan did. I feel better knowing that Aunt Alma sent the cushions. I've worried about them so. After all, what happened to his men?"

"Many died at Ardnamurchan. You know that."

"But not all. There were some I wondered about. The one who barked orders during the attack on our village is still walking free. He was not at Mingary. I looked for him." She stared at the flames in the hearth. "I'll never forget the coldness in his eyes."

"He could have been killed at any of the other minor battles. You know that's possible, Merryn. How is Shealee?"

"She's fine, Tristan. She has no memory of all that happened. It saddens me, yet I know it's a good thing."

"It is. We'll help her remember her mother." Tristan patted her forearm. "You're taking good care of her."

"I'll feel better after I speak with Uncle Neil and Aunt Alma. While we're crossing, we'll check along the way for anyone who may have seen Rut, Dermot, Sheona, or Taskill. I cannot believe they are all missing at the same time."

The three munched on the food for a bit, all lost in their thoughts. Finally, Tristan sighed and said, "I have to ask. Everyone I speak with is all upset and on edge, just as they were when Kelvan was about. As far as we know, other than one man who Merryn remembers on the mainland, Kelvan's group is gone. Why are so many acting oddly? There must be something I'm not aware of yet."

Broc looked at Merryn and gave her a small nod. Then she added, "It's Tora. You know how she has consistently proven to be a seer."

"Aye, with amazing accuracy," Tristan agreed.

"She's been telling Dyna's father that bad men are after Sheona."

"Oh, heaven above us," Tristan whispered. "Hell's fury find them first."

"And worse. During the storm," Broc said, taking Merryn's hand, "Dyna and Avelina had horrible headaches. They are both seers. They claim Taskill and Sheona were in a boat that broke apart. Please keep an eye out for any survivors or pieces of boat onshore."

"I'll say my prayers that they landed safely. That's a tough swim, though I imagine they're both strong swimmers."

Broc nodded. "We hope to find good news in our travels."

"May God be with all of them."

"Dyna is staying at Duart while the rest of us search for the four or any news of the evil fools after Sheona. Have you heard anything at all of some questionable men? Have you noticed anything unusual across the water?" Broc asked.

"Nay, naught. But now that I know, I'll start asking more questions when the boats arrive. The one for you should be here shortly. Once we unload the goods, it goes right back. I'll ask the men what they know or what they've seen, and then you can see what you learn from Uncle Neil."

"Many thanks to you, Tristan. What goods are coming this time?" Merryn asked.

"Linens, I believe. And we've been promised smoked beef too. When you return, I hope you'll see if you can land me a pheasant or two with your bow. Have you caught any yet, sister? You've done so well with archery."

"Nay. Shealee keeps me busy. I've practiced, but I'm not skilled like Dyna and Eli yet. Mayhap I can send them this way before Yule for you."

"That would be wonderful."

The door opened, and one of his men shouted, "Ship is nearly here, Chief."

Broc said, "We need to ready our saddlebags, Merryn. You'll take care of our horses while we travel, Tristan? We should be back in a sennight."

"I'll take good care of Midnight Majesty, I promise."

"You may ride him, but no one else, if you please," Broc said with a grin. "He is verra special to me."

"My thanks to you for all you've done for Merryn and for me," Tristan said with a small bow. "I'll care for him myself."

"He loves to run down the coast. Something about the sand he likes."

The three headed outside, Tristan going straight to the ship while Broc led Merryn to the stables. All along, her gaze locked on every man she passed, looking for that one who she hated so, the one who'd helped her sister's husband murder her family. He needed to be brought to justice just as Kelvan had.

She'd seen so many at Mingary and watched them die in battle, but the one man who rode behind Kelvan when he'd driven his sword into Nara's back she'd never seen again.

She vowed to bring him to justice.

She'd find the bastard.

CHAPTER FORTY

TASKILL

TASKILL AWAKENED WELL after dawn, the sun rising. All was silent outside, to his relief, and Sheona slept soundly on the bed. He'd taken the floor and slept without moving.

They'd been through a harrowing and exhausting experience, something that made him look at things differently. He peeked at Sheona, noting how lovely she was even in her sleep, her braids in disarray, but her lips plump and pink, a shade darker than her cheeks.

He opened the door as quietly as he could, an intense need to relieve himself overtaking any other thoughts for the moment. Once he completed that task, he made a point of wandering back to the shore, keeping an eye out for a wee lass of around six summers. He recalled some of the guards arguing about Erraid once, some claiming it was an island and others saying it wasn't, but he hadn't paid them much mind at the time.

Had they both been brought here by a guiding angel, as Sheona called Lia? He'd seen her with his own eyes and seen that odd contraption that helped to keep Sheona afloat so they could make it back to shore. He even recalled Maeve saying she saw something similar when she'd been in the sea near Ulva.

What exactly was Lia?

He wandered down the coast, noting it was low tide on Erraid, an island he was unfamiliar with but couldn't be too far from Mull or Iona. He climbed a crest and when he reached the top, he nearly took off on a dead run, but he laughed instead.

There, a short distance away, stood the back of Tristan MacClane's castle. He noted the sea and the tide and figured that in high tide, he'd have to take a boat to the castle from here.

Thus, the reason Erraid was called an island when it wasn't.

He hurried back to their small cottage, because he'd have to awaken Sheona quickly so they could walk to the castle instead of being forced to swim over when the tide rose again.

But she stepped outside just as he approached. "Come," he said. "You'll not believe it until you see it yourself."

"Where did you go?"

"Down the beach. Over that crest. You have to see it yourself," he said with a grin, taking her hand in his. "I'll show you."

He broke into a slight run, wishing to hurry before it was too late. Helping her up the sandy incline of the crest, when they finally reached the top, he turned to watch her face.

And he loved seeing the delight, knowing exactly when she recognized the view in front of them. "Is that Tristan MacClane's new castle?" she squealed. "It is! I think it is! We're saved!"

"Aye, but when the tide comes up, you'll have to swim over there. We can grab our things and go. I wouldn't recommend waiting too long."

"I'll race you back!" she said, taking off down the dune, squealing as she slid in the sand to the bottom.

Taskill laughed but took off running behind her, enjoying the view. She ran like the most graceful creature in the forest, glancing back over her shoulder with that sparkle in her eye.

He'd let her win just for the joy of racing behind her. He loved watching Sheona because of the way you always knew her mood. She was the happiest bairn he'd ever met when she was small, her smile lighting up the chamber or hall she stepped into, the lilt of her laughter turning heads.

Sheona had been his favorite to swim with, to hunt with, to race against. She had a way of turning every task into something magical, her curiosity at whatever they set against always offering a different view of life. She never hunted, but she rode her horse like a royal princess and could ride as quietly as a mouse sneaking in for a crumb of bread, calming everything around her so she could hear where the pheasant or deer were.

Everyone followed Sheona's lead, even the animals.

He loved Sheona, always had, and a small part of him always knew it. He preferred her company to any others. She was always honest and true, not the kind to flatter him with falsehoods or even truths to gain his attention.

She didn't need trickery or false flattery to gain anyone's attention.

Perhaps it was time to tell her the truth, tell her the real reason he'd never marry.

"Where are you, Taskill? Are you that slow?" She stood on the stone step in front of the cottage, looking into the copse between them.

He thought of hiding, making her come back searching for him, but he couldn't do it. They'd been through enough.

Sheona had been through enough. "I'm coming. I just can't keep up with you. When did you get so fast, lass?" He burst through the trees, laughing.

But the sight in front of him caught him short. Sheona held on to her mantle as if it might disappear.

"Taskill?"

"What the hell?" was all he could get out. "What happened?"

She looked back at him, wide-eyed. "Naught. I opened the door and the entire cottage disappeared. Am I daft?"

Taskill did what he wished to do. He strode up to her and wrapped his arms around her. "You are the farthest thing from daft I've ever met. It's proof that the cottage was arranged by an angel. That guardian angel, Lia."

"And she took it back."

"Those are our bags, though I know not how Lia saved them from the sea, so we head to Tristan's land. Agreed?" His arm dropped and reached for his saddlebag. "And here are my boots! All dry."

"Are we both daft, Taskill? No one will ever believe us."

"Nay, we're not daft. And I know two people who will believe us."

"Who?"

"Avelina and Dyna. Let's go before anything else happens." He took Sheona's hand in his and they headed back toward the sand dune, one they climbed much slower this time. Probably because he had a growing fear deep in his belly.

Would Tristan's castle still be there?

Or had they imagined that too?

CHAPTER FORTY-ONE

TRISTAN

———✦———

TRISTAN MACCLANE KNEW something was going on among his men. He hadn't determined who yet, but he knew they had something planned.

He needed to find out exactly what it was and which guard was guilty.

After his sister Nala had been murdered by her husband, alongside every other villager in their small grouping outside his uncle's mainland castle, Tristan always looked over his shoulder, afraid one of Kelvan's evil men had taken over the dead man's position.

The clans on Mull had banded together to put an end to Kelvan's attack on bairns, but strange things were happening again, and he didn't like it. Merryn had left with her husband for McLean Castle, somewhere she would be safe, but she still had to get there without any delays.

Losing her in addition to Nala and his parents would be more than he could bear. Nala's daughter was at Duart Castle with the Granthams, one of the safest places of all in his mind.

But things were off again, and he had a bad feeling deep in his belly.

Merryn and Broc had gotten off without any problems in his uncle's galley ship, one that would get them there without issue.

Then why were the men not acting right? He leaned over the parapets, a good place for him to hide because he could overhear much of their conversations without them knowing it.

"What are you always looking over the sea for?" the first guard asked.

A second one said, "The fool is always dreaming of some daft way to make coin. Do you think it will rise up from the sea?" He chuckled heartily.

"We have to find her," one said, an evil lilt to his voice. One Tristan did not like but could not recognize since he was too far away.

"Why?"

"Because I can get lots of coin. One or the other. He wants the sister of Kelvan's wife or the other one at the nunnery."

"Who?"

"The man in charge. You dinnae need to know who."

"What if we get both?"

"If you find both, I'll double your part."

"I'll help, but only if I can sample the flesh myself first."

"Nay, hands off. You do not wish to become the enemy of the chieftain of this group."

"What group?"

Tristan heard at least three different voices. Were they all guilty participants or some just listening?

"The Dubh group."

That sent a shiver down his spine. He'd been at Duart Castle one eve when Connor Grant had told the tale of the Channel of Dubh years ago. How they'd funneled bairns from all corners of the land over to the east. No care as to who they stole the bairns from, but Connor had reported that they'd killed or arrested everyone involved.

Perhaps they hadn't caught everyone. He'd pass on what he knew to the Granthams on the next visit.

Until then, he'd find out who was involved here.

"I'm not joining any Dubh group."

Good for one guard, Tristan thought.

"We have it good here. I'll not do anything to jeopardize it," a second man said.

"Fine. I'll do it all myself."

"Who the hell is that?" the third man, the evil one, asked. "I like the looks of her." Tristan wondered who he referred to because he didn't see anyone. He moved around the parapets so he could see in a different direction.

"Where are they coming from?" the second one asked.

First one said, "They're coming from Erraid. Low tide."

Tristan stepped away, moving to the edge of the wall where he could peer toward Erraid. He leaned forward, pleased to see who he thought was Taskill. He wasn't sure of the lass but guessed it could be Sheona. Both looked hale and were happy, but he had to get out to them before either of the guards reached them. "Taskill!" he shouted as he ran down the staircase and headed toward the pair.

Before he caught up with them, he turned back to look at the three guards who stood behind him: Percival, Roger, and Fitz. Which one was planning to go after Sheona?

He'd not allow it to happen.

"Taskill, is that Sheona with you?"

"Aye, we've had a rough time of it, but we are here and hale."

"You must be hungry. Come inside for a brief repast. Tell me all that transpired."

He took in the two and their clothing, which appeared dry and in good shape, though Taskill was not wearing his clan's colors, instead a tunic and trews. Tristan had many questions, but they could wait until they were inside.

Once he stepped into the keep, the three guards followed and Percival asked, "May we join you, Chief?"

"Nay, you may not." He was not willing to let the traitor he'd discovered be a party to whatever was going on with Taskill and Sheona. "Percival, I'll update you all later. Go fishing, then go search for apples knocked down by the storm. Find another basket before they rot. Then you can hunt or fish. We need a stew for the morrow, and there's no more meat."

"We'll gladly go fishing," Roger said, and the three departed.

Tristan stoked the fire and pointed to the sideboard. "Grab a bowl. There's enough left for three."

Taskill said, "Are we eating everything you have? We had food last eve, but not yet today."

"Nay, we have plenty. Help yourself. I have cheese and apples yet." When he finished banking the fire, he moved into the kitchen and came out with a platter of cheese and fruit.

Sheona moved over to the hearth, shivering as the warmth hit her. "It is cool, but better than the water."

"What happened? Everyone is looking for you both."

Sheona glanced at Taskill, who explained, "We headed back from the nunnery just before the storm hit. We were in the middle of the sea when the worst came upon us. The squall came up so quickly and we had no idea. The sheeting rain, the wind, the rolling water was too much. The boat eventually broke apart from a rough wave. I'm sorry, but we have no boat to return to you, Tristan."

"No worries. I'm just glad to see you survived. The boat was one I found here when I arrived. We have many more and can build more too. But how did you make it through? That storm was rough."

Sheona took a goblet of wine and sipped it, taking a seat close to the fire. "I thought we were going to die. It was only because of Taskill that we survived. I swam for a while, but I lost all my strength. That odd thing in the water kept me afloat while Taskill tugged on my tunic and swam."

"Odd thing?" Tristan asked.

Sheona glanced at Taskill, making Tristan wonder exactly what had happened. Both were quiet, then Taskill sat forward, setting his bowl on a table and clasping his hands together. "Look, Tristan. I doubt everyone will believe us, but some odd object helped us stay afloat, and when we finally made it to shore, that lass, Lia, was waiting for us. Told us she knew where we could ride out the storm."

"Lia? The one known as the angel?"

Sheona nodded furiously and then stopped, her hand covering her mouth. "Taskill, I just thought of something. It didn't dawn on me before because I was so grateful to be onshore I didn't notice, but …" She glanced over her shoulder as if someone were there.

"But what?" Taskill asked. "Just say it, Sheona. There were many odd things about our experience."

She glanced over at Tristan, so he nodded, hoping she would speak her mind.

"Lia … She wasn't wet. Did you notice? She stood in the rain, yet she was completely dry. Or was I seeing things?"

Taskill closed his eyes, then rubbed them lightly with both palms. He let out a huge breath and said, "You're right. I didn't notice either. She led us to that cottage on Erraid, and she was dry as could be while we were soaked through."

Tristan thought he heard wrong. "Cottage on Erraid? There are no cottages on Erraid."

Taskill said, "We know that now. It disappeared in front of our eyes. Never mind. I don't wish to talk about this anymore. Tell me about my mother. Has she been found? Or Dermot?"

"I have not heard anything, but I saw them run across the beach and get on my uncle's boat that was heading back to the mainland. I'm quite certain it was them. They looked hale."

"My sire was with Rut? And they went together?"

"Aye. Merryn and Broc just headed that way. They're going to Clan MacLean on the mainland to visit our aunt and uncle."

Taskill glanced at Sheona, then subtly nodded to her. "Shall we?"

Sheona nodded. "We must follow them. When's the next ship arriving, Tristan?"

"Probably within the hour. My uncle was sending four boats within a short time because he had so much furniture custom-made for the keep now that it is completed. He wishes to beat the winter."

Taskill asked, "May we jump aboard on the return trip of the next boat?"

"Of course," Tristan replied. "But I need to make you both aware of something."

"What?" Taskill asked, Sheona also giving Tristan her full attention.

"Be careful. Merryn suspects one of the men involved with Kelvan may still be out there, and I've heard some suspicious conversations between my guards. I hate to admit it because some have been with my uncle for a long time, but one is not to be trusted."

Sheona stared at her hands, looking guilty.

"What is it, Sheona? This should have naught to do with you."

"But it might. Two men were seen on a boat at Iona, looking for a lass much like me. They were sent away, but they are still out there somewhere. They planned to return to the nunnery after the storm."

Tristan looked at Taskill and said, "What the hell is wrong with all these men?"

Taskill explained, "One was named Clyde, from Clan Rankin. Have you seen him?"

"Nay, but I would not know him if I did. I've not heard the name, but I've overheard my guards discussing some business that doesn't sound right, though they keep it from me."

Taskill said, "If you hear more, please let us know. And please send a messenger to Clan MacVey about my mother and Dermot. Lennox and Sloan are both waiting to hear any news."

"I will." Tristan stood. "I'll be back in a bit." He had to check on his men again, then look for the arrival of the boat so he could hold it for Taskill and Sheona.

And he'd be watching to make sure none of his guards went along.

CHAPTER FORTY-TWO

RUT

RUT SAT IN the back of the boat enjoying the scenery. After all, it had been a long time since she'd been on the mainland, especially in this direction. She'd been to Lochaline not long ago, but not toward Oban, though she had to admit she wasn't exactly sure where they were headed. She really didn't care.

Dermot Rankin had surely lost his mind. Of that she was certain. She glanced over at him, standing tall in the wind, the harsh planes of his face holding strong. If she stood, the wind would blow her over, but not Dermot. He had an inner strength most men lacked, though both his son and her son carried similar constitutions.

He wouldn't back down to whatever he had planned, but she intended to give him as much grief as possible. How dare he try to tell her what to do!

Reviewing their situation, she thought about the good parts. She did trust Dermot, and she'd enjoyed their time together during the storm. The empty cottage of Tristan's had suited them perfectly. They were headed on a boat to Clan MacLean, or so the ship's captain said, and MacLean was a former ally of her dear husband. No one there would pay them much mind, far better than being on Mull where everyone knew everyone's business.

She'd tried to find out what Dermot had scheduled for the two of them once they landed, but he wouldn't talk. It could be he just wished to go on a small journey.

Or it could be that he'd lost his mind completely. Perhaps he was going daft and planned to go to London. She hated London. All those people with their noses up in the air like they were better than the Scots.

But her mind took her further. What if he was truly losing it and was thinking of going to Europe? While she'd loved to go, she surely wasn't interested in traveling in a galley ship without any of her belongings. She had only one other gown with her, one night rail, and a few things to take care of her basic feminine needs.

He wouldn't do such a thing, would he?

He glanced over at her and winked.

Rut stuck her tongue out at him.

Dermot's head fell back in a guttural laugh that nearly sent her into hysterics, but she had an image to uphold, so she glared at him, narrowing her gaze in the haughtiest look she could summon.

"We'll see, my lady. We shall see!" He chuckled again, this one a husky sound that conjured up images of bodies with limbs intertwined in nearly impossible ways.

Rut wished to throw a stick at him, hit him in the head with a giant boulder, kick him in the shins, slap him until he begged for forgiveness. But then again, she thought about kissing him in some unfamiliar places.

But for now, she was on an adventure. She had no idea what was about to happen.

And she felt more alive than she'd felt in a long, long time.

CHAPTER FORTY-THREE

SHEONA

SHEONA RODE IN front of Taskill on
a powerful chestnut stallion, glad to see
MacLean Castle up ahead, sitting majestically on
the approaching hill. The torches lit the castle
since the dark of night was nearly upon them.

Taskill had suggested they travel as husband
and wife to keep men from considering bride-
stealing. That had been difficult for her to accept,
but ever since they'd traveled down the paths
toward the castle, she'd been glad he'd called her
his wife.

She'd had the feeling that someone was
watching her ever since they left the ship. Sholto
was the only man who'd come from Tristan's
land, and they didn't know any of the others, but
she'd had this strange inkling all along.

It hadn't been bad on the ship since the men
had jobs to do, but since then, she'd been uneasy.
Even with Taskill, men had stared at her along
the way.

At one point, Taskill had said, "Sheona, you've
not been away from home much, have you?"

"Nay. Not since I was young."

"They stare because you are beautiful, but I think it surprises you. Does it?"

She nodded, but waved her hand, not wishing to continue the discussion. "I don't like it."

"I don't either, but it's best that you stay close. I won't let anyone touch you."

"My thanks to you. My apologies if I've caused any problems, but I wish to see that my sire is hale. Why do you think he and Rut travel together?" She'd had thoughts but dismissed each one as ridiculous.

Taskill gave a small shrug. "I'll tell you what Meg suggested, though Lennox and I dismissed it. That Dermot and Rut had some intimate moments when they were arguing. She claims they are attracted to each other. She suggested there was some tension between them that wasn't true anger, if you understand my meaning. I didn't like it, and Lennox laughed at Meg, but now I wonder. What say you?"

"Romantically? That kind of interest?" She couldn't have been more stunned.

"Aye."

"Nay." She shook her head without thinking.

"Aye, I think Meg might be right."

"Da still thinks of Mama all the time. He's always mentioning her."

"Because he misses her. Misses the companionship. As Meg reminded Lennox, just because they are old doesn't mean they don't have needs."

Sheona recoiled at the thought. Her father and

Rut? Not that they didn't suit—they did. But thinking of them committing the act was … well … something she didn't wish to think on.

They arrived at the castle just after dark. Sheona was exhausted but pleased to be there finally. She had only the clothing on her back, which embarrassed her, but they'd been shipwrecked, so what options did she have?

Neil MacLean greeted them, and Taskill gave him a letter penned by Tristan. Once they were seated in front of the hearth with a goblet of mead, the hall mostly empty, Neil read the note and said, "I'm sorry to hear of your troubles. I will find Alma, and she'll settle you each in a chamber. On the morrow, I will help you with whatever you need. And you may find some clothing in the chest in your chambers. You're welcome to use whatever fits your needs. I understand you've been traveling as a married couple, which I think was a wise choice, but I will give you your own chambers." He nodded and took his leave.

Sheona's gaze scanned the beautiful great hall, now empty except for the two of them. "I'm tired. I'll look for Da on the morrow, Taskill. I'm too exhausted to look for them now."

"Agreed. They are adults. We'll search later."

Alma came in shortly thereafter, introduced herself, then led them to two chambers above stairs that were across the hall from one another.

Sheona was more than grateful for the warm welcome. "Many thanks to you, my lady. These accommodations are lovely."

"I'll send a tub up on the morrow for you.

There's a basin with linens to refresh yourself this eve. You'll find a night rail in the chest. I hear you've been through much, so fear not. Have a restful night. Is there anything else I can do to assist you?"

Sheona shook her head. "Nay, this is lovely, and I'm exhausted."

"I have a goblet of broth next to the fire along with some bread for you. If you need anything else, just go to the kitchens. Someone is always there. Until the morrow." And Alma left.

Sheona fell into the chair, taking swigs of the warm broth, enjoying the way it heated her insides. She got up to wash her hands and face but froze in the middle of her ablutions. She heard laughter coming from down the passageway.

Doing her best to ignore it, she found a night rail and changed into it, but the laughter continued, and it began to sound familiar.

What. The. Hell?

It sounded exactly like her father and Rut.

She opened the door and peered down the passageway, seeing no one, but then Taskill's door opened.

"You heard it too?" Taskill whispered.

She nodded and pointed down the corridor. She tiptoed out, still in woolen socks, and headed toward the laughter, frowning as the sounds continued.

When Sheona and Taskill stood outside the door, they both paused to listen, and when she heard her father's sultry voice, she couldn't stop herself. She burst into the chamber and shouted, "Da?"

There stood her sire, his arm leaning against the hearth mantel, clad in just his dress plaid. Seated nearby was Rut MacVey, rose-colored cheeks and a cup of wine in her hand.

"Mama?" Taskill yelled. "What the hell is going on?"

Both stupefied and shocked, they looked at the two elders who didn't look the least bit out of sorts or guilty, both wearing smiles that Sheona hadn't seen in years.

His mother said, "Don't get upset, dear. We made Neil and Alma promise not to tell anyone we were here after Broc and Merryn arrived. We had no idea you would be here."

Taskill bellowed, "What the hell did you drag my mother here for, Rankin?"

Sheona said, "Taskill, you cannot yell at him. He's my sire. It's my job to yell at him. Da, what the hell is going on? Do you know how many people are searching for the two of you? Do you know we could have lost our lives looking for you?" Her hands settled on her hips.

The only reaction they received was more laughter.

Dermot came over, rubbed her cheek with the back of his hand, and said, "We'll talk in the morn, lass. You look exhausted."

"Nay, you'll disappear again."

Everyone quieted around her, and she did her best to hold her tears inside, successful for now but probably not for long. "You left me, Da." Her voice came out in such a whisper that the facade her sire usually wore crumbled.

Rut said, "Dermot, we're leaving soon. You need to talk with her."

"Nay, I'll escort her to her chamber, Rut. You stay here with Taskill. I'll have a conversation with your son on the morrow. That much I promise."

Rut climbed out of her chair and her arms waved over her head at him. "Oh, stop with that intimidating act, Dermot. Enough is enough. Can you not see that both of our bairns are exhausted and discouraged? Go speak with your daughter."

Her father set his hand on Sheona's back and ushered her toward the door. "Which chamber is yours?"

Unable to speak, she pointed two doors down the passageway.

Once inside, she took a seat next to the hearth, sipping on her barely warm broth. Her father grabbed a blanket from a basket nearby and settled it on her lap. "Now, tell me how you ended up here instead of at the abbey."

"Nay, you first. Why are you here with Rut?"

Her father sighed and sat down. "It's a simple answer, lass. I'm lonely. I miss your mother, but she's no longer here. I was looking for some female companionship and there was Rut. I've known her forever, and she's been alone over two years. Why not the two of us?"

"You should have told someone where you were going. Lennox, Sloan, Eva, everyone is looking for you."

"You're right. I'll have MacLean send a message to Mull on the morrow. Now, I need to hear about you. You look a mess, lass. What happened?"

"You mean besides being left alone at the abbey, and having two men come to the holy place searching for me who were stopped by a friend because she hit them with a dagger and sent them away, and then running into Taskill who said you were missing so we left, and then we got stuck in a storm and our boat was crushed to pieces, and we had to swim to shore and we ended up on Erraid where there are no cottages, but Lia led us to one where we spent the night?"

Her sire bolted out of his chair. "You spent the night with Taskill? I'll kill him!"

She jumped up. "Da! The hell you will. After all we've been through, I'd be dead if not for Taskill. He got me to shore. I couldn't swim anymore and he barely made it. And after everything else I told you, that was the only thing that concerned you? Not the fact that we nearly died or two men tried to kidnap me? All you're worried about is Taskill? And something else … Stop yelling at me, Da. I've had enough of your bellowing. I'm old enough to make my own decisions now, and I'm confused. I needed you, and you left me." And that did it. The tears came out in full.

"Ah, lassie. I'm sorry." He lifted her and set her on his lap. "Stop your tears now. I don't know what to say to you. I need Ailis here. I'm sorry she's gone."

"I miss Mama," she wailed, a bit too loudly, but then she slowed her tears. There, it was said. Then she whispered, "I miss Mama, Da. If she were still here, she'd tell me what to do."

"I miss her too. I'll help you if I can. In fact, I'm not hiding any longer. The abbess said she thought someone might have abused you. I need to know if there's any truth to that statement, Sheona. Did anyone abuse you or force themselves on you?"

"Rinaldo. He did." She sighed, wiped her tears with a linen square, and then told him about Rinaldo. She'd held it in long enough, and now he needed to know.

"Did he rape you?"

"Nay. He said he would. That it was his job to do so as my brother, to take my maidenhead, but you killed him first." She waited, wondering how her father would feel about her admission. Would he be upset with her? Mad at her for telling him the truth? "I'm sorry, Da."

Her father kissed her forehead and said, "Do not apologize. I'm sorry I didn't protect you from the evil soul. I should have, but I never would have guessed that I needed to protect you from your own brother. I wish he were alive right now to stand in front of me ..."

She stared at him wide-eyed, that thought so terrifying that she wished not to think on it.

"Nay, lassie. I wish I had the good fortune of being able to stab his dark soul again. He's a liar among other things. I'm sorry."

They sat together near the hearth, her tears now spent. Her father finally said, "I love you, Sheona. Always remember that. And I miss your mother too. I'm sorry she wasn't here to help you with such a thing."

"I love you too, Da. And I think I love Taskill, but I'm not sure. I'm still confused."

"You take whatever time you need. I'll not push you anymore." He lifted her and set her on the bed, pulling the coverlet back and tucking her in. "You need rest. We'll talk on the morrow."

He moved over to the door, but she had to catch him. "Da?"

He stopped, looking older but still as strong as ever. "Aye, Sheona?"

"You aren't leaving, are you?"

"Nay. I promise I'll be here in the morn. One more question, daughter. Who were the two men looking for you at the abbey?"

The look in her sire's eyes was one she was more familiar with—one that sent men running years ago. "Clyde. That was the only name my friend heard."

He took that information and left, the click of his boots ringing out down the passageway.

She closed her eyes and thought of Taskill. They definitely needed to talk on the morrow.

CHAPTER FORTY-FOUR

SHEONA AND MERRYN

MERRYN CAME INTO the great hall in the morning, pleased to see Sheona Rankin seated by the fire, chatting with Rut and Dermot.

She approached right away. "I see you've found your sire, Sheona. How did you get here? We were not expecting you. Broc and I arrived two days ago. Everyone was looking for you and Taskill along with this lovely couple. We just learned they were here this morning. Apparently they wished to keep their arrival a secret! I'm glad you are here. And is Taskill here too?"

"He is. We were caught in the storm when we were returning from Iona Abbey. The waves split the boat in two. We ended up on Erraid, which was near your brother's place, fortunately. When Tristan said he'd seen my father and Rut get on a boat, we had to follow."

"Broc will be down shortly. Where is Taskill?"

"Aye, he should be down soon."

Rut stood and said, "Dermot, I'd like to go for

a stroll on the courtyard and the parapets. Would
you escort me, please?"

Sheona caught the look that passed between
the two, and she had to force herself not to stare
at her own father. He acted like a lad in love.

"You know I would love to escort you
anywhere, dearest Rut." With a smile, he found
a fur to wrap over her shoulders and led her
outside with a smile.

"Were you surprised?" Merryn asked.

"Completely!" Sheona didn't know what else
to say. She'd met Merryn but didn't know her
well. "You are enjoying your trip?"

"Anywhere I go with Broc makes me happy."
The staff were busy cleaning up the trestle tables
and ignoring them. Merryn leaned toward
Sheona and asked, "I need to ask you a question
that's a wee bit different. Do you mind?"

"Go ahead," she replied, wondering what she
could possibly be considering.

"If you haven't heard, I saw the evil Kelvan kill
my sister with my own eyes, and I heard him kill
my parents. He was with a small group of men,
many who I saw at the battle at Drimnin, and thus
saw them meet their death in battle. But there is
one man who I recall well, and he was not there.
I'm here to see if he is one of my uncle's guards.
I still have fears."

Sheona's mind filled with images of watching
someone kill Marta or her mother and father,
of how she would feel after witnessing such an
atrocity. How could she continue to function?
"How did you ..." Unable to put her thoughts

into words, she fumbled for the right way to ask such a thing.

"I continued because Shealee needed me, and Nala had put her into my arms just before her husband killed her. She begged me to save her daughter, so that's what I did. There is no other explanation. I had to protect that beautiful wee bairn, and she remembers nothing."

"Of course. Forgive me for my rudeness." She wished to hug the lass, not just sit in a chair and stare at her.

"You are not rude. I'm wondering if you've seen any men behaving oddly. Not doing what they should? Someone different who doesn't belong? He has to have gone somewhere, and I have not seen him here yet. I thought of all the guards on Mull. Could he have gone to one of your castles?"

Sheona thought for a moment, considering the men on Iona. "I don't know them well enough, but I can tell you that two men were searching for me at Iona Abbey. One of them was Clyde, an unsavory character who is a guard of my brother's, though once I tell Sloan what I've learned, he'll be gone. And your brother said that everything is not as it seems. I'm not sure what he means by that, but possibly there are some evil guards on his land? He overheard a few talking, and it wasn't something he approved of. I'm not sure. Ask Taskill when he arrives."

Merryn whispered, "The unsavory character was looking for you specifically? Does that not unsettle you?"

"It does. I wish I could protect myself. I was learning how to use both a spear and a dagger at the abbey. A lass whose mother was Norse taught me the techniques for a spear, but the enormous weapon isn't something you can carry around with you. I had a dagger that I practiced with a wee bit, but I lost it in the sea. I had it in a sack tied to my waist, but it was gone when we landed." Along with her dear mother's necklace, though she didn't mention it to Merryn.

"Come with me. I'll teach you how to use a bow, if you're interested."

"Truly?"

"Aye. It will give you a feeling of power that nothing else can. It truly will ease your worry not to be solely dependent on a man. My aunt Alma had an archery field set up just for me after everything happened. I love it." Merryn got up and took Sheona by the hand, leading her out the door through the kitchens.

And Merryn was right. Sheona fired off three arrows before she found her rhythm and fell in love with archery. It was difficult and she wasn't verra good at it, but she would persist until she could use it well enough to scare someone away. A dagger worked, but she'd have to be close to her attacker to use it. This gave her a better weapon. They practiced for quite a while before Merryn froze.

"What's wrong?" Sheona asked, looking over her shoulder.

"Hush for a moment, please." Merryn crept around the back of the curtain wall, following the sound of men on horseback outside the castle. They were a distance away, but the lasses could overhear the men yelling because they were galloping so fast.

All of a sudden, Merryn took off toward the staircase at the rear of the fortress, running up so she could follow the curtain wall around. "It's him. I've heard that voice before."

Broc came flying out of the keep, chasing after her. "Merryn, what is it? What's wrong?"

"Hush, Broc," she called back. "It's him."

The horses followed a path toward the front of the castle but then headed in the direction of the village.

Merryn was overcome with emotion, more than she could handle. Sheona's insides twisted with the pain Merryn carried inside her. What a horrible situation. Taskill came behind Broc and caught up with Sheona as she followed Merryn.

Merryn screamed, "You bastard! Come back here and I'll fight you!" She leaned over the wall too far, nearly losing her balance.

Broc bellowed, "Merryn! Be careful."

One man looked at her and cackled, an evil laugh unlike she'd ever heard before. Then she scowled. The man looked familiar. Sheona's knees buckled and Taskill caught her.

Dermot appeared behind Taskill. "Who was that?"

Merryn still hollered as loud as she could. "Come back here! Are you afraid of a lass?"

But the other men on horseback ignored her,

instead the group of seven horses continuing on their journey. Who were they all?

"Sheona!" her father bellowed. "Who was it?"

She turned around to her father and said, "One man was Clyde. I think it was Clyde. The other was one of Tristan's guards. His name is Percival or Roger, I think."

Dermot turned around and hurried down the staircase.

"Da! Where are you going?"

"I'm going after that bastard Clyde. I'll string him up by his bollocks, then cut them up and stuff them in his mouth. Make him chew on his own in front of me. Then I'll kill him slowly. How dare he try to touch my daughter."

Rut whispered, "Oh, Dermot ..." She fanned herself with a linen square.

CHAPTER FORTY-FIVE

TASKILL

WHILE THE GROUP waited for Dermot to return, Taskill paced in the great hall. Here he was, a failure again. Why did he hate confrontation so much? He was Lennox's second-in-command, at the ready with his sword at all times, yet confronting Clyde turned his belly inside out and upside down.

Lennox had always told him not to worry about it, that he'd been the same when he was younger. "When the situation matters to you, you will not back down. It's youth, that's all, Taskill. When it's about someone you love, you'll step up."

But would he? Here he was, trying to decide whether to ask Sheona to marry him, and Clyde was just outside the castle, and he should have gone after the fool, but he hadn't moved, instead her sire was chasing after the piece of slime.

Taskill was the fool. How was he ever to right this situation?

Should he marry Sheona or not?

Indecision had tormented his every waking moment ever since they'd walked out of the cottage on Erraid. The one that disappeared in front of their eyes. Or had they just been exhausted?

Nay, he could recall the fragrant smell of apples baking in a pot when they entered. It had been real. Just as real as their boat exploding and that odd thing that helped to keep Sheona afloat.

Rut came to the balcony and yelled to him, "Taskill, meet me in the solar."

Taskill didn't know what to make of the situation, but he did what his mother asked, going up the stairs to the MacLean solar, holding the door for her.

Once they were alone, he waited for his mother to take a seat, which she did behind the desk, so he took a seat opposite her. "Mama? Is something wrong?"

"I wish to know what you think about my relationship with Dermot." She crossed her arms and leaned back in her chair, waiting.

Waiting.

Hell, but he hated being put in these situations.

"It's fine. Whatever makes you happy is fine with me. I wish you much happiness, Mama." Satisfied that his reply would surely garner no rebukes from the woman, he leaned back and sighed with relief. One argument avoided. He certainly was not about to answer honestly.

Though he wasn't even sure what his honest answer would be. He had too many other things on his mind. There was Sheona and Lia and Sheona and Clyde and Sheona and so many other things to consider. Sheona had almost died in front of him, and it would have been his fault for taking her across the water in a storm, and if that had happened, who knows what he would have done because he'd loved Sheona all his life and he'd …

His mother jumped out of her chair and grabbed him by the collar, yanking him to his feet. "What the hell is wrong with you? Something is going on in that head of yours, and it's not that everything is fine because it's not. You don't like me being with Dermot, but I don't even care about that. What is bothering you?"

Wide-eyed, he pulled back and stared at her. "I don't know what you speak of, Mama."

"Enough, Taskill. You are my son, blood of my blood, and it's time to stop lying. What is going on in that mind of yours? Something has you all tied up in knots, and I want to know what it is." She shoved him back in the chair and straightened her gown, smoothing the wrinkles with her hands. "Now out with it."

"Mama, I really don't know what you mean. Why do you think something is wrong with me?" Then he had a sudden thought. "Wait, I understand now." He paused and smiled, nodding because it all made sense. Why had he been so blind?

"I think I understand. It was the boat exploding and the lightning and Sheona going into the water. Then I couldn't see her, but then she came up for air and we swam for quite a while in the storm, the lightning over our heads, but we made it. And Lia sent that odd object to help Sheona float, so we made it, though I was exhausted and …" His mother came toward him again, so he stopped speaking and stared up at her.

"Not that. I know it was upsetting, but this has been bothering you for a longer time, and I know you won't speak of it around Lennox because you think he doesn't know. Speak!"

"Mama, with all due respect …"

And she slapped him across the back of his head with such vigor that he jumped out of his chair. "Ow …"

"Are you awake now?"

"I've been awake …" He rubbed his head and stared at her.

"Listen to me. Ever since your sire passed, there's been something bothering you, and I wish to know what it is. Why would you be happy to see me with Dermot? You don't like the man. He tried to force you to marry his daughter, so that's a lie, and a big one. What is it about your sire? Something is there, and it's tied to you and the idea of staying single. I have no idea what is nagging you, but we will remain in this chamber until you tell me the truth. No more lies, no more smiles of false happiness. It's eating your insides, Taskill, and I'll find out what it is if I have to get Lennox to hold you down and beat it out of you."

He gaped at his mother, taking two steps back and away from her arching arm.

She knew.

How the hell could she know? He couldn't tell her. It would break her heart. This was something he vowed never to tell anyone, and one little slap in the back of his head would not change that.

"I'll hit you again. You've got until I count to fifty to tell me. One, two, three, four …"

"All right. I'll tell you." What the hell. The man was dead, so what did it matter? He stared at his mother, tears brimming his lashes as he tugged on his sheath, wishing to hold his sword in his hand to feel better. He spun around and faced the back, pacing, then turned to face her. "I'll tell you everything." Perhaps it was time to stop keeping secrets, but he didn't wish to tarnish his father's image. Yet since he was dead, why not tell his mother the truth?

She came toward him, her arm outstretched again, so he blurted it out.

"Da was a cheating man. He took a lover."

There. It was revealed. The secret he'd kept for nearly four years was finally known. He'd never told his mother or Lennox or Eva or Jasper or anyone.

"That's it? That's what's bothering you? Is that what keeps you from a betrothal?"

"Aye. Of course. I don't wish to marry someone if it's in my blood to be a liar and a cheat."

She walked forward and nearly slapped him but stopped and grabbed his collar. "Never say that again about your sire."

"But he was. A liar and a cheat. He was married to you and carrying on with another woman. I saw him, Mama. I heard him speaking with her, making their … arrangements." He strung out the last word as long as he could.

"Sit down, Taskill."

"Not unless you promise not to hit me again."

A very unladylike snort came from his mother, something he hadn't heard before. "I promise." She moved back to the seat behind the desk. After she sat down, she folded her hands on the surface in front of her. "Taskill ..."

"There's nothing you can say to excuse it, Mama. And why is this not bothering you more than you are saying? I thought you'd be in tears by now, learning the truth of your husband. Why aren't you upset?"

"Because I knew, Taskill. It's not a surprise to me. I don't know if you've ever noticed, but your mother is no fool." She drilled the fingers of one hand on the desk in a perfect rhythm.

"You did? I've kept this for so long and you knew? Why? Why didn't you hate him for it? I don't understand you at all."

"Because it was an arrangement we had. We were a married couple and our relationship had nothing to do with our job as parents. We both supported all of you, but we had different ... needs. And we both did it willingly."

"Wait. What? You did what willingly?"

"We did it as quietly as we could, made sure to use discretion, but if he was with a woman, then I was with her husband. It's what we did as a couple, Taskill. We both agreed and enj—"

He covered his ears. "Nay, nay, nay. That's enough. I don't wish to hear anymore."

And he ran out the door.

CHAPTER FORTY-SIX

SHEONA

~❧~

SHEONA ENTERED THE great hall as Taskill came barreling down the staircase with an expression on his face that she couldn't fathom. "Taskill, are you hale?"

"Nay. Please. I just need some time alone. I'll be back in an hour, Sheona. I must have private time." He looked upset, so she let him go without further questioning.

He hurried out the door. As soon as he left, Rut came out of the solar and down the stairs. "Where is Taskill?"

"He left."

"Where is he going?" Rut's rich blue skirts swirled around her ankles as she descended.

"He said he needed private time." Sheona had known Lady MacVey all her life, but she'd often been a wee bit afraid of her. Sheona had always thought her tall, but when she came down and approached her, she realized they were about the same height.

Her father came in the door and said, "Rut,

what the hell did you do to your son? He looks a mess."

"Where did he go?"

"Toward the stables is all I can tell you. Do you want me to get him?"

"Nay, let him be. He needs some time alone. Did you find that bastard, Dermot? These poor lasses are always worrying about one evil soul or another."

"Nay, he got away. But there were seven of them. Merryn thinks one is the man who took part in killing the MacLean village, and Clyde is one of his men. That's seven men either looking for lasses to abuse or people to rob or something else unsavory. We have to put an end to this. I'm going to speak with Neil, see what he knows of it."

"Fine. I'm going up for a brief rest. I'll be down for a wine later."

Dermot squeezed Rut's shoulder, then kissed her cheek before she left the hall. Then he gave his full attention to his daughter. "You are hale, Sheona?"

"I'm fine, Da. I'm going out to practice archery with Merryn."

"You're learning archery?"

"Aye. Do you mind?"

"Nay, I'm proud of you, lass. Go work with Merryn. I'll see you at the evening meal. I have things to do."

Her father left, so she headed out to the archery field in the back. She didn't know what was next.

She and Taskill had found their parents, so would they go back home? Go their separate ways? Was her father going to force her to marry? Last eve, he did tell her to take her time, so she hoped he meant it.

She greeted Merryn out on the field, picking up a bow and practicing stretching before firing her first arrow.

"Did they find him?" Merryn asked.

"Nay. My sire said they couldn't catch them. Is Broc still out there looking?"

"Nay, he's at the gates talking with the guards, trying to determine who all the men were."

They practiced for a while before Sheona stopped and turned to her new friend. "I thank you so much for volunteering to teach me. I love this more than anything I've ever done."

Merryn said, "I feel the same. I wish they'd allow us to compete in the archery tournaments, but they don't let lasses in these contests."

"Won't your uncle see it changed for you?"

"I've asked Aunt Alma to talk with him, but it doesn't matter much because I'll be on the Isle of Mull with Broc."

"Is that where you think you'll stay?" Sheona wasn't sure if she'd prefer to live on Mull or not. Iona was beautiful, but she also admired MacLean land too. Though there wasn't much of a chance to swim here, and she loved the water. Sitting on a nearby log, she took a sip from the water skin, watching Merryn for a bit. Her stance was powerful, and that alone made her proud. Proud to know a lass who could be strong like a man.

She hated that men's concerns were always considered more important than a woman's.

"I think so. I love Mull, I love Broc, I love Shealee and Tristan. My brother says he'll stay on Mull because he likes fishing and boating. So, we'll stay too, I think."

One of her brother's guards hurried over to them and said, "My lady, your brother is looking for you out the back entrance. He just got here and he's a mess, so he wished to come in where he wouldn't be seen by everyone. And your sire is there with him, Sheona."

Recognizing him as one of Tristan's loyal guards, Merryn set her bow down and moved over to the rear entrance. Sheona dropped her bow but grabbed a dagger and shoved it into the fold Gwyneth had sewn into the leggings she wore.

Merryn said, "My thanks, Roger. I can't wait to see my brother again. Uncle Neil will be so happy to see him."

Merryn reached the door, and Roger held it open for her while the two lasses stepped through the narrow opening. Sheona didn't see Tristan or her sire but rather three horses without mounts.

Roger shoved her forward, and a man grabbed her from behind, stuffing a dirty cloth in her mouth. "You've been naught but trouble, bitch."

Clyde shoved her toward another man and the two tied her hands behind her back, another man helping Roger to do the same with Merryn. Sheona and Merryn tried to scream, but it was impossible with the rags in their mouths.

Sheona kicked and fought her captors, but they were stronger. They tossed her up on a horse and she tried to jump off the other side, but something hit the back of her head.

Darkness claimed her before she could fight any more.

There was just a whisper on her lips. "Taskill …"

CHAPTER FORTY-SEVEN

TASKILL

———————⋙⋘———————

TASKILL HEADED OUT toward the gates to see what was going on. No one was in the hall, so he thought this would be the place to learn what was happening. He spied Broc leading a horse into the stables and strode up to him.

"Anything new on the attackers?"

Broc turned back to him. "Nay. The men who went after them lost the bastards. They were too far ahead by the time we readied the horses. Dermot went in to speak with Neil to see what he knows of the gang."

"Where's Merryn?"

"She's working with Sheona on archery. She says Sheona is a natural." Broc brushed the horse down.

"I believe it. She's always been able to accomplish whatever has been on her mind." Now only if he could do the same. He still hadn't been able to reconcile that his parents often took other lovers. What did that say about the two of them?

He tried not to think too hard about it, instead

focusing on the fact that he was not likely to be a liar and a cheat since his sire wasn't. After all, that was the issue that had eaten away at his insides for nearly four years. Something else popped into his mind.

He was free to marry. No reason not to anymore.

Roger, one of the MacLean guards entered, looking around for something. "What do you need?" Broc asked.

"I found it." He reached onto a shelf and grabbed two pieces of cloth and a length of rope. He headed out without a comment.

"May I ask a personal question, Broc?"

"Sure. I'll answer if I can." He reached for an apple and gave it to the horse when he finished his task.

"How's married life? Better or worse than you thought?"

"I didn't expect that!" he said, smoothing his hair back in place. "But it's easy to answer. I love married life. I had always been a wee bit jealous of all the others who married, especially watching Alaric with his new wife. But every day it gets better. Merryn is not the type to stick to my side all the time. That's the only complaint I ever heard from some guards after they married. Some couldn't get their wives to leave them be to hunt and fish as they wish, but Merryn has her own interests. We like it that way. She loves archery and spends time with Shealee. I like to spend time with my cousins, and I love to hunt. Though I think she'll be hunting pheasant soon enough."

"Good to know. My thanks for sharing." Taskill wasn't sure how he felt now, except for two things. First, if Dermot forced him to marry Sheona, he'd accept it without complaint. He'd come to admire her more than he ever did when he was younger. She was much stronger than he would have guessed, stronger and kinder. In fact, he was quite certain the way he felt about her might be considered love. And second, he no longer held the belief that he was destined to become a liar and a cheater like his sire.

But how did Sheona feel? He still was unsure. He'd thought himself in love with her at times, but did she reciprocate his feelings?

What did love involve? He didn't know. "Can I ask you an even more personal question?"

Broc nodded.

"How did you know she was the right one?"

"Well, I do know now that I love Merryn, though I wasn't sure about it before."

"What changed your mind?"

"The first time we were in battle and she was taken, I was angry, furious at Kelvan and his men. But the second time? When we were at Drimnin, and I thought someone was going after her? I had such a fear that I thought I might heave out my insides. I had to conquer that feeling to keep moving." He paused for a moment and said, "When the thought of living without her scared me, I knew we belonged together. Does that make sense?"

"I guess. So, for you, love is worth it?"

"Absolutely," he replied with a grin.

Taskill nodded, noticing that a man sounding like Tristan was outside the stable. "That sounds like Merryn's brother. Was he coming?"

Broc shook his head, tossing the brush into the nearby basket. "Nay. I'll go see if there's something wrong. He wouldn't come unless there was important news." He headed outside without hesitating.

Taskill followed, his gaze scanning the area but not seeing the lasses anywhere, though he knew the archery field was inside the wall behind the castle, a distance away from the stables. Tristan saw Broc and headed straight toward him. "I had to come as soon as I found out who the evil seed was."

"You know?" Broc asked. "Besides Clyde?"

"Aye, I had to put pressure on some of my guards, but I found out that Roger has an evil soul, and he's trying to make as much coin as he can in the next fortnight before he goes back to London." Tristan panted, out of breath from hurrying so. "Where's Merryn?"

"In the archery field behind the keep. Inside the wall so she's safe. Where is the evil seed?"

"That's why I'm here. Roger disappeared from Mull."

"I think he was just here," Broc said, looking around him and back at Taskill. "Wasn't he?"

"Aye," Taskill said just as the thought occurred to him. "Shite."

"What?" Tristan asked.

"He came in for cloth and rope." Taskill took

off on a dead run toward the archery field, Broc and Tristan behind him.

The door in the gate was open, the lasses' bows on the ground inside the wall. The men stepped outside and found something more frightening than anything.

Naught.

No sign of Merryn or Sheona and numerous horse hoofprints in the dirt.

Broc let out a wail that brought ten men toward him.

Taskill couldn't believe it.

One thought of Sheona being gone, and he felt like vomiting all over the ground.

He was in love.

CHAPTER FORTY-EIGHT

SHEONA

SHEONA WOKE UP in a dingy old cottage, her hands still tied behind her back, on her side on a bed. The disgusting cloth was out of her mouth, one small improvement with their predicament. She peeked around the chamber, rolling from one side to the other, happy to find a lump on the bed next to her. "Merryn," she whispered. She was certain it was her friend.

No reply. She used her shoulder to push against the person's back. "Merryn, wake up."

A muffled sound told her this person was indeed Merryn and while she could be badly hurt, she wasn't dead. Sheona could see the lass's hands were tied behind her back as well.

The lump moved and rolled over to face her. Merryn's confused face stared at her. "What happened?"

"Roger and Clyde. I saw them both with two other men. I don't know where they are, but we're in some small cottage." She pulled and tugged against the bindings on her hands, but they didn't budge.

But her feet were not bound. Thank the Lord above, she could climb off the bed.

She did, moving over to the door and leaning her ear against the worn wood. She heard voices but couldn't make out anything. Merryn sat up, staring at her wide-eyed, so Sheona moved over next to her. "Don't say anything. We don't want them back in here."

"What exactly happened?" Merryn whispered. "Tell me everything."

"Roger hit me over the head. Clyde was there too. Threw us both on horses. I'm trying to listen to what they are saying so I know what they have planned for us. I have no idea where we are."

The voices grew louder, more heated, so Sheona said, "Hush! I'll go listen."

The one she knew as Clyde said, "I'm going in to sample my wench. You do what you wish, but I've waited long enough."

"The chief will make you pay. She's merchandise now."

"She was promised to me long ago."

"That was one mean brother she had," the second one said.

The door flew open and a voice she didn't recognize said, "The ship has arrived. Bring them down now."

Clyde said, "We'll bring them in half the hour. They aren't awake yet."

"Nay, you'll get them now. I have a cart, and my orders are to see them to the sea. To keep an eye on you two. He doesn't trust you, and I can see he was right. Get them now."

"What are you going to do with them? I'd like to travel on the ship with you," Clyde declared.

"They'll be sold across the sea. That's why he has the biggest ship ever, and he's going to have three other lasses too. So, get them up and get them to the ship. It's not far. Straight west from here."

"I said in a wee bit," Clyde shouted, but then a loud smack sounded after that.

"What was that?" Merryn asked, standing next to Sheona at the door.

"A fist, I would bet. Hush." She again leaned her ear against the wood.

"Fine, I'll get them now."

The two jumped back just as the door opened. Clyde grabbed Sheona's arm, and Roger came in behind to grab Merryn. Sheona kicked Clyde in the shins but got a quick slap for it.

Merryn said, "Don't anger them."

The men put the two in the cart, the third man watching their movements. He was huge, almost as big as Broc, but not quite as tall as Connor Grant.

"Aye, don't get us pished," Clyde drawled.

"Fear not, the Grants will be coming for us."

The third man snorted. "You think the Grants care about you? They care naught about a couple of lasses. We'll be gone before they hear anything about you missing."

Merryn said, "Did you forget that I'm married to a Grant?"

The man who brought the cart grew wide-eyed but said nothing, getting back on his horse and leading it away, the two girls jostled uncomfortably against the bare wood.

Clyde said, "I'll gladly let the golden-haired one ride with me."

"You'll keep your hands to yourself, lying bastard."

"You don't know me."

"I know enough. Is she married to a Grant, Roger?" he asked.

Roger cleared his throat and said, "Aye."

"Shite. We're moving."

The cart bumped and rattled along, but they saw no one else on the way.

Merryn said, "We just have to wait until we're near the ship. There will be others there who might help us. We must be patient."

Sheona nodded, recalling that she had one dagger still in the pocket of her leggings, but she couldn't get to it until her hands were free. "I can help if I get the chance."

"We will. We'll fight, but not until we're on the water. Sound carries far on the water."

Sheona had to pray their absence had been discovered already.

But how the hell would they know where to find them? She couldn't help but whisper to herself, "Mama, help us."

CHAPTER FORTY-NINE

TASKILL

TASKILL WAS SURPRISED to see the number gathered outside the stables, planning their rescue of the two lasses. He was even more surprised when Lennox and Sloan appeared at the gate, Meg and Eva with them.

"Lennox? What the hell?"

"They said Mama was here, so we came. What's going on? I don't like this."

Broc said, "Merryn and Sheona are missing. Roger, Clyde, and a few others kidnapped them. The problem is we don't know where to look for them."

Dermot, Neil, Rut, Broc, Taskill, and ten guards stood near the gates. Lennox and Sloan dismounted, helping their wives down, waving to their respective parents along with a shake of a few heads, but they focused on the rescue operation.

Tristan flew through the gates on his horse, panting. "I know where they are."

"Where?" Dermot asked. "Where's my wee lassie? I'll kill that bastard Clyde."

"When I came across, I noticed a larger ship down the shore. I just checked with someone heading along that path, and they are preparing to leave. He said there have been others, though I did not see our lasses. From what I could hear, that ship will be sailing across the sea soon. Mount up, whoever is going. We don't have much time."

Dermot pushed five guards out of the way. "I'm going. Tristan, Broc, and I will go with Sloan and Lennox. The rest of you can wait here. And Rut—don't you dare leave this castle." He gave her a pointed look, then headed to the stables as the group broke up.

Taskill found a horse and mounted.

Dermot said, "You aren't going, MacVey. No reason for you to go."

"The hell there isn't. I'm going. Whether you like it or not, I'm in love with your daughter, so I'm going."

Dermot snorted. "You have an odd way of showing it. Stay back with the rest of the bairns."

Taskill jumped back off his horse and stood face-to-face with the old warrior while everyone else stopped to observe. "If you weren't her sire, I'd put my fist in your face. But you aren't going to stop me, old man. I'm going after Sheona."

Dermot laughed, the rumble starting from his belly. "Punch me? You don't have the guts." He turned away from him and headed to the stables.

Taskill grabbed his shoulder. The old chieftain turned back to look at him and found a fist in his face. Taskill knocked him on his arse. Then he held his hand out to help the old man up.

Rut clapped.

Dermot smiled.

Taskill said, "You'll not stop me, old man."

Once Dermot was on his feet again, rubbing his face, he muttered, "Rut, I'm starting to admire your son after all."

Taskill mounted up and headed out directly behind Tristan. "No one is stopping me."

CHAPTER FIFTY

SHEONA

SHEONA AND MERRYN were thrown onto a large ship by two men, not Roger or Clyde, and found themselves seated next to three other lasses. To Sheona's surprise, their captors removed their bindings, but then again, their only chance of escape with nearly a score of men nearby was diving over the tall side of the boat into the frigid water.

"How old are you?" Sheona asked one as soon as the men left.

"I'm ten and three."

"And I'm ten and four. Where are we going?"

"And I'm ten and five. Be quiet, Jeanie. They'll come back and hit you again."

"Where did you come from?" Merryn asked.

"They stole us away from home when Papa went to market. Mama died last year. Where are they taking us? I want to go home," Jeanie wailed.

"Shut your mouths or we'll gag you," Roger stopped to yell, but then went on his way, loading items into the lower part of the ship where the rowers sat.

Other men worked the sails, but most ignored the lasses.

"What are we going to do?" Merryn asked.

"I know," Sheona said in a low whisper. Then she said to the sisters, "Keep an eye out for horses coming or for any men watching us."

The eldest lass nodded. "I will."

"What are you planning, Sheona?"

"Didn't you notice? When they're not looking, peek at the sack at the end. I saw two bows at least. And I think I see fletchings sticking out. If we can get them, we can shoot our way out of here."

"How are we going to get them?"

"I'll do it. Give me a moment. Do you have any daggers?"

"Nay," Merryn said. "You?"

"I have one, but I'm saving it for Clyde. When he tries to touch me, he's a dead man. I need you to be able to hit someone with an arrow. Can you do it, Merryn? I doubt I'll be efficient at all. I just started."

"But you can scare them."

Jeanie whispered, "I hear horses."

Sheona said, "If it's true, then as soon as the men notice the horses, I'm running for the bows. Listen."

The five quieted and sure enough, the very distant sound of pounding hooves could be heard. How she prayed they were coming for her and Merryn. "Merryn, when they all look that way, we run. Ready?"

"I'm ready."

They waited, and within moments, one of the men shouted, "Horses coming! Ready yourselves!"

The men scurried and shoved, grabbed weapons, hid crates, and threw stuff everywhere, just enough confusion for Sheona to hurry over to the sack and lift it, pleased to see three bows and probably a dozen arrows. She tossed one to Merryn, who took a stance and aimed at the men, now off the boat and preparing for battle.

Sheona moved next to her and said, "You shoot that way and I'll aim in the opposite direction."

A man yelled, "The lasses grabbed the bows. Get them!"

Clyde yelled, "They can't shoot those. I'd worry about the dozen men coming up on us with their swords unsheathed already. Forget the lasses."

And they did.

Sheona fired, missing everyone, but enough for one man to move away from her.

Merryn shot next and hit Roger in his arm.

"Bitch!" he yelled, coming at her. But Merryn was faster. She fired again and hit him in the leg. He fell to the ground, yanking at the arrows.

Sheona took another shot and hit a different man in the leg. At this point, the horses were close enough to attack, and she nearly shed tears of relief.

"Merryn, I see Broc!" And then she saw Taskill right in front, his sword arm ready and taking out two men immediately.

"Tristan, be careful," Merryn yelled. "Broc, kill the bastards!"

Sheona laughed because she felt the same way. She wanted to tell her father to be careful, but to tell Taskill to kill the bastards too.

The clash of metal rang out, screams echoing around them as men were pierced by the Highlanders' sharp blades. The men around the boat fought for a bit, but many ran off, one crying out, "I didn't sign up to die!"

Those who stayed didn't last long before a sword ended their fight, and for a few, even their lives.

The battle finished quickly. Merryn went to free the three lasses just as a man they didn't know came along and shouted, "My lassies?"

The girls ran to their father, while Merryn ran to Broc. Sheona stood on the edge of the boat because she could see better from the higher vantage point.

Taskill shouted, "I love you, Sheona. Are you not going to come down?"

Her gaze scanned the area, not seeing the one she wished to see. She had to see him. The bastard was going to harm her. Do what her brother did to that poor girl.

Her father yelled, "Sheona, get your arse down here now."

But she couldn't. Frozen, she searched frantically for his body, finally seeing him hiding behind a boulder. "Come out of there, you piece of shite." She nocked her arrow and waited.

Clyde stood up, grinning, arms outstretched. "You think you can hit me? Go ahead and try."

So she did, catching him low enough in his

belly that it was nearly in his private area, his hands going to cover them. He cursed, so she came down from the boat, Sloan going after him. "I'll finish him, Sheona."

"Don't you dare, Sloan."

She strode toward Clyde, then kicked him in his bollocks, smiling when he screamed in pain. Then she looked at her father and brother and said, "Now he's yours."

And she ran straight into Taskill's arms.

He caught her, solid and warm and *real*, his arms closing around her so tightly she could barely breathe. But she didn't care. She wound her arms around his neck and buried her face against his shoulder, breathing in the scent of him—leather and sweat and steel and something uniquely *Taskill*.

"You're safe," he whispered against her hair, his voice rough and broken. "Thank God, you're safe."

"You came." Her voice cracked. "I knew you would. I knew—"

He pulled back just enough to frame her face with his hands, his blue eyes blazing with an intensity that stole her breath. "Did you think I wouldn't? Did you think anything in this world could have stopped me from coming for you?"

Before she could answer, his mouth on hers.

The kiss was nothing careful or restrained. This was desperate and fierce and filled with five years of longing, weeks of fear, and the overwhelming relief of finding each other whole. His lips moved against hers with a hunger that made her knees weak, and she kissed him back with equal fervor, pouring every ounce of love and terror and joy into the connection between them.

When they finally broke apart, both gasping for air, Taskill pressed his forehead to hers. "I love you," he said, his voice raw. "God help me, Sheona, I love you so much I can't breathe when you're not near me. I love you, and I'm done pretending I don't. I'm done running from it."

Tears spilled down her cheeks. "Say it again."

"I love you." He kissed her forehead. "I love you." Her temple. "I love you." The corner of her mouth. "I'll say it every day for the rest of our lives if you'll let me."

"I love you too." The words came out on a sob. "I've loved you since I was nine years old, and I never stopped. Not for a single day. Even when I hated you, I loved you. Even when it hurt, I loved you."

His thumb traced the line of her jaw, gentle despite the calluses on his hands. "I was so afraid for you."

She grabbed the front of his shirt and pulled him down for another kiss, softer this time but no less intense. "You're mine, Taskill MacVey. You've always been mine. And I'm done letting you decide what I deserve."

A sound that was half-laugh, half-groan escaped him. "Fierce lass. Mine," he agreed, and kissed her again.

This kiss was different—slower, deeper, a

promise of everything to come. His hands slid from her face down her neck, his touch reverent, as if he were memorizing the feel of her. She shivered when his fingers traced the line of her collarbone, then gripped his shoulders when his lips left hers to trail along her jaw.

"Taskill," she breathed.

"Hmm?" His hands had moved to her waist, pulling her impossibly closer.

"Everyone's watching."

That got his attention. He lifted his head, and sure enough, her father, Sloan, Broc, Tristan, and at least a dozen guards were all staring at them with expressions ranging from amusement to exasperation.

Dermot crossed his arms. "About damn time."

Sloan grinned. "I believe there was a betrothal agreement, wasn't there, Da?"

"Aye, there was. And I expect MacVey here to honor it." But Dermot was smiling—really smiling—for the first time since Mama's death.

Taskill's arms tightened around Sheona's waist. "I'll marry her right now if she'll have me."

"Now?" Sheona pulled back to look at him. "That's a bit rushed, don't you think?"

"I've waited five years for you." His eyes were soft, vulnerable in a way she'd never seen. "I'm done waiting. But if you need time—"

"I don't." She cupped his face in her hands, marveling at the freedom to touch him like this. To look at him without hiding. To love him without fear. "I don't need time. I just need you."

"Then you have me." He caught one of her

hands and pressed a kiss to her palm. "All of me. For as long as you'll keep me."

"Forever, then."

"Forever," he agreed, and pulled her close again. This time when he kissed her, it was tender and slow, a seal on the promise they'd just made. His hand cradled the back of her head, fingers threading through her loosened braid, while his other arm wrapped around her waist as if he'd never let go.

Sheona melted into him, into the warmth and strength and love of him. She'd dreamed of this moment—of being held by Taskill MacVey, of hearing him say he loved her, of kissing him without reservation or fear—but the reality was so much better than any dream.

Because it was real. He was real. This love between them—this fierce, impossible, beautiful love—was real.

When they finally parted, both breathless and smiling, Taskill rested his forehead against hers once more. "No more running."

"No more hiding."

"No more distance."

"Just us." She smiled up at him. "You and me, together."

"You and me," he echoed. Then his expression turned serious. "I meant what I said, Sheona. I want to marry you as soon as possible. I want everyone to know you're mine and I'm yours. I want—" He stopped, swallowing hard. "I want to spend the rest of my life proving that I'm worthy of you."

"You already have." She rose on her toes to kiss him softly. "You came for me. You fought for me. You loved me even when you thought you shouldn't. That's all I ever needed."

"Marry me now." It wasn't a question this time, but a plea. "Please. Let me stand before God and everyone and claim you as mine. Let me give you my name, my vows, my whole heart."

"Yes." The word came out choked with tears. "Yes, I'll marry you. On the morrow, next week, whenever you want. Just don't let go."

"Never." He kissed her forehead, her cheeks, her nose, her lips. "Never again."

Around them, their clan and family cheered, but Sheona barely heard them. All she could feel was Taskill's arms around her, his heart beating against hers, his love wrapping around her like the warmest plaid.

They'd fought so hard to get here—through misunderstanding and fear, through years of distance and weeks of danger. But they'd made it. Together.

And now, finally, they could stop fighting and just *be*.

"Take me home," she whispered against his lips.

"Home," he repeated, and kissed her once more. "Wherever you are, that's home."

CHAPTER FIFTY-ONE

TASKILL

———— ❧ ————

THE GROUP SAT around the warm hearth at Clan MacLean that night, enjoying wine and a bit of Dermot's finest brew. Lennox looked at his brother and said, "I can't believe you took Sheona straight to the kirk and asked the priest to marry you right away."

Taskill broke into a wide grin. "I love her. Things in my mind had cleared considerably on this journey, and I didn't wish to wait." He kissed Sheona's cheek. "She was ready."

She nodded, an odd misting in her eyes. "I was. I am. Forever." She leaned against her new husband, still in disbelief that she was so happy.

"What convinced you?" Lennox and Sloan asked in unison.

"Swimming in a storm," Taskill said.

Sheona nodded, agreeing with him. "Seeing our boat explode in the middle of a raging sea. Changes the way you look at things."

Dermot said, "I can't believe the priest married you that quickly. I got there just in time to see my lassie marry. Marta will be furious."

Rut added, "You could have waited for me, Taskill, but I'll call you out of your mind and in love. Lennox, it's your fault."

Lennox said, "Don't worry. There's still a sizable party to come to celebrate their marriage. Your place or ours, Sloan?"

Eva said, "I still don't understand why Clyde was so daft."

Dermot hung his head. "Rinaldo. He was an evil man. I'm ashamed to admit that he belonged to me. Poor Ailis. If she only knew."

"She knows, Da."

Everyone gave Sheona their full attention. Dermot looked at her and said, "You say that with conviction, but I'm sure you're right, if only you could ask her."

"Nay, Da. I know. I spoke with Mama."

Eva and Alma both gasped, while Sloan sat up and leaned toward her. "What do you mean, Sheona? How could you possibly talk with Mama?"

"Lia. When I was on Iona before Taskill came for me, Lia told me someone had a message for me. Mama told me to go with Taskill. She said there were men coming after me."

Sloan said, "I know you believe that it was Mama talking through her, but it could be Lia just guessing. Or maybe she knew about the men somehow. It doesn't mean you were conversing with Mama, Sheona. I'm sorry."

"I have to agree with him, daughter. Mama is gone."

"It was Mama. She said she wished she hadn't

let me have the third cinnamon cake. That I wouldn't have gotten sick if I'd stopped at two. Do you remember, Papa?"

Her father paled, his voice coming out in a low tone. "Heavens above. It was Ailis."

Rut came over and clasped his shoulder.

"What else did she say?"

"She said she was sorry about Rinaldo. That she wished she had been here to stop him, that his soul was evil. And she told me to go with Taskill. So, I did. Mayhap we shouldn't have gone then because of the storm."

The door opened, and a wee lass of six winters walked in, dressed in green and gold. She came into the group and folded her hands, waiting for their full attention.

"Chief MacLean and Alma, this is Lia," Sloan explained.

"Greetings to you all. You stopped an evil group from their task, and you did it so well. The universe is grateful. Roger was interested in the coin. Simple greed." Then she strode over to Taskill and Sheona, one small hand resting on each of theirs. "You needed to go then because they arrived on Iona shortly after you left. But it is over now, and you will have many happy years together with many golden-haired bairns to watch over."

"Why are you here, Lia?" Taskill asked.

Lia smiled, then replied, "I have messages for Dermot and Rut."

Dermot fell into a chair, his hand gripping the arm as he sat. "Ailis? Truly?"

"Aye, Ailis said she wishes you and Rut much happiness. And Rut," Lia said, turning her attention to the tall woman who stood next to the chair, "Douglas said you deserve happiness too. Love him with all your heart."

Lia took Dermot's hand. "Love your grandchildren for her since she cannot, Dermot. Ailis says Rowan needs you more than ever. That Rinaldo was not a fault of either of you. That the universe has ways that no one understands at times. She says to let him leave your mind and enjoy the ones you have who are so wonderful. And Rut, Douglas says to love with that big heart. That you'll have two grandbairns within the next year to love, and it's your job to help raise the new MacVeys in the world."

Dermot reached for Lia's hand and said, "Ailis, are you angry with me? Do you forgive me?"

Lia laughed and said, "Ailis says you need to tell your bairns that you and Rut married. They need to know. And she's surely not mad. Who do you think shoved the two of you together? Ailis and Douglas have been working on you for the last six moons."

Lennox asked, "Mama? You married him?"

Sloan only mumbled, "Da?"

The group erupted in congratulations, but Dermot followed Lia to the door. "Many thanks, wee lassie. Tell Ailis I'll always love her."

Sheona stood behind him, her hand on his shoulder.

Lia said, "She knows that. Oh, and I have something for you, Sheona. I found it in the sea."

She held out her mother's pearl necklace. "Ailis wanted you to have it back."

Sheona took the necklace and clutched it to her chest before putting it on. "Many thanks to you, dear Lia."

Lia turned to Dermot. "These words come from me, Chief. Will you do me and Ailis a favor?"

"Of course. Anything," he replied, wiping the tears from his eyes.

"Recognize that lasses are much more capable than you think." Then Lia winked and said, "Because we are."

EPILOGUE

THE MAN WOKE up on a pallet in a squalid cottage, so weak that he was unable to lift his head from the flat pillow he lay on. Wiping the drool from his mouth, he rolled onto his side, searing pain from the wound in his leg shooting through him, a moan erupting from deep in his insides.

What the hell had happened? Bits and pieces of the last few days gathered in his mind until he recalled almost everything.

A woman came into the chamber and said, "So you've decided to live, aye?"

"Shut up and bring me an ale."

"I have water, and that's all you'll get." The woman he married long ago, before he left her, gave him a dark look before turning away, her wide hips hitting the door on her way out.

How had he ended up back here? He hated the old witch and hadn't been around for years. Pushing himself to a sitting position, he groaned again at the pain from the wound. He looked at the bandage saturated with green pus. Disgusted, he ripped it off and tossed it into the corner of the chamber. The wound looked raw still, but most of it had healed, only a small section still oozing.

The door opened again, and his wife entered with a goblet of water. While he preferred to toss it against the wall, his mouth was so dry that he desperately needed fluid, so he took the proffered beverage. "How long have I been here?"

"A sennight. You came in feverish, so I called a healer. She's been here three times putting ointment on your wound." She glanced down at his leg. "It does look better. You're lucky to be alive."

He brushed his brown hair back from his face.

"Have you no sense to appreciate what I did for you? I could have left you out there to die."

She probably would have done him a favor then, but instead, he said, "My thanks to you. What have you to eat? Any bread or meat pies?"

"Some bread. If you don't toss the water up, I'll bring the bread."

"Just get the bread," he bellowed, sick of the way the bitch always did what she wanted instead of what he told her to do. "For once, just do what I say."

She gave him a wry smile and said, "Fine. I'll get your bread. Then you're to get your arse out of my cottage."

A knock sounded on the door, and a man's voice rang out. "Is he here?"

His wife stepped into the main chamber and said, "He is. He'll be leaving soon. Take him this hunk of bread, then get him out of here."

The man chuckled. "He won't shut his mouth, will he?"

Sholto said, "Bring me the bread, then get me out of here. We have work to do."

The visitor entered Sholto's chamber. "Whew, does it smell in here. You need a bath."

"I'll take one later. I have things to do."

"What exactly?" he asked, handing Sholto the bread after taking a bite.

"I have a wee lass to kill."

"Which one? You have enough enemies out there."

"I'm going to put my blade in the heart of the one who did this to me." He chewed on the bread and forced himself to a standing position, swaying a bit, but managing to take a few steps. "I just need my breeches, and I'll get dressed."

"I don't think you'll be swinging your blade yet, old man."

"Mayhap not yet. But I'll get her soon enough. I'll not stop until she's dead, and I'll have my way with her first."

"I'd wager you'll have to wait a day or two with that thing on your leg."

Sholto snorted, then grinned. "You make a good point, but I'll still find her."

"Where are you going? Who is she?"

"We're going to Iona to the nunnery. She's the

one with all those braids, making her look like a Norseman."

"You're sure she's there?"

"If she's not, I'll find her. I'll not stop until she's dead."

THE END

DEAR READER,
Thank you for enjoying my books. Especially to those of you who have been with me through all my novels. I appreciate you so much.

Next up? A wee Christmas novella.

Happy holidays to all!

 Keira

NOVELS BY KEIRA MONTCLAIR

<u>CLANS OF MULL</u>
THE PLIGHT OF A SCOTTISH LASS
THE BURDEN OF A SCOTTISH
CHIEFTAIN
THE ANGUISH OF THE SCOTTISH
LAIRDS
THE TORMENT OF A SCOTTISH
WARRIOR

<u>HIGHLAND HUNTERS</u>
THE SCOT'S CONFLICT
THE SCOT'S TRAITOR
THE SCOT'S PROTECTOR
THE SCOT'S VOW
THE SCOT'S DESTINY
THE SCOT'S WARNING
THE SCOT'S RECKONING
THE SCOT'S LEGACY

<u>HIGHLAND SWORDS</u>
THE SCOT'S BETRAYAL
THE SCOT'S SPY
THE SCOT'S PURSUIT
THE SCOT'S QUEST
THE SCOT'S DECEPTION
THE SCOT'S ANGEL

FALLING FOR THE CHIEFTAIN-3RD in a
collaborative trilogy
HIGHLAND SECRETS -3rd in a collaborative
trilogy

THE SUMMERHILL SERIES-
CONTEMPORARY ROMANCE
#1-ONE SUMMERHILL DAY
#2-A FRESH START FOR TWO
#3-THREE REASONS TO LOVE

ABOUT THE AUTHOR

KEIRA MONTCLAIR IS the pen name of an author who lives in South Carolina with her husband. She loves to write fast-paced, emotional romance, especially with children as secondary characters.

When she's not writing, she loves to spend time with her grandchildren. She's worked as a high school math teacher, a registered nurse, and an office manager. She loves ballet, mathematics, puzzles, learning anything new, and creating new characters for her readers to fall in love with.

She writes historical romantic suspense. Her best-selling series is a family saga that follows two medieval Scottish clans through four generations and now numbers over thirty books.

Contact her through her website:
www.keiramontclair.com

www.ingramcontent.com/pod-product-compliance
Lightning Source LLC
Chambersburg PA
CBHW070534260626
47161CB00002B/378